A SECRET GUIDE TO FIGHTING ELDER GODS

CHESYA BURKE   J. C. KOCH

JONATHAN MABERRY   SEANAN MCGUIRE

PREMEE MOHAMED   LISA MORTON

WESTON OCHSE   STEPHEN ROSS

LUCY A. SNYDER   JOSH VOGT

TIM WAGGONER   WENDY N. WAGNER

DOUGLAS WYNNE

Edited by
JENNIFER BROZEK

PULSE PUBLISHING

A SECRET GUIDE TO FIGHTING ELDER GODS

Copyright © 2019 by Jennifer Brozek.

Cover art image by Peter Tikos.
Cover design by David Allan Kerber.
Book layout by Stonehenge Editorial.

Published in the United States by Pulse Publishing.

First edition / April 2019

Trade Paperback ISBN: 978-1-950701-00-1

Introduction © 2019 by Jennifer Brozek.
"Away Game" © 2019 by Seanan McGuire.
"The Icarus Club" © 2019 by Weston Ochse.
"Stormy Monday" © 2019 by Chesya Burke.
"Pickman's Daughter" © 2019 by Gini Koch writing as J.C. Koch.
"Us and Ours" ©2019 by Premee Mohamed.
"The Art of Dreaming" ©2019 by Josh Vogt.
"Visions of the Dream Witch" ©2019 by Lucy A. Snyder.
"The Tall Ones" © 2019 by Stephen Ross.
"Just Imagine" © 2019 by Tim Waggoner.
"Holding Back" © 2019 by Lisa Morton.
"The Mouth of the Merrimack" © 2019 by Douglas Wynne.
"The Geometry of Dreams" © 2019 by Wendy N. Wagner.
"Being Emily-Claire" © 2019 by Jonathan Maberry Productions, LLC.

CONTENTS

Foreword   vii

Away Game by Seanan McGuire   1
The Icarus Club by Weston Ochse   19
Stormy Monday by Chesya Burke   40
Pickman's Daughter by J. C. Koch   60
Us and Ours by Premee Mohamed   77
The Art of Dreaming by Josh Vogt   95
Visions of the Dream Witch by Lucy A. Snyder   116
The Tall Ones by Stephen Ross   133
Just Imagine by Tim Waggoner   153
Holding Back by Lisa Morton   168
The Mouth of the Merrimack by Douglas Wynne   187
The Geometry of Dreams by Wendy N. Wagner   206
Being Emily-Claire by Jonathan Maberry   223

About the Authors   251
About the Editor   259

Dedicated to all of us who fight monsters every single day.

FOREWORD

The monsters have always been here. Sometimes hidden. Sometimes obfuscated by a polite or respectable veneer. Sometimes standing in light of day or shadow of night. But always there. Always seeking to take what is not theirs; to damage the mind, body, or soul.

It used to be that monster hunting was an adult's responsibility; they were to protect the young, the old, the sick, the infirm—the most vulnerable among us. The most likely to be attacked; to be killed or worse. The adults failed.

Today's teenagers are fierce and savvy. In this modern era, they speak up and fight for what they believe is right. They have tools at their disposal—knowledge, weapons, experience —like none of the previous generations. They have not yet been chained by familial duty or jaded by exquisite heartbreak. Even if they've experienced both, they still have the energy of youth to buoy their step.

In truth, there is no greater zealot than a teenager who *believes*; who has seen the light or the darkness and knows what goes bump in the night. It is these teenagers who will save or destroy us.

H.P. Lovecraft created a marvelous Mythos. The creator

himself was "problematic" at best; racist, bigoted, and misogynistic in reality. Because of this, the Lovecraft universe was rife with such problems in the early days. His lush prose was marred by hateful speech. It turned many readers away.

Lovecraft did do one thing right. He opened his universe to other authors to make of it as they will. It is a decision that gave the world another chance to tell Mythos stories without the same problematic attitude. To use the Old Ones and Elder Gods as metaphor for more earthly problems that many of us face every day.

In *A Secret Guide to Fighting Elder Gods*, thirteen authors bring the Mythos stories into the new millennium with a youthful perspective. Magic, mayhem, and murder no longer reigns just in dusty books in decrepit libraries. Monsters can be called by more than incomprehensible rituals in candlelit basements. Today, madness is hidden within the internet and lives on the football field. It breeds in the backyard parties and ambushes its victims outside the club. It finds the cracks in the mirror and it does whatever it can to break through—often with complicit adult help.

Teenagers, from every walk of life, use whatever they can to defend our world. Sometimes they win. Sometimes they lose. Sometimes...they give into the temptation of power.

—JENNIFER BROZEK

AWAY GAME

SEANAN MCGUIRE

The sky above the athletic field was hazy with clouds, painted gray on gray on gray. The threat of rain hung heavy in the air, damp and chilly and clinging to the skin. Despite the weather, the field was alive with moving bodies. Football players ran scrimmages at one end, while on the other a group of cheerleaders in orange and green skirts jumped and danced and flew like bright birds, almost shocking against the monochrome that was the rest of the world. Even the grass seemed muted, dulled down by the fog and the clouds and the impending storm.

"Ready?" shouted one girl, clapping her hands together. "Okay!" The other cheerleaders began to move in tempo with her, letting her guide them, their ponytails and skirts swaying in their self-generated breeze.

Becoming captain of the Fighting Pumpkins cheer squad was not something that came easily, or without effort. Jude had been studying videos of the team since middle school, when she'd cheered for touch football games as a member of the Johnson's Crossing Middle School Scarecrows. All she'd ever wanted was to graduate from Scarecrow to Pumpkin, and once she had achieved that glorious brass ring, she'd pushed herself, and her squad, ever higher, ever harder.

They jumped and cheered and tumbled and moved as one being; a single beast made of many bodies, sometimes in unison, other times breaking into disparate but complementary parts as they went into their acrobatic routines. It was the sort of performance that would never win so much as a participation trophy at Nationals, but would wow the crowds at the night's away game, which was honestly all that mattered. The more impressed the crowd was, the louder they would cheer. The louder the crowd cheered, the more they would inspire the football team to greatness. On the field, the role of the cheerleader was facilitation, inspiration, muse. Jude didn't believe in fielding a team that gave anything less than one hundred percent.

Normally, Jude would have been moving with them, performing her own tumbling passes and assisting Heather in stabilizing the pyramid, so that Colleen and Laurie could perform the sort of terrifying flying moves that got the crowd on its feet. At the moment, a cool assessment of the squad's skill was more important than her own place in the pattern. They were cheering against the Morton Goats tonight, and they needed to be perfect. No—more than perfect. They needed to be on *fire*.

Marti had tripped at the start of practice, skinning her knee against a rock hidden in the grass. The smell of blood was still hanging in the air, putting Jude's nerves on edge and making her skin jangle with little pinpoints of heat, like ants were walking all over her. The others noticed, she was sure of that; it was why they'd been so willing to agree to do the routine without her, letting her observe until she got herself under control.

Ordinary cheerleaders couldn't smell blood. Their teeth didn't ache at the thought of it. But since when had the Fighting Pumpkins been willing to settle for *ordinary*?

"Miss Feldman!"

Jude turned. The team's staff sponsor, Coach Harrison, was walking across the field toward her. As always, Ms. Harrison was dressed in clean blue jeans and a Fighting Pumpkins sweatshirt. Jude wondered sometimes if the vague disdain the other teachers seemed to have for the gym teachers was less related to any slight on their intelligence, and more sheer jealousy of the fact that the gym teachers were allowed to wear things that looked like they were actually comfortable, and not just on casual Friday.

"Yes, Coach Harrison?" The rest of the squad kept moving. They had performed this routine so many times that they could probably have done it in their sleep.

"How's your team?"

"They're good," said Jude, and smiled, the ingratiating smile she always used when Coach Harrison seemed to be taking too much of an interest. They needed a coach. The law said so, and so did their need to grow, improve, and learn. No one could be an athlete without someone to teach them what not to do.

At the same time, the routine they were doing tonight had been developed under Coach Harrison's supervision, rehearsed while she sat in the bleachers reading romance novels and amiably ignoring them, and refined in a hundred practice sessions while Colleen checked their physics and Heather broke their falls. They were a single organism now, and as any sideshow manager could easily explain, most organisms functioned better when they only had one head.

Coach Harrison turned an assessing eye on the cheerleaders, taking their measure. "Do you think you're ready for tonight's game? The Goats have been undefeated all season."

Part of Jude wanted to point out that the football team was really going to be in charge of beating the Goats at their own game: her cheerleaders were there to jump high, yell loud, and try not to break their own necks. The rest of her understood that talking back to the woman who was legally in charge of her squad was probably a bad plan.

"Yes, Coach," she said firmly. "We won't let you down."

The routine was over. The other Pumpkins began drifting over, drawn by the nerve-racking sight of their captain speaking with their coach.

Marti was the first to reach them. Looping an arm around Jude's neck, she put her chin on the slightly shorter girl's shoulder, batted her eyelashes, and said, "What's up, coach?"

"Checking in before the bus leaves," said Coach Harrison. "You'll all be on your best behavior tonight, correct? I need you to make me, and your school, proud."

"We're always on our best behavior," said Colleen indignantly. "It's just that sometimes the world decides it should behave badly around us, and we have to make it stop."

Coach Harrison looked at her flatly. "See that it doesn't happen tonight."

"Yes, ma'am," said Colleen, shrinking back.

Coach Harrison returned her attention to Jude. "We're going to have a good, clean game, and I need you to be a large part of that. I'm putting my faith in you. Don't let me down."

"We won't, Coach," said Jude.

Coach Harrison nodded before turning and walking away across the field.

Above them, the sky finally fulfilled its promise of rain and tore open, dropping a fine drizzle down on them. The Fighting Pumpkins didn't move. All stereotypes about broken nails and hairspray aside, they were competitive athletes: they understood that sometimes, they were going to get wet, and dirty, and less than poised and perfect. Most of them had been covered in blood or worse at one point or another. On one remarkable occasion, Laurie had broken her nose on her trip up the pyramid, only to complete the stunt she'd been on her way to perform, resulting in her effectively transforming into a blood sprinkler as she spun. The entire squad had come away looking like extras in a production of *Carrie: The Musical.*

"Well?" demanded Heather. "What was all that about?"

"I don't know," said Jude, with a thoughtful look at Coach Harrison's departing form. "She said she wanted to be sure that we'd cheer a good game."

"We *always* cheer a good game," said Marti. "We've cheered for every game this season, and we've never cheered a bad one. The football players are another story."

A murmur spread through the rest of the squad as they agreed, with varying degrees of conviction. In the end, it was Laurie who summed things up:

"She looked like she didn't trust us tonight, and that doesn't make me comfortable."

"I agree," said Jude. She looked up and squinted, seeming to notice the rain for the first time. "Oh, for...let's get inside. The last thing I need is to be down a girl because we were too stupid to get out of the rain."

They trailed toward the waiting gym, a stream of girls in orange and green, and no one seemed to notice them going. The rain continued falling on the field, washing the imprints of their feet away, until nothing remained but the muddy grass where they had been.

As a rule, the cheer squad preferred to avoid the team buses when they were going to away games. There were always cheerleaders with licenses, and the football team could get downright gross when they were trying to pump themselves up for the gridiron. It only took one spitting contest for the most team spirit-oriented new girl to flee for the relative comfort and safety of someone's back seat.

If they had been in the bus, they would have been safely lifted above the landscape, able to tune out and focus on the little pre-game rituals, like doing their nails and adjusting their spirit bows. As it was, they had to watch where they were going, which meant paying attention to their surroundings.

Colleen, sitting in the passenger seat next to Jude, frowned as the car rolled past a small barn with a sign identifying it as an independent butcher shop and meat market. "That's the fourth non-chain butcher I've seen since we reached the city limits."

"Are they 'city limits' when you're talking about a sign in the middle of a field, without a visible house in any direction?" asked Heather. "I'm asking for a friend who'd really rather not wind up missing the football game in order to star in a horror movie."

"Who?" asked Laurie guilelessly.

Heather scoffed and rolled her eyes.

"Morton has its own style," said Jude. She glanced uneasily at a copse of trees that looked distressingly like screaming human forms, somehow elongated and wrapped in gowns of bark. It was an eerie trick of light, shadow, and geometry, and she couldn't blame people for refusing to build houses within a mile of them. She would have spent all her time checking the locks on the windows, making sure the trees couldn't get in. Not exactly the sort of thing that leant itself to a good night's sleep.

"Is that style 'early Addams Family'?" asked Heather.

"I think the Addamses were less evil than this," said Colleen. Something flashed across the road, all long legs and bristling fur, there and gone before Jude even had time to slam on the brakes. Colleen grimaced. "I don't like it here."

"That makes four of us," said Jude. She squinted at the GPS. "I think our turn is coming up."

"Is it a U-turn?" asked Heather. "Because we could turn this car around and head straight home. I have a box of microwave popcorn with our names on it."

"The rest of the squad is probably there by now," said

Colleen. The car grew very quiet. "They're probably wondering where we are."

"Crap," said Heather.

"Fighting Pumpkins forever," said Jude, and hauled on the wheel, sending them down another narrow, tree-choked street.

The town began to appear. Slowly at first—one or two houses slotted in amongst the trees—and then with more and more frequency, until they were driving through a normal-seeming neighborhood, with normal-looking homes and small businesses to every side. There were even flowers blooming in the yards, although they looked somehow wrong, like brightly colored bruises nodding on long green stems.

Jude found herself staring at one bush covered in leprous roses and shuddered, looking away. Morton was a town like any other. It was perfectly normal. She was being silly to think anything different.

"How far to the school?" asked Heather.

"Not far," said Jude.

"Isn't it weird that we've never had an away game against these people before?" asked Laurie abruptly. Heather and Colleen both turned to look at her. She shrugged. "I'm just saying. We've been playing the Goats forever, but they've always come to us before. Everybody else, we take turns. Why is this the first time we've been to their school?"

"I—" Colleen began, and stopped, frowning. "I don't know. The rules say that we should have been there before now, but I'm sure we haven't been. I have a list of all the games we've attended off-campus, and Morton isn't anywhere on it."

"Of course you have a list," said Heather.

"How else would I know if someone had been messing with our memories?" asked Colleen matter-of-factly. "Writing things down is a level of protection against an uncaring universe, as long as you're sure nothing's changing what you wrote."

"This is where I feel like I'm supposed to say something about normal cheer captains not having to deal with this kind of crap, but since I'm pretty sure normal cheer captains don't exist, I'm going to say this instead: we're here."

The girls turned. The girls stared. An uncharacteristic silence fell over the car, heavy with the things they weren't saying, as all-encompassing as the Morton fog...the Morton fog which had, inexplicably, disappeared as they came around the final curve, leaving their destination framed by the sun, shining like a jewel in the brightness of the autumn afternoon.

Morton High School, home of the Black Goats, was built along the same level, open design philosophy as their own Johnson's Crossing High. It was a West Coast thing: never construct a building intended to house children any higher than absolutely necessary, since earthquakes are real and insurance rates are unforgiving. Roofed corridors connected the various buildings, which lay like a child's discarded Lego bricks around the wide, airy campus. Trees grew between them, their branches twisted and somehow warped, like they had been shaped by an unkind gardener. The grass was green. Very green. Too green, almost. It was like the color balance had been turned up on the landscaping, hiding something darker and less kind.

The longer they looked at the school, the more uneasy they felt. In the end, it was Laurie who put words to the sensation: "I don't think the walls are right."

"The town records say the school underwent earthquake retrofitting ten years ago," said Colleen.

Laurie frowned. "That's not...I mean, that's not what I meant. The walls aren't *right*." She looked around the car, seeking support from her teammates. None was offered. Heather and Jude looked as uncomprehending as Colleen.

Being a cheerleader sometimes meant walking into danger with chins and pom-poms high. Laurie was used to danger. What she wasn't used to was being the only one who saw it. She considered the virtue of trying to explain and dismissed it.

If no one else saw what she saw, well, maybe there wasn't anything to see after all. Maybe it was okay.

"I guess it's just their terrible color sense," she mumbled, hunching a little in her seat. "I'm sure it's fine."

Jude flashed her an encouraging smile. "If it's not, we'll kick its teeth in. Come on. I want to see the field."

Somehow, Jude's encouragement made Laurie feel even worse, like she was being childish when she ought to be brave and stalwart and true, like the rest of the Pumpkins. She bit her lip as she slid out of the car, smothering the rest of her objections, the small, still voice that said something was terribly wrong here. Something about the way the walls fit together, or didn't, made her mind itch, shunting her thoughts down channels they didn't want to follow.

They're just walls, she told herself firmly. *Walls can't break rules. Walls have to stand around holding things up all day. Walls can't do anything.*

Jude was already starting for the front of the school, with Heather and Colleen close behind. Laurie realized that the only thing she wanted less than being here was being here alone. She hurried after them, ponytail flipping from side to side, and she didn't look back. If the fog was rolling in to cover the parking lot again, she didn't want to know.

LAURIE ISN'T WRONG. As reassuring thoughts went, this one ranked right below "it's probably not infected," and right above "nobody's called my parents yet." Jude kept her expression composed, even as her eyes searched the edges of the buildings around her, looking for the key to their subtle wrongness. It was something in the angles, she supposed; some intangible, indefinable problem with the way the corners came together. The whole thing was probably riddled with asbestos; their earthquake retrofit must have been a rush job.

Heather and Colleen were sticking close, the one narrow-eyed and scanning her surroundings for signs of danger, the other with her nose buried in a rulebook. Colleen was the best when it came to dealing with dusty old books and terrible tomes, but she wouldn't notice actual danger until it bit her head off. Sometimes that was useful. While the rest of them were panicking, Colleen would still be calmly reading about possible threats. It was always good for someone to stay calm.

Laurie, though.... Laurie was another matter altogether. Laurie didn't usually panic about anything that wasn't actively trying to kill her. For her to be this uncomfortable meant that something was really *wrong*, and the fact that Jude could barely see it—that Heather and Colleen didn't seem to see it at all—was worrisome.

The distant tromp of feet and murmur of the crowd told her that they were heading in the right direction. A football game was a beast in its own right, made up of the combination of players and spectators and yes, cheerleaders. They were the soul of the creature, the roaring spirit that combined the body of the crowd with the leashed, furious mind of the team. This beast hadn't fully come together yet, wasn't awake and tearing at the sky, but it wouldn't be long. It just needed the last few pieces of itself to wake, and rise.

"Come on, girls," said Jude, picking up her pace. "The others will be here soon, if they're not already, and I want to go over our game plan for the night."

"Jump high, don't fall, don't break our necks," said Heather.

"Basically that, but with more synchronized chanting," said Jude mildly. She had long since learned not to argue with Heather when the sarcasm came out. It didn't do any good, and it could slow them down. She didn't want to be slowed down, not here, in these subtly misshapen walkways, where the corners seemed to watch her in some indefinable way.

"They sure do have a lot of murals," said Laurie. Her voice was shaky. "They really like goats."

"We have a lot of murals, and we really like pumpkins," said Colleen.

"Sure, but our murals are...they're different."

Jude glanced at one of the murals in question and looked quickly away as the painted goat seemed to look back at her, surrounded by a tangle of painted ivy that looked almost like a web of chains, holding the animal down, rendering it motionless.

The hall ended at the gym, and beyond that stretched the football field, wide and so perfectly green that it hurt to look directly at it. Heather, whose sense of smell was distressingly sharp, stopped and sniffed at the air before bending and plucking a single blade of grass. She rolled it between her fingers and dropped it, holding her open hand out toward the others. There was a smear of green on her skin, as vivid as the grass itself.

"It's been painted," she said.

"There's a drought," said Colleen. "Maybe they're following proper water conservation standards."

"I don't think it's following any proper environmental standard when you paint your entire football field the color of Ireland's nightmares," said Heather dubiously. She wiped her hand against the side of her skirt, leaving a streak of virulent green across the fabric. The Pumpkins wore orange and green daily. There was no way the stain should have clashed. It did. It stood out like a bloodstain, like something terrible and impossible and unwanted.

Jude looked uneasily at the field, which suddenly seemed less like a welcoming expanse of curated lawn and more like a trap. But it was between them and the bleachers, where the lights were going on—and where she could see their buses, parked in a lot she hadn't noticed when approaching the school. Well, of course she hadn't. If they wanted people to park by the football field, they needed proper signage. Otherwise, they could deal with people wandering aimlessly around their campus.

That seemed wrong, too. At home, they would have locked the front gates of the school. and festooned the main parking lot with signs and volunteers to make sure the away team went where they were supposed to go. It wasn't that they didn't trust visiting football teams to be smart enough to find a parking lot. It was that they didn't trust those teams not to indulge in a little recreational vandalism if left unsupervised on a "rival" campus. Someone should have been at the front of the school to direct them. Even if that person had directed them to go the way they'd gone, there should have been something.

The four of them trudged across the painted grass, toward the waiting bleachers, and it was impossible to shake the feeling that something was wrong. It tingled on Heather's skin, burning where she had touched the ground; it flickered at the corner of Laurie's vision, twisted and wrong and unable to reconcile itself with the world around them. For Jude, it was a lingering scent in the air, like the hot iron smell of her mother's cooking. Even Colleen looked up from her rulebook, frowning.

"Where's the rest of the squad?" she asked.

"There." Heather pointed to a smear of orange and green. They were too far away for any details to be really clear, but it was apparent, even from this distance, that they were standing motionless, pom-poms hanging limp at their sides.

"Come on," said Jude, and broke into a run.

The field seemed to fold beneath their feet as they ran, four bright birds racing toward the rest of their flock. In half the time it should have taken, they were running into the shadow of the bleachers. Colleen, who so rarely seemed to pay attention to anything other than the rulebook and the squad, stopped just shy of the line that separated the rest of the area from the field of play.

"Don't!" she yelped, spreading her arms wide.

Laurie and Jude stopped. Heather, carried forward by her

longer stride, didn't. Her foot touched down on the other side of the line. She froze for a moment, looking perplexed. Then she shook herself, like she had walked through a cold patch in the air, and trotted onward to the rest of the squad. She didn't look back, not once. She just kept going.

"What the—" Jude began.

"There hasn't been an away game in Morton in twenty-one years," said Colleen, holding up her book. "I was checking the schedule. Every time they've been assigned to host, something's happened, and they've had to either relocate or forfeit. Every time. Until this year, when they requested a change of schedule because they didn't get to host last year."

"Okay...." said Jude slowly. "Why is this important?"

"Because the last team to play against them was Mill City. The Mantises."

"That's not a real team," said Laurie. "Mill City has the Muskrats and the Sparrow Hawks."

"The Mantises never returned from the away game," said Colleen. "Their bus disappeared on the way home. The high school closed down later that year, and never reopened. Twenty-one years before *that*, the Black Goats played against the Oceanside Otters."

"Same thing?" asked Jude.

Colleen nodded, expression grim. "Same thing," she said. "Look at them. The rest of our squad is right there, and they don't even seem to realize that we exist. Something is really wrong here."

"Yes, it is." Jude took a deep breath. "Laurie, stay with Colleen. If the two of you need to step onto the field for any reason, I want you to order her not to be affected by whatever's going on before you do."

"Okay," said Laurie, in a small voice.

When Laurie gave orders, it was almost impossible to disobey them. No one knew for sure why it was like that: she had always been able to command people to do her bidding.

The fact that she was one of the sweetest, least malicious people any of them knew was most of what kept her on the squad, and off the list of things the squad had to deal with.

"What about you?" asked Colleen.

Jude smiled grimly, and her teeth were very white, and it would have been easy for someone looking at her from the wrong angle to get the impression that something was wrong with the shape of them; that they, like the hallways of Morton High School, didn't quite adhere to the rules of what they were supposed to be, even as they defied exact categorization.

"I'm going to remind them who my mother is," she said, and stepped over the line onto the football field. She took a long step toward the rest of the squad. Then she froze, going deathly still, her hands clenched at her sides and her chin dipped slightly forward, like she was attempting to rest it on her own sternum.

"Jude?" said Colleen worriedly.

"I'm okay," said Jude. Her voice was far away, watery somehow, like it was traveling through peat and bog to reach them. "Stay where you are. This is...not so good."

"I could tell you to come back," said Laurie. She made no effort to hide the fear in her voice, or the way it trembled.

"Don't," said Jude. Her voice was still far away, but it seemed to be getting closer, even though she never moved a muscle. "There's something here. This whole place belongs to something. Something that isn't supposed to be here. It makes the streets bend when people get too close. It makes the fog. Not just outside. Inside, too. But it doesn't...it's not here. It's here, but it's not here. This place, it's not big enough for what owns it, and so it only pays a little attention, every twenty-one years, when time comes to pay."

"Pay for what?"

"Not being eaten." Jude raised her head, glancing back over her shoulder at the others. She could taste blood, bitter on her tongue. How she loved them. "Stay where you are."

"But—"

"*Stay*," ordered Jude, and returned her attention to the field. The rest of her squad was so close. They were so far away. She began to run.

The bleachers were crammed with bodies, all of them wearing Morton black and red. Where were the Pumpkins supporters? But that was a silly question, really: they were somewhere else. The roads had bent, turning them away from the school, away from the site of a slaughter they weren't meant to witness. The thing that owned this place was terrible and vast, but wasn't *here*, although its presence permeated everything, distorting the flowers, the grass, even the air they breathed.

Breathing. Now there was a thought. Jude stopped breathing.

The world wobbled for a moment, her cells screaming a sharp reminder that she was technically a living thing, and living things needed oxygen. Then the part of her that was only and ever her mother's daughter rose sluggishly from sleep, yawning, and shunted those screaming cells aside. If Jude wanted to run without air, there were ways for that to be arranged. The taste of blood grew sweeter in her mouth, reminding her of the cost of moments like this one, the consequence of calling on her heritage more than absolutely necessary.

But the ground wasn't bending under her feet anymore, and in only a few long steps, she was standing behind Heather. Jude took a breath, dulling the taste of blood, and pushed her way into the huddle.

Coach Harrison was speaking, eyes sharp and animated. "—if you jump high enough and cheer loud enough, you'll drive our boys to greatness. Now, I want you all to look over these new cheers—"

"Coach," Jude interrupted. Coach Harrison turned to look at her with open surprise, like Jude was the last person she'd been expecting to see on this field. Jude took another breath. "I didn't approve any new cheers. We can't do them."

"I'm your staff advisor. I think you'll find that you don't have a choice."

"Cheerleading is a student-operated elective, thanks to budget cuts," said Jude. *And thanks to Colleen, for making sure we all knew that,* she added silently. "You supervise us and escort us to competition, but we choose our own material. My squad can't do any cheers that I haven't approved."

"Then I suppose you'll have to approve them, won't you?" Coach Harrison took a step forward. There was malice in her eye.

She had a red scarf tied around her neck. Bright red, arterial red...school color red. Just, well, for the wrong school.

"This was your high school, wasn't it?" asked Jude. She cocked her head. "You're too young to have been a student here last time they hosted a game, unless time bends here, too. But this was your high school. They sent you out into the world to bring them back a sacrifice."

Coach Harrison paused. Only for a second. That was long enough.

"What?" Heather shook her head like she was trying to throw off a fog—one that clung to thoughts, rather than to landscapes. She took a step toward their coach, and her gait was that of a predator, a lion stalking its prey, and not a teenage girl. "You brought us here to sacrifice us?"

"Not just us," said Jude, putting a hand on Heather's arm before she could get any closer. "The football team, too. They disappear along with the cheerleaders. Coach, why would you bother with Johnson's Crossing? You know what we are. You know what we do."

"Because our Lord doesn't like the competition," hissed Coach Harrison, and leapt.

Cheerleaders are athletes. Anyone who would contest that has never seen a cheer squad at the height of their skill, moving as one entity, a smaller beast inside the greater beast-body of the football game. Their captain and her presumptive second were standing against their coach, and that alone was enough to let the others throw off their confused tractability and move into position, surrounding and supporting Jude and Heather.

Coach Harrison found herself grabbed by a dozen pairs of hands, flung backward, away from the group of girls in orange and green, brightly colored birds showing their talons at last. She hissed, snarling something in an unspeakable tongue.

Jude sighed. "The Black Goats," she said, sounding disgusted. "We should have guessed. *I* should have guessed. Shub-Niggurath owns this school, doesn't he?"

This time, Coach Harrison recoiled. "How dare you speak his name?" she demanded.

"Easy," said Jude. "He doesn't own me. He doesn't own any of my family. He's the servant of a different darkness." Her teeth ached. Her skin buzzed. It would be easy to kill this woman, so easy to surrender to what her body wanted and her heart denied. "When you see him, ask what he knows of Yibb-Tstll. Ask him what he knows of blood."

Five Pumpkins held Coach Harrison back as Jude turned to the rest. "Get the football team on the buses. They should be pretty easy to convince. Tell them we won. They'll believe you."

"What if the other team fights us?" asked Marti.

"They won't." Jude glanced at Coach Harrison. "They know they can't win without messing with our minds. They didn't want a real game. They wanted a slaughter."

"We'll have it," hissed Coach Harrison.

"Sure. If you're not all fired when your boss realizes you forgot to bring him his morning coffee." Jude smiled at the slowly dawning horror in Coach Harrison's face. She could feel the points of her incisors digging into her lip. Damn. She'd allowed too much of her mother's influence to show through. It would be weeks before she could handle direct sunlight again.

It was worth it, though, f it meant they all walked away alive.

Jude turned her back on their protesting coach and walked back to where Colleen and Laurie waited, offering them a reassuring look that kept her teeth covered.

"Come on," she said. "Let's get out of here before the unspeakable terror from beyond time and space tears a hole in reality and eats the home team to punish them for their failure."

"Okay," said Laurie amiably. "Can we go for Dairy Queen?"

Jude—cheer captain, vampire's daughter, and most importantly of all, Fighting Pumpkin—nodded. "Sure," she said. "Just...not in Morton, okay?"

"Okay," said Laurie.

There was a mighty cheer from the field as the football team was persuaded of their victory. Jude relaxed a little. "All right," she said. "Let's go home."

"Go Pumpkins," said Colleen, and followed her to where the rest of their squad was waiting.

THE ICARUS CLUB

WESTON OCHSE

I t had once been such a crowded sky with Brandy, Nero, Andi, and all the others who had come before. They used to all fly, high, unlimbered, free to do in the night sky what one could never do in the day. But now Egan is the last of them, grounded and strapped like a human anchor to the impossible. Landlocked, and so far, no longer willing to convince the Old Ones to let him fly as well. Where once he'd been the leader of the Tecumsa School *Brokens*, now he remains the exclamation point of a grand idea, the anticlimax left behind to something no one really ever believed could happen.

Everything had started when he'd dreamed of Icarus. It wasn't a hint of something. There was no whisper of flying through the air, wind whipping his hair. The dream wasn't his brain twisting something he'd learned into a mind-warping multi-colored live-action Manga. In fact, he'd never heard or read of Icarus or any other Greek mythology before he'd had the dream. No, this was a dream of prophecy and just as every prophet who'd ever walked the earth knew that they'd been spoken to by the divine, he also knew that the Icarus dream was incredibly special.

It had all begun with a whisper.

Excerpt from Police Report from 3 August - Tuesday - 0614 Hours:

I then met with Sister Lucretia Santos who'd been present for final lights out. She insisted that all residents of Tremblay Hall had been present, including Nero Panousis and Brandy Scoggins, who are now whereabouts unknown. When asked if they are romantically involved, Sister Santos and the other residents who are interviewed (see addendum) informed this officer of each of the missing persons' physical issues. Nero NMN Panousis, Age 14, Ward of the State of Tennessee, Cerebral Palsy, able to walk short distances with the aid of crutches. Brandy Renee Scoggins, 15, victim of fire with third degree burns over one third of her body, but able to walk short distances with the aid of canes (crutches reportedly too painful to use). Both missing persons current location unknown. Investigation currently awaiting the results of cellular forensics to see if any local numbers are in use at time of disappearance.

"Mr. Egan, if you please. Inform us about the relationship between Phaethon and the other children with whom he associated."

Egan glances at the other kids in the classroom, but no one dares meet his gaze. They are equally afraid that they'll be next. Egan's nemesis for as many years as he's been going to Tecumsa

School, Brother Amos, has a way of asking questions that seem too close to home, almost as if he knows more than he should.

"Mr. Egan. We *are* waiting."

Sixteen years old last month, Egan should have had a normal life in a normal home with normal parents. He should have been driving a car, friends in the backseat, and a girlfriend in the passenger seat. But that isn't the way his life has been laid out. His is something different. His is a life with *gravitas*. He adjusts himself in his wheelchair so he is sitting up straighter and decides to go along for the ride.

"Phaethon had been told that he was the son of the Greek god Helios, who was responsible for driving the sun across the sky. The other kids didn't believe him, even though it seemed that every Tom, Dick, and Agamemnon was the bastard of one god or another."

"Careful, Mr. Egan."

He nods, inner smiling knowing he'd gotten away with one.

"Why do you think the other kids didn't believe him?" Brother Amos asks.

"He had no proof."

"Can a son of a god have proof?" Brother Amos paces to the chalkboard, then spins, his robes sweeping around him. "Does a son of a god even need proof? Or do you think the son of a god should show proof? After all, if he's the son of a god, does he need to?"

Egan considers the question, "To set him apart. To make him feel important, maybe? In Phaethon's case, he stole his father's chariot and drove the sun across the sky. One doesn't always know who their parents are—even back then—so to know yours is a god definitely gave you bragging rights."

"Tell me this, Mr. Egan. If you are the son of a god, would you keep your powers secret, or would you feel the need to prove it? To act out?" Brother Amos presses.

"I don't think using powers is acting out. Just because a

human doesn't understand what a god has done doesn't mean there isn't a good reason for doing it."

Just as Brother Amos seems ready to ask another question, the bell rings. Everyone averts their gazes, grabs their books, and leaves.

"Why does Brother Amos have it out for you?" Zane asks, an hour later, shoving the second half of a bologna sandwich into his mouth. The food makes a ball in his right cheek that bobs up and down as he chews.

That's a question Egan has been asking himself for years. "Maybe he's jealous of my mad wheels," he says, deflecting, gesturing towards his wheelchair.

Zane, and another of the newly arrived *Brokens*, sit on the grass leading up to Coolidge Hall—one of the three buildings used for classrooms and administration by the Tecumsa Home for Wayward Children, or as it was renamed by a committee of forward-thinking, grant-leaning donors, The Tecumsa School.

Zane, who has cerebral palsy like Nero had, sits beside his crutches on the grass. A half-eaten sandwich lay in his lap.

The girl is another thing. Her name is Andi and there's something about her that makes Egan nervous. She has a wandering eye and a clubfoot that makes her limp and look like a hunchback, but if she sits still and her eyes manage to focus, she is the most beautiful thing he's ever seen in a purely organic sort of way.

"Anyway, the bell rang, so I wasn't able to finish talking about it," he says.

"Do you really believe that?" Andi asks. Rumor has it that she's been tossed around schools in New England for a time which explains the razor edge to her speech. "What you said about gods acting out?"

He scoffs. "Are you asking if I believe that there are gods and goddesses who fly about and cause things to happen?"

"You seemed so certain." She pauses. "You have conviction about you when you talk."

Her innocence makes him smile. "I don't believe that there's a pantheon of gods waiting around to do things. But I do believe that we all have the potential to be like gods."

She glances sidelong at his wheelchair.

"Ever want to do something greater than yourself? Ever want to belong to something greater than you ever dreamed of?"

"I wanted to join the Boy Scouts," Zane says, "But my fosters wouldn't let me."

Egan nods to Zane, then turns back to Andi. "Have you ever wanted to fly?"

A brief millisecond glance at her foot says it all. She'd probably give up the world just to walk straight so the idea of flying is preposterous. If she'd had parents and a decent healthcare plan she wouldn't have her problems anyway. Both of her issues are correctable, which probably infuriates her.

"I'm serious. Have you ever wanted to fly?" he presses.

Her face turns red, but she eventually looks at him. "Fly. Like with wings and stuff?" she asks.

He leveled his gaze and lowers his voice, summoning the same authority he'd had in the classroom. "You don't need wings to fly."

Just then, Crespo runs up, out of breath, eyes wide with excitement. He is one of the few who'll associate with the *Brokens*, but only because he knows his escape is so narrow. "D-d-did you hear? They f-f-found crutches on t-t-top of the water tower. They're N-n-nero's and Brandy's and n-n-no one can figure out how in the h-h-hell they made it up there."

The mystery of it is impossible. Two kids on crutches just gone with the only evidence as improbably as the explanations.

"Anyone ever consider that they might have left them there?" Egan asks.

Crespo scoffs. "How would they even g-g-get up there to leave them?"

Which is the wrong question, but Egan lets it sit there and

fester. He merely nods and wheels away. A better question would have been *where did they go?*

Historians never understood the reasons man needed to be higher. They turned man-made rockpiles into places of unnecessary mystery. The great pyramids of Egypt—Khufi, Khafre, and the Red Pyramid—became mausoleums by short-sighted and tone-deaf historians rather than the stairways to the gods that they'd been meant to be. Modern Buddhists utterly failed to learn the obvious lessons of their worshipful ancestors, pretending that they actually heard something while sitting in the lotus position on mats in Iowa, Oklahoma, or California, fingers touching thumbs as they made noises together. They forgot that the original Buddhists lived in the mountains. The Maya Devi Temple in Nepal is the oldest of them all. Rongbuk Monastery rests on the back of Mount Everest at sixteen thousand feet. The Tiger's Nest hangs on the edge of an eleven-thousand-foot cliff in Bhutan.

Theologians would have one believe that it is the remoteness that is the governing principle of their foundings. Except the remoteness is but a symptom of those who'd built the places and their need to go higher and higher to find places where they could constantly hear the voices that are ever-present in the clouds. The deep thrumming words that made bones hum and organs quiver, words like *N-Ver* and *Hammom* repeated over and over, until the monks joined them in a multi-octaved chorus that echoed and endured through the ages.

Egan had first heard the words at thirty thousand feet during a thunderstorm. He'd been a mere boy of seven, moving from the Cascades in Washington to a home in Western Kentucky before he made it to the Tecumsa School. One more shake of the dice. One more roll of the bones. His young heart sent from one more foster family to another, forever in search of someone or something that would claim

him as their own. *Perhaps that is why he'd been so keen to hear the words—his need. Or perhaps it is because he is chosen—a reason he more firmly believed, shoving the embarrassment of not belonging aside, relegating it to an inadequacy he had no power over, like walking.*

The first crack and sizzle of lightning snapped across the portside wing. Passengers screamed as a fist of thunder enveloped them. Lights flickered. The plane shuddered. Overheads opened, spilling luggage and jackets into the aisle. Almost everyone had their eyes closed, hands white knuckling their armrests.

But Egan's eyes are wide and searching, wondering who'd said the word and made his body tremble.

Then it came again.

A sizzle and crack.

A fist of thunder.

And the words—N-Ver, N-Ver, N-Ver —repeated over and over by a voice that felt far older than anything he'd ever known.

It isn't until they landed in Lexington that he'd stopped listening and by then, he'd understood, nodding to himself, nodding to the unseen, that yes, he would do as he'd been asked. He'd be their messenger. He'd explain their needs to the world, even if it took one person at a time.

THE NEXT MORNING IS SATURDAY. They didn't have any classes until after lunch, so Egan spent the day as near the water tower as he dared to go. Yellow police tape still fluttered in the breeze. Even the bright sun couldn't destroy the memory of the others flying, their arms wide, eager laughter falling from their lips, as they did only what they'd dreamed. This is what Egan's life has become and he is proud of it. He is a messenger. He is a giver of the air. If only they'd listen, he'd send them high, pirouetting, swooping, diving above the water tower, into and out of the clouds, the words powering them, the wind propelling them, the—

"Hubris," comes a voice from behind him.

Egan's memory melts as reality burns through. He's been caught daydreaming, returning to the scene of the crime. He grabs his wheels and turns around.

Brother Amos stands with a hand up to shade his eyes, staring towards the top of the water tower.

"What did you say?" Egan asks.

"I said hubris." Amos lowers his hand and levels his gaze at the boy in the wheel chair. "I was trying to get you to understand hubris. You do know what it means, right?"

Egan regards the brother. About thirty and a dozen or so pounds above two hundred he wears his usual black cloak. Black sandals adorn his feet. The hair on his head is closely shaved. Even if he hadn't shaved, it is clear he is already going bald. But it is his eyes and mouth that consistently grab Egan's attention. The man seems to always be in the middle of a smile, as if there is a joke for which only he knows the punchline.

"It means bragging about something, right? We were talking about the young gods. None of them could keep their power secret. Is that what you meant?"

"Hubris is more than that. It's more than foolish pride. It's more than arrogance. It's doing something knowing that it will bring down the ire of those around you. Even the gods sometimes can't appreciate hubris."

"The gods were once young themselves," Egan says. "They probably bragged when they were young."

"Some gods were never young, Mr. Egan. Remember that. The gods are older than anything we know." He resumes looking at the top of the water tower. "Where do you think they went?"

Egan stares at the brother, wondering at his response. Then he realizes he's been asked a question. "Do you mean the gods?"

"The gods haven't gone anywhere. I was talking about dear Brandy and dear Nero. Where do you think they went?"

Which is the right question. Egan smiles. "Don't you mean how did they get up there? That's what everyone wants to know."

"We know that's not the most important question."

"But they are broken. Not even regular people," Egan says.

"Come now, Mr. Egan. I know you've created this whole mythology that you and the other kids with disabilities are broken, but we know that's far from the truth. I have a feeling you can do very much whatever you want to do."

Egan doesn't know what to say. No adult has ever addressed him with such aplomb. He ignores it. "The police think that the crutches and canes were left on the tower as a decoy."

Brother Amos grunts and shrugs. "Interesting speculation. Did they say a decoy for what?" he asks. He turns on his heel without answering. "Decoy," he says to himself. Then he chuckles and walks away.

THE NEXT DAY is the fourth Sunday of the month which means a field trip. They leave in three busses for Lookout Mountain to learn about its rich history during the Civil War. Egan and the *Brokens* ride on the handicapped bus. He'd hoped Andi would have ridden with them, but she is still trying to assimilate with the normal students. When they arrive, he makes sure to find a place beside her for Sister Santos' presentation, who begins by telling of the *Nickajack Expedition* against the Cherokee Indian, then moves on to talk about the major Civil War battle in 1863. Behind her, the Tennessee River meanders lazily in an arc past Chattanooga and around a spit of land called Moccasin Bend —where the Tecumsa School once threatened to send him to a mental health facility.

He has little time for the presentation, instead, watches the way Andi tilts her head as she listens as if she is an animal trying to understand a different language.

He is just getting up the nerve to speak to her when she leans towards him and asks, "Why do you want to be called *Broken*?"

He hesitates, then answers, "It's not what we want to be called, it's who we are."

She flashes her eyes at him, then resumes watching Sister Santos. She says, "Bullshit," and nothing more.

Egan stares at her. No one has ever called him on this before so he doesn't have a frame of reference to argue. Luckily, she saves him.

"No one calls you that except you. Why do you want to be a *Broken*? It's such a derogatory term."

"Maybe I just want to call us something before others get the chance," he says. "They could call us gimps or something worse."

"Do they?"

"No." But then he adds, "but there is this one boy who did. He used to make jokes about me like, *What do you call Egan when he's sitting on the front porch?*"

She glances at him and when it became apparent that he is waiting for her to ask the question, she raises an eyebrow instead.

"Matt. As in door mat. You call him Matt." When this gets no response, he says, "Or *what do you call Egan when he's floating in the pool? Bob. Get it? Bob? Or what do you call Egan when he's nailed to a wall? Art. Get it?*"

She grins a little, but it isn't what he is looking for. "Those are dead baby jokes," she says. "Like, *what is red and sits in a corner playing with razor blades? A dead baby. What's red and green and sits in a corner? The same baby two weeks later.*"

"That shit isn't funny," he says, smiling.

"Some people think it is," she says. "Ever hear the one

about how to tell the difference between a baby and a bowling ball?"

He can't help but grin wider. He knows the joke. They all know the joke. For some reason he's surprised she knows the joke. He gives her a grudging laugh as he shares his unusually candid thoughts. "It's really crazy the sort of things we find funny. I wonder if our parents ever had jokes like these."

"Of course, they did," she says.

"And I suppose they found them funny, too."

"Given the right context. So what happened to this boy who made fun of you?"

"Ronnie? He aged out at the home I was in. On the day of his eighteenth birthday, he just got up and walked away."

"So your whole life has been changed by that one boy," she says. "He must have some powerful magic."

Sister Santos ends her presentation. She tells everyone they have thirty minutes to look around and then back to the busses.

Without a word, Andi stands, goes behind Egan's wheelchair, and begins to push it.

He can feel her limp behind him, but it is ever so slight. Holding onto the handles helps her keep weight off her bad foot. She is probably using him as a cover.

He has nothing to counter what she's said. It takes him awhile. But as they approach the edge of the bluff, he asks, "Don't you think one boy can change a life?"

"If he has powerful magic he can, I suppose."

The curve of the river is becoming obscured by low clouds. At three thousand feet above the valley floor, they are high enough up and soon, find themselves in a white bubble of muffled cloud cotton.

"What do you know about hubris?" he asks, his voice deadened by the air.

She shrugs as she pushes the chair to a stop near a stone bench.

He engages the wheel locks.

She sits beside him. "I know it has something to do with pride."

"Brother Amos thinks that it's foolish pride. But what if you are so certain about something and we showed pride in that? Is it foolish? Or is it knowing more than anyone else?"

"Knowing more than anyone else? *Sounds like something a teenager would say*, is what a grown up's response would be."

"But it can happen." He knows he shouldn't say anything more, but he can't help it and feels the words leave his mouth of their own volition. "A teenager can know something...something special...something magical."

"You'll have to stop vague-booking and tell me what you're really talking about."

He cocks his head and listens. They are there. The words of power. N-Ver. N-Ver. His spine vibrates with their bass. And something else behind them like the sound of children playing. At first it sounds like glass falling on glass, but if he listens closely, he can make out individual laughter.

"I can't really explain it," he says. When he sees her about to protest, he holds up a hand and says, "But I do promise that there is great magic. You just need to listen."

"Listen to what?"

"If you're talking, you aren't listening," he says. "Now, just listen."

She shakes her head as she stares into the clouds. "But I don't hear anything."

"You will if you just keep quiet."

"But what is it I'm supposed to hear?"

He uses his hands to encompass the clouds. "This. Now. Everything."

He watches her stare blankly into the clouds until a breeze comes and they part. The bend in the river appears, and with it, the place where the crazy people live. All the while, he stares at her as she sits with her eyes closed. He doesn't dare move as his gaze redraws the curve of her jaw and the way her closed lips seem as if they are telling her cheeks a secret. He imagines her sitting closer to him, feeling her breath on his cheek. He imagines it smelling sweet. Not like candy, but something more organic, like the palm of a hand after a vanilla bean is crushed within.

They sit there, him watching her as she sits with her eyes closed, listening to everything he hears, the words of the Old Ones even now should be coursing through her. They sit as one perfect pair until Sister Santos rings her old fashioned, silver bell to call them back to their busses.

Her eyes snap open and she turns to him, a hint of a smile playing across her features.

A surge of something delicate fills his chest. "Did you hear it? Did you hear them?" he asks.

Sister Santos rings the bell again.

"Come on," she says, standing. She unlocks his wheels and turns him around. "Time for us to go."

He can no longer see her, but he still whispers, "Did you hear them?"

Five. Ten. Twenty feet. And she says, "No, Egan. Sorry. I didn't hear anything."

The delicate thing inside of him shatters.

Then they are on separate busses, each on their own journey back to the Tecumsa School.

The rest of the day and night pass in miserable silence. By the time he is back in Brother Amos' classroom for third period on Monday, he's barely able to contribute. For the first time in his life, he thought he'd found someone to share his connection with the voices of those who lived in the clouds. He felt so sure about her, but replaying everything they'd said, he realizes how mistaken he's been. Who is she anyway? Pretender. If the best she could muster are dead baby jokes, then what good is she?

The problem is that she and Zane have been assigned to his classes and they now sit a few rows in front. He can't help himself as he watches her back, longing for her to turn and regard him. But the best she can do is turn to Zane and laugh at something stupid, or raise her hand and answer one of Brother Amos' stupid questions.

"Mr. Egan, are you with us?"

He realizes that all eyes are now on him. He's been so lost in his love-hate that he's missed the question.

And there she is, turning around, eyes appraising him, inspecting him, analyzing him, and for the first time in years his face turns red. He opens his mouth to speak but feels like Crespo and knows he can't get the words out.

Brother Amos's voice surrounds him. "I was asking about James Matthew Barrie, Mr. Egan, and his most well-known work, *Peter Pan*."

Egan feels the buzzing of everyone staring at him and grinds his teeth together. He hates the feeling. He fights against it. He exhales and forces his mouth to enunciate the words, "*Peter Pan*?" And of course as soon as he says it, he feels ridiculous. He has his own love-hate relationship with *Peter Pan*. He remembers in the Cascades with Mother Dixie and how she liked to sit them in front of the television with her library of Disney movies while she drank wine all day. Two of the older kids fought over what they'd watch. It was either *Lion King* or *Peter Pan* and he'd been forced to watch them until he was sick of them.

Brother Amos sighs in exasperation. "Mr. Egan. *Peter Pan*. We're waiting."

The memory of the older boy named Ronnie and the girl named Jess and their pinching and punching and stealing of his food avalanches back on him with the music of *Peter Pan* and *Lion King* as the sound track.

He says the words again, "*Peter Pan*."

The eyebrows arched. "Indeed. Sure. Tell us about the hubris of Mr. Barrie."

"Back to the Greeks then." Egan clears his throat and sits up straighter. "Pan is the God of the Wild. Barrie named his famous character after Pan to display Peter's nature. In both mythology and Barrie's story *The Little White Bird*, Peter is wild and is able to communicate with otherworldly beings and travels to Neverland."

"And his hubris? You were asked about his hubris," Brother Amos mentions.

Just as Egan is about to speak, Sister Santos comes to the door, her face pale.

Brother Amos meets her in the hall.

Crespo being Crespo listens at the door, then crabs to the middle of the room.

"They found them."

"Who?" several students ask.

"B-B-Brandy and Nero."

"But that's impossible," Egan says.

"No. That's what the Sister is explaining They found their bodies in a field near Pikeville."

"Are they dead?" Zane asks.

Crespo nods. "She said it is as if they'd fallen from a great height."

Egan can't keep his mouth from slamming open.

As BAD AS the previous night was, this night is even worse. Storms rage outside, and he hears himself being called. But he is too confused to go to them. He'd thought that he'd freed the others of their earthbound dramas. He'd never meant to send them to their deaths. The voices never promised—never told him what they were going to do with the others. They just made them fly and let them join them in the clouds.

And to think that Brandy and Nero fell from the sky like a pair of modern Icarus.

There has to have been some mistake.

There's been repeated knocking on the door, but it isn't until well after midnight that he finally relents and opens it.

Zane stands in a puddle, soaked with rain. His face is red with tears and something else. He slumps on his crutches. "She won't come down. She wants you."

"Who won't come down? Who wants me?" Egan asks.

"Andi. She says to come and get you. She said that she lied. She *can* hear them." Zane's eyes grow wide. "What can she hear, Egan? What did she lie about?"

Egan ignores the questions. He rolls past and into the storm.

Zane shoves his crutches aside and begins pushing Egan. Soon they are in a loping run. Zane seems to be holding on as much as he is propelling them.

The storm lashes at his face and torso with wicked slaps of rain. The sound assaults him on multiple levels. Thunder booms and wind roars. Beneath it all comes the voices, stentorian, anguished, starving. They want more to fly. They want more to come to them. The entire way to the water tower Egan wonders what he is going to do.

Then he sees Andi, standing on the edge of the tower, arms raised to the sky, shouting into the wind.

"I hear you. I hear you talking. Take me. Take me now."

Zane pulls Egan to a stop, then lets go and limps to the tower. He pulls himself up to the top. When he joins Andi, he points, and she follows his gesture.

She sees Egan, then steps to the edge and shouts. "I lied to you. I heard them." She spins, slipping on the wet metal surface and almost plummeting below. She catches herself at the last moment. "They won't stop talking to me, Egan. They want me. They want to make me fly."

He shouts. "Don't do it. Andi! I was wrong. Don't listen to them."

Egan's chair jerks around violently.

Brother Amos holds the arms of the chair, his face inches from Egan's. "What are you doing?"

"Andi. She's going to get hurt."

Brother Amos' gaze pierces him. "She needs your voice. She needs your connection."

Visions of her falling thousands of feet in some lonesome field flood him. "No. I can't. I don't want her to die."

"This is not yours to decide, Egan. The Old Ones have claimed her. They've made their voices heard through you, their conduit. They want her."

Egan shakes his head and struggles to be free of the brother's grip. "I thought all they did was fly."

"You didn't want to know. You were so happy being a ringmaster you didn't take time to learn what it is they did. Nevertheless, we are here, and you have been long ago chosen. The Old Ones need to be fed. What lives in the cloud is but a memory of them. A whisper of what they once were. To keep them alive they need ones such as yourself."

"But why me?"

"You came from nothing. You have nothing. Nobody wants you."

"But that's not true. I had a mother."

"That picture? I gave you that picture. I found it in a frame I bought at the store. It means nothing."

Egan screams at Brother Amos. Unintelligible. Primal.

But the brother ignores it. "I tried to give you hints. I tried to warn you, but you wouldn't listen. Remember when I asked you to tell me about the hubris of Mr. Barrie? Why would he have any hubris if he is merely telling a story...a fiction...something he'd invented whole cloth from nothing. What amazes me is that regardless of how smart you are, you still don't get it. You still haven't made the connection."

"This can't be true. All they ever wanted to do is fly. All any of us ever wanted to do is fly."

"Barrie couldn't help but brag. His hubris is incredible. He put everything in plain sight, albeit hidden behind a pleasingly youthful narrative."

"Shut up!"

"*Peter Pan* is real. Neverland is real. It's not some place for lost boys and girls to go to live a life of freedom from responsibility. Neverland is above us. We see it every day. The sky is Neverland. The clouds are Neverland. They're where the Old Ones live. You've heard them. I know you've heard them. You wouldn't be a Pan without hearing them."

Egan reels from it all.

"The irony of the real story is that the real *Peter Pan* couldn't fly. He couldn't even walk. Pans by their very nature are only half human. Just as you are.'

"I'm human. What are you talking about?"

"Your upper half is. What about your lower half?"

Egan stared at his useless legs. They are worthless for what they are. The wheels of the chair are his real legs. Like a modern Pan. The body of a human, the legs of a goat.

"Tell us about Pans, Mr. Egan. What is their lineage?"

"I d-d-don't know." But he did know. He'd studied and studied well. He knows the answer.

"Come now, Mr. Egan. Enough of this. Tell us about the Pans."

"They preceded Apollo. The Pans came before any of the Olympians. They were here before any of the Greek gods. Pans were here before anything else."

"Why were they here, Mr. Egan? What was their reason?"

Egan glances at Andi who seems to be levitating above the water tower, her arms raised into the air.

"Don't you want to know the reason, Mr. Egan? Don't you want to understand why Pan is written into *The Wind in the Willows* as a *Piper at the Gates of Dawn*? Don't you want to know why Peter is a Pan and why he needed children to follow him? It's all the same. Peter makes them fly and the Piper makes everyone forget. It's all the same. It's all connected."

The sky suddenly booms.

Then Egan's legs begin to move, not as legs should move, but as strange spongy appendages, as if they belong to a different creature, like an octopus or a squid. They pull him from his chair and beneath the police line.

Brother Amos shouts into the heart of the storm. "I've been waiting for someone like you. When you came, I knew what you were. It just took time to make you into what you could be."

Egan glances wide-eyed at Brother Amos as he is pulled towards the tower. He opens his mouth to scream, but nothing comes.

"Who is it that pushed you? Who is it that fed you all the information? I knew when I saw the way you looked at the clouds. Normal people don't look at them that way."

"Help me!" Egan manages to scream. His legs begin pulling him up the ladder, wrapping themselves around the bars and dragging him up and up.

"You looked at the clouds as if they spoke to you and they did. *Peter Pan* is never about the myth of eternal youth. It is about eternal life. Living as one with the Old Ones. Feeding them. Become one part of them. The Aztecs had it right. So did the Egyptians."

Then Egan is atop the water tower. He's never been up there but has always dreamed of it. His legs move beneath him, pushing him to an improbable standing position.

"Egan. This is wonderful," Andi screams. "Can you hear them?

N-Ver! N-Ver!

"They want me. They will fix me, Egan."

N-Ver! N-Ver!

She reaches out to touch him.

He grasps at her.

Just as they are about to touch, she shoots into the sky with such speed that she is gone in an instant.

Egan sways and Zane steadies him.

Brother Amos arrives on the top of the water tower, huffing. Still, as out of breath as he is, he finds a way to continue lecturing. "Carved on a rock at the apex of the Red Pyramid is a series of hieroglyphics that have been translated. *To fly is to cry, reliving the tears of joy and sorrow of everyone who has come before, the clouds a repository of all human emotion, controlled by something older, wiser, and wanting. It is to you we feed. It is to you we pray. It is to you we heed.*"

"I want to fly," Zane says.

Egan now knows. He realizes what is job has been. He'd thought he was there to free his *Brokens*. And he was. But the freedom he thought he was giving them wasn't the same.

The sky booms again.

Lightning strikes the tower.

Egan feels himself pulled into the air by an unknown force.

"No! Not him! Never him!"

Brother Amos lunges at Egan's legs and grabs them, holding him down like an ecumenical anchor.

Egan stares into the clouds, white and gray and ablaze with the storm. They are alive. He feels the Old Ones. He can almost see an echo of their presence...images in the clouds of the great monsters they once were.

Lightning smacks the tower.

Zane and Brother Amos go flying.

Egan feels as if his legs are on fire.

Thunder booms once more.

N-Ver! N-Ver! shouts the sky.

DAYS, weeks, months later, Egan remembers that for one brief moment he flew. He thought he'd love it. It was all that he'd ever wanted to do. But what he discovered was that the feeling was less one of freedom and more being at the end of someone else's line. Brother Amos saved him in those final moments, whether he knew it or not.

Egan is supposed to return to Tecumsa School. He's not looking forward to it. He has a long road to recovery, both mentally and physically. The lightning did something to him. When it struck, it changed the shape of his right foot. It's more like Andi's now—but not a club foot—more akin to a hoof. Still, he accepts it gladly, for as strange as it seems, he can walk now. Physical therapy has been the most painful thing he's experienced, but to leave his wheelchair behind is something he'd never once imagined.

He's seeing counsellors as well. They want to know what happened up there on the water tower. They want to know how he got there. They want to know what happened to Andi. The more questions they ask, the fewer answers he has. Ultimately, they blame it on Brother Amos who will never be able to answer their questions. His body was found at the base of the tower, smoking, charred, and broken.

Egan has been searching the internet. He's looking for Andi's body. So far he's yet to discover it. He could have missed it. Or she still could be flying. He doesn't know, but he wants to.

Soon he will walk out of there.

He's not sure what's in store for him.

But when it storms and when the thunder booms, he can hear them calling for him.

N-Ver! N-Ver!

And he says it right back at them.

But one day.

One day he just might find her.

STORMY MONDAY

CHESYA BURKE

My name is Stormy Monday, and I'm a ghost.

As far as anyone in the outside world knows, I was never born. I don't have a birth certificate. Don't have a social security card. I don't exist. I can't walk through walls, but sometimes I wish I was invisible.

I have this ugly mark splitting me literally in half. I'm two different people. One is black, dark skinned, coarse hair, a lovely hazel eye. The other half of me is white as snow. You wouldn't believe it to see me. Most people just gawk. A large green eye staring from my socket, and straight, platinum-blonde hair that belongs on a white woman.

I am a freak. Hell, I'm a freak, among freaks. My home is a carnival. And we kill people. That's our job.

This is our story:

The Mysterious Macabre. We focused on the horrific, the ugly. The only modern-day Freak Show still in existence. The Macabre was like a great big traveling sideshow. Our people are odd and wild; free. Walking through our doors was like stepping back in time. The isolation—that's what hits you first. You'd leave knowing, if nothing else, your life was secure, meaningful. Because you knew that you were nothing like "those" people.

You are nothing like us.

We die every day...to satisfy your need to feel worthy.

Large tents full of larger than life people afflicted with larger than life problems would stare at you as you pass. You would see June, the crystal ball reader. Her eyes are her loveliest feature, but they're always sad. Her son died several years ago— it shows in her eyes the most, I think. Then there's Katrina, the legless woman who was pulled around the park on a red wagon by her twenty-year-old, deaf and mute son, Pat. There were many people with gifts in the Macabre. Everyone was welcome.

WE'D PLANTED ground in Sun, Kentucky. It was like every other town we had been to over the years. The buildings sat a little too close together in town, and a little too far apart outside. It wasn't big, but it wasn't too small either. The population poster that I read coming in said 4,000. Once we'd set up, the doors always open promptly at 6pm.

At sixteen years old, my only job at the carnival was working the kiddy worm. It had a big huge sign over it proclaiming *Wiggly Worm*, in squiggly, neon lights. It was boring and a pain in the ass most of the time, but hey, it beat the hell out of cleaning out the trucks, or taking down the rides.

The best part about the ride was that I got to work with children. I love children. Kids are such wonderful beings until adults get their hands on them.

As I was opening the ride for the day, a little boy walked up to me, and pulled my shirt. I jumped back before he could touch me. I must have scared him because he jumped too, and looked up at me, hurt. Black curls framed his round face, his skin was about the color of my dark side, and his eyes were wide with wonder.

I started to reach out to him before I stopped myself, "I'm sorry," I said and I held up my left hand, which had a glove on it, "I just don't like to be touched. It's not you. It's me." I smiled trying to reassure him.

"What's wrong with you?" He asked. Kids are filled with wonder. And I don't mind them asking, as long as they *do* ask, instead of just pretending that my white half is not there, or even worse, my black half.

"I have a skin disorder."

"Dis—dis—what?"

"Disorder." He smiled along with me, trying to say it. He couldn't have been older than five or so.

"And it makes some of you white?"

"Yes." I knelt down beside him, careful I wasn't close enough for him to touch me, looked around. "Where's your mommy?"

He looked in the same direction as I did and shrugged his shoulders. "I lost 'em." He seemed not to even care that he didn't know where his mother was. "That's funny. Can I be black and white, too? No, I wanna be green like the Hulk. That's what I want."

I smiled at him again and pulled down my shirt sleeve so that it covered my entire arm, and then I reached out to him. "Come on, let's find her before she loses her mind."

Before he could even grab my hand, a woman rushed up, and *touched me*. Her hand found the only uncovered spot on my body; my neck. She pushed me out of her way; discarding me like a piece of trash. I fell back, on my butt as a flash of pain gripped me. My whole body spasmed and the left side of my head pounded with pain, as the world around me swam beyond my control.

I hadn't realized her other arm was in a cast until I felt the pain of my wrist bone crack within my skin. I scream from the sudden rush of agony flooding me. The fracture seemed to resonate from deep inside my mind, as if it had told my body itself to break. Layers of bone shattered under tender pale skin until my hand simply hung from my arm like a limp sausage.

Visions of memory flashed before my eyes. They weren't my memories. They were the boy's mothers. I saw her standing in a doorway to a large home. Behind her, her son was staring, wide eyed. She began moving, as if in slow motion, looking behind her. A tall man, with hairy hands reached out to her, but he wasn't trying to help her. He smacked her hard, and I felt a twinge of shock across my face. The woman tried to protect herself, but the blows were coming too fast, and one knocked her down on her butt. She fell hard, bouncing down the stairs leading into the house.

But that wasn't what had broken her arm. No, I saw what was coming before it even happened. The woman had fallen with her arm propped halfway on the step and the ground. The big man stomped down, stood on the last stair, staring at her, with a crooked grin on his face. I watched in terror as he placed his boot on the woman's wrist forcefully. Screamed in pain as my bone shattered into a thousand pieces. My mind reeled; I had never seen such pure hatred in my life. But then I noticed something strange about him. It was hard to see it through the filter of her memories, but there was something off about his face. It was monstrous, literally.

When my brain finally calmed down a bit, I was sprawled out on the pavement, barely conscious. They tell me that my eyes roll into the back of my head, when I have these fits, and once I bit my tongue so hard, I had to have several stitches.

I guess that must have been the case here, because all of a sudden the woman broke out in this horrendous scream that stilled everyone around her. I guess she really thought I was dead because when I moved she jumped, and ran away, pulling her son behind her.

Breathing heavily, I looked around me and the first thing I

saw was an old woman. A small bit of pepper was sprinkled throughout her ever growing main of salt white hair. Her eyes were intense, but they seemed to show that nothing was there —as if she were seeing through glasses that were not her own. A younger woman pulled her along, and she followed, without a word.

But it wasn't the old woman that had caught my eye. It was the thing *within* the woman. Like it was riding her soul, as if hitching a ride on the back of this poor, defenseless, old lady. It was just there. Watching everything that the woman watched, hearing everything she heard. I could see sorrow on her real face, as if she knew something was wrong, like she could feel this thing, but she wasn't quite sure what it was. I stared into the face of the creature, and I grew cold. Because it was cold, unfeeling, uncaring. It was ugly. Disfigured. The face of nothing I have ever seen before.

I couldn't move, couldn't speak, as the creature gradually moved the old lady past me her white gown flowing behind her. I pointed to the old woman, my finger shaking. Everything seemed to move in slow motion. Its staleness lingered over me and a wave of nausea choked its way into my throat.

Suddenly it turned to look at me. It *saw* me. And the worse part was, that it knew that I knew it was there. It looked right into my eyes, measuring my fear, as if feeding from it. A wicked grin spread across its face, and it winked. *Winked* at me.

I wanted to scream, but I couldn't. The woman leading the old woman stopped and asked if I needed help, while the creature never took its eyes off me.

The Human Pin Cushion ran over, scooped me up in his arms.

"Look at her! Do you see it?"

He looked around and whispered in my ear. "Can you see something? What is it, Stormy?"

The old woman came closer to me and reached out her

hand to touch me. But I knew it was really the creature that wanted to *feel* me. I recoiled away.

Pin Cushion stopped her, and told the woman leading her that I would be fine. He looked at me again, and then back at the old woman, "Is that your mother?"

"Yeah, I thought I'd get her out today. She hasn't been to a carnival in ages."

He nodded his head as if he understood completely. "She's sick?"

"Yeah. They say it's Alzheimer. Sometimes she's completely out of it, but sometimes she's like this, *clear*, and sees everything that's going on around her. She even noticed your friend was in distress. I just don't get it."

"Neither do I," Pin said.

I did.

THE HUMAN PIN Cushion stared down at me as I awoke. Pin always had that smile plastered to his face. It's so funny to look at, I couldn't help but smile back.

"Hey. She's awake. How ya feel, Stormy?" His voice was as smooth as woven silk, as was his bald head that shined in the evening sun.

Pin's a nice guy, despite his hardcore rep that he put on for his show. He was double jointed and swallowed swords—which at that time would give me all kinds of interesting dreams at night. It was an act; it usually was. He put his hand on my forehead and brushed the hair from my face, without dropping that beautiful, bright smile. Sure, he was a "made" freak, but I didn't care. I could have fallen in love with him right there; I was sixteen and romance novels were my life.

"...Okay, I guess." My voice sounded strange in my ears. I tried to sit up, but my head swam so fast it knocked me back down.

"Oh, there. Hold on. Don't try to move, Sweetie." He wrapped his arms around me, and I breathed in his smell—cool water cologne—and he helped me sit up.

My arm was in a cast with a sling wrapped around my neck. I looked down at it and frowned. Everything came rushing back to me. My head pounded again remembering the pain that had seized my body. *God, I hate this shit.*

"How ya feelin', Bit?" Momma Mae appeared in the doorway with Doc Mayer at her side. She wasn't my birth momma, but she was as good as any I could hope for.

"You gave us all a scare." He felt my wrist, pushing on the cast. I winced in pain. "Totally fractured." Doc always used gloves when he worked on me. I hadn't known then, but he had taken me to the local hospital, to have me fitted for a cast. He knew of my white side's aversion to touching people, everyone in the carnival did. There was no doubt that Doc would have insured that the hospital doctors not work on me unless they were also wearing gloves. He sighed, "Can I ask what happened?"

"I...I don't know. I think I might've fell." I tried to lie, but he saw right through it. They all did.

I COULDN'T WORK, and after what happened, I was scared to be around people at that time, so I spent the next couple of days with my best friends, Annabel and Margie. They were conjoined twins and they were glorious.

I couldn't wait to see my friends' show and there was nothing in the world that I loved more than seeing them perform. It was so elegant and beautiful. There weren't any tricks, no fire breathers came out to precede them. They simply performed for the world to see, and what a sight it was.

The show followed like this: Annabel and Margie would walk onto stage, one foot at a time. This in itself was a marvel to see. If ever there was a question that their minds worked as one, it was when they took the stage, one step at a time, and strolled to the center of it.

If they regretted for a single moment what fate had done to them, there was no hint of it. Life, chance, time; none of it seemed to matter to them when they took the stage. It was as if they had lived only for this purpose.

I hurried to my seat in the back, to watch, for like the thousandth time in my life. Once, when I was little, I had told the twins that I wished I had talent like them, that all the world were a stage for me to play for them, but they simply laughed.

"You don't want to be us, Sweet Stormy, we die every night on stage. Fate is against us."

I think I had cried then. Nothing is sadder in the world than to see two such beautiful creatures as tormented at these twins. I cried again watching them that night. They took the stage in classic form, their gorgeous, turquoise gown flowing behind them. Their eyes were wide, all seeing, staring at no one and everyone in the crowd at the same time.

They stepped to the edge of the stage in front of Andre and began the most touching song that my ears have ever heard. They were marvelous and hit the high notes like seasoned pros. Opera, with the unique flair of the mysterious.

They were synchronizing perfectly with each other, both taking all the notes at the exact same time. They held their hands up high and bobbed their heads with soulful movements of the youth. Time stood still, everyone held their breaths just as the last notes came to an end.

But the two were not finished. Just as the last sounds came flowing from their tongues, they flapped the dress behind them, headed to the back to the stage and took to the piano, with gusto. Playing like two possessed souls, they stood, feet pounding on the hard-wood stage, fingers dancing on the keys, heads bouncing to the rhythm.

They'd stand there, playing, until the last bit of life left their bodies and melted into that piano. Until nothing but the twins and it existed, nothing else mattered in the world. Nothing could get them to stop. No one ever tried. No one wanted to.

The crowd was spellbound. It was the most amazing thing they had ever seen, or ever would.

Finally, after an eternity, they stopped. Standing, waiting. Their heads hung low, their feet barely able to carry them, their arms like lead pipes. They stood there, crying. Every night was the same. Every show, every time. Crying.

You don't want to be us, Sweet Stormy, we die every night on stage.

AS THE CROWD FILTERED OUT, I sat there, waiting. I don't know what I was waiting for, but I just could not get up. Every time I saw Annabel and Margie, there was the same effect. Always the same feeling: helplessness. I think most of the crowd felt the same way, because about half of them still sat there, their backs to me, just staring at the empty stage.

Finally, after a few moments, they stood up and began to march out. Still I couldn't move so I just sat there. That's when I noticed something about all of them. Something that should have caught me before, but I was too wrapped up in my own misery to see. Something that was so obvious to me now that could have been smacked over the head with it.

I sat there holding my breath as the people marched out. None of them really paying any attention to me, and not really caring one way or another who I was. They were too full from their lunch of heart-broken, pain-driven twins.

They were all monsters.

I'd realized something else. They were feeding from the pain of the twins, as if their song had been a meal to them. They savored every moment of it.

There had to be at least twelve of them—all of the faces

inside the faces distorted and ugly; all of them marching to a somber beat.

One of the things looked over at me, but I didn't move. I was frozen, I couldn't look away. I wished I could have just turned and pretended that I hadn't seen them, but I couldn't.

This one seemed to realize that I could see it, just as the other had. He stopped, looked at me, and then smiled. It was a horrific sight, seeing that thing smile at me. The face of the man that he inhabited, didn't change at all. In fact, it didn't act as if it even registered where the hell he was.

Soon another walked up and joined him, they exchanged words, and the first one pointed at me. They both just stood there staring, and smiling this wicked smile. My heart stopped. The new one came forward, slowly.

I stood to my feet and looked around. No one was there. Even the twins had exited the stage, and were somewhere behind the curtain. Usually they would have come out by now. But tonight had seemed to be especially hard on them, so they may have taken longer to get over it. It always took a while, but never this long. The first thing was walking toward me. I just stood there, watching.

One of the things walked toward me, staring, smiling. I was frozen. It walked up, within inches of my face, cocked its head, examining me.

As he reached out to touch me, I heard Pin call out to me. You can't know what a relief that sound was to my ears. I turned to look and he was running up behind me, as if he knew something was wrong. Maybe he did. At that moment I didn't care.

I looked back at the two monsters. They were gone. I sighed.

What the hell are they? I thought. *Why were so many of them here, tonight? And most of all, why the hell was I just now seeing them?*

I guessed I might know soon enough, because whatever they were, they knew I had seen them. I shivered.

"ARE you sure you saw what you think you saw?" It wasn't that Mr. Macabre, the owner, didn't believe me, it was that he was scared.

I shook my head. "No...I don't know."

"She's sure." Pin had been there, both times. He knew something had been wrong and most of all he trusted me.

The entire carnival was there, from Pin to Momma Mae, to the twins. We were family and we made decisions together as a unit. Was it time to pick up stakes and leave or time for more drastic measures. Carnies do what they must.

"What are they, Stormy?"

How could I know the answer to that? I barely even knew if I was seeing what I thought I saw. "I...I don't know for sure. But I think they need our pain. Like they feed from it or something. Nothing else makes sense." I think hard trying to make sense of everything I had seen and experienced from those things. "Maybe they're what's wrong with people, ya know? I mean, you hear about all of the evil things that we do to each other. Maybe it's not us...maybe it's them."

"We're bad because there are monsters inside us?" Pin shook his head. "Naw, they feed from us because we're bad. Not the other way around."

Momma Mae stood up and looked around the room. She had presence and everyone respected her. "They know Stormy can see them. They tried to attack her once. Are we gonna let them do it again? Are we going to let them hurt the children? Are we those kinds of people?"

"So, what do we do?" One of the younger carnies asked from the back of the tent.

Mr. Macabre sighed, stood to his feet. "We're going to do

what we do best. We're gonna have a show. A show to end all shows."

IT WAS DECIDED. There would be one final hurrah for the Mysterious Macabre. It would be a grand finale of the great show, with all the acts performing to a spectacular climax of the Gods. Or something like that. We needed to pump it up to be huge, gigantic, and colossal. Like that damned car had been. And we wanted just as many people to show up.

Annabel, Margie, and I had printed up some flyers for the great show:

GRAND FINALE
OF THE
MYSTERIOUS MACABRE!
BE THE HUMAN; BE THE MONSTER
BE THE SMALL; BE THE TALL
COME ONE; COME ALL
SEE THE
DEATH OF THE
MYSTERIOUS MACABRE!

I thought it was a bit melodramatic, but it would get the job done. We wanted those things to be intrigued by the promise of death and danger. Hell, I didn't even know what "The death of the Mysterious Macabre" meant. It was just designed to get as many of those things to fill the seats as possible.

It worked.

THE HEADLIGHTS POURED through the tree line, creating a striped outline of light through the forest wall. We watched as a caravan of cars came up the hidden road that lead to the park. At the last minute, Pin called out to everyone, "K, all, take your places. And good luck." Everyone scattered, each running their separate ways. I stayed for a moment with Pin. He looked at me, smiled and kissed my forehead on the good side. Then he shooed me off.

I hid from sight as the cars pulled up to the gate. They stopped in front of Pin, the headlights casting him in a brilliant hue.

Pin spoke, and he actually sounded excited, "Hello all. Welcome to the final show of the Mysterious Macabre." Then he opened the gate to let the devil in.

I WASN'T privy to everything that happened that night. A lot of the time I have to use my imagination, but a lot of things I witnessed firsthand, myself. I saw things that night that I can't seem to get out of my head. Other things I knew would happened, because we'd planned it that way. Of course even the best laid plans never work out the way you expect, and this night was no different.

It went down something like this:

They filled into the tent, anxious to see the show. All of them were monsters. Searching the crowd, from behind stage, I didn't see a single human face. The tent was huge, but it wasn't big enough to hold all of those things. At last count we had sat out two hundred and seventy-five chairs. They were standing, lining the walls and crowded toward the back in groups of ten or more. At least three hundred monsters were in our mist. At best count we were a hundred and forty. Three to one.

June took the stage first. Her act was mellow, and she was more soft-spoken than usual. I think it was because she was scared. But she didn't really seem afraid, just sullen. That was part of her act. She spoke to the dead and read people's auras.

The crowd just stared, but for some reason they were entranced with June. They couldn't take their eyes off her. I think it was because of the sadness inside her. I think depression and pain drove those things, they lived for it. And they felt it in June. Her son had died many years before from pneumonia.

Outside, Pin and I made our way around each of the cars, flattening the tires. We didn't stop with one, we punctured all four of them. I had a large hunting knife that Pin had given me, and Pin used a carving knife from Momma Mae's kitchen. It wasn't easy trying to get that knife inside that thick rubber, and it took me several tries before I got it in the first one.

INSIDE THE TENT, June was just finishing up her story, as all eyes were on her. She had been crying. Though she had tried hard not to, it had happened anyway. She hadn't wanted to give those things the satisfaction, but she said that it had all been for the group. Of course, that didn't make her feel better. She ended, asking for anyone from the audience to come forward for a reading.

None of the monsters came up. We had expected this. If you fed from something, would you put yourself out there as food? Nope, them either. We had placed a few people in the crowd, just for this purpose. Tammy came forward. Her mother had died the year before, and it had destroyed Tammy.

The things ate it up.

AFTER WE WERE DONE with the tires, we headed back inside, I stood in the rear, watching the crowd as I always had. The tents had precut holes so that the carnies could see out into the audience, but they couldn't see back to us. We use it to check out the marks, to make sure that certain shows were crowd pleasing. If there were no smiling faces, or if no one cried or laughed, then we would consider revising the show. That was the nature of the business. It was a great tool, and boy did it come in handy that night.

As I watched, I saw one of those things give a sign to several others, and they quickly got up from their seats and left the tent. I wondered what they were up to. I pointed it out to Pin who said that he'd seen it too. We ducked, and rolled under the tent, back out into the night.

It was a hell of a lot better inside the tent. Because in there as least you could tell yourself that everything would be okay, that we would get through things just fine. But out there, in the night, with the moon shining like a spotlight, it was harder to lie to yourself.

Outside, Pin and I peeked around the corner of the tent, trying to see where they were going and what they were up too. I counted a lot of them, maybe forty. I knew they were definitely up to something. Maybe they were trying to catch us off guard, get us before we tried to get to them.

The monsters moved off in different directions, each searching the wooded area around the park. One headed toward the back, toward me and Pin. In the distance, Annabel and Margie lit up the night with their melody and I thought for sure I would just lay in the grass and die, right there. The man moved closer, and Pin nudged me to move back. I walked backward, looking back to make sure that I wasn't gonna walk into anything. Just as I looked up, another one rounded the corner, and was walking along the tree line. He hadn't seen us yet, but as soon as he turned, he would. I touched Pin to make him aware, and then I pointed to the tent again. Maybe we could get back under there before either of them saw us. I leaned down, and lifted up the curtain, as I did, Pin grabbed me. The thing had spotted us.

He smiled, turned in our direction. I froze. Pin stepped

forward, his knife hid behind him, getting ready to strike. Just as he did, another monster grabbed him from the back, and pinned his arms to his sides.

Pin struggled with the thing, and it lifted him off the ground and dropped him, hard. He fell, landing on his ankle, as it twisted beneath him. He crashed to the grass, holding it.

Suddenly, two soft, missile-like sounds sliced through the air, and the thing above Pin, bounced twice and then fell to the ground. Before the other could react, another shot hit him in the back of his head, and blood sprayed from a hole in the center of his forehead. Many more shots rang out, and I knew more monsters were falling under fire. I heard a body or two fall to the ground, but after that, it was silent. From inside, Annabel and Margie sang the last note, and everyone clapped. I mean everyone, even those things. Hatred at its fullest. We listened to the twins, and enjoyed them despite the pain; they listened enjoying *because* of the pain.

I guessed because of the applause that no one had heard. One of the young carnies, Sammy, ran out of the tree line, all but screaming, "We got 'em. We got 'em!"

His father shushed him, covering his mouth. But they were still clapping inside and I knew they hadn't heard. Mac and Little John followed and began dragging the bodies back into the woods. Sammy grabbed one leg, the big gun hanging from his tiny shoulder, and his father grabbed the other, taking away the monster.

We went back inside, and left the others to their dead. I helped Pin walk, him leaning on me. He was limping pretty bad, the pain showing on his face. I took a look at it once we got inside, and it was beginning to swell and bruise. I was worried, but he said he'd be fine. I grabbed a cloth, ripped it into smaller pieces and wrapped it around and around his foot, pulling it as tight as possible. He winced a bit, but told me to try to make it even tighter. He said it would keep the swelling down.

The monsters seemed not to even notice their missing

comrades as Annabel and Margie left the stage. Pin was up next, and he gave me a wink before he climbed on stage.

He pushed on a large spinning wheel with him, and his back was to me, but I knew what he was doing. Pin was a sword swallower and sometimes he sharpened his swords on stage for dramatic effect. He never used the swords he'd sharpened, he always switched them first. And this would be no different.

He sharpened them, showing the gleaming blade to the crowd. Pin said it was always uncomfortable when he put those 50-inch swords in his throat. Pin did his sleight-of-hand thing, switching the dull blade for the sharp one, and proceeded to stuff it down his neck and into his stomach, teasing his rib cage.

Just as Pin finished his show, several Fire Eaters and Fire Breathers ran on the stage. They twirled the doubled edge baton, and flipped across the stage, landing on the other's back. There were six twirlers. Many of them had been with the carnival for several years. There was Morgan, Sondra, Patina, Donald, Swan, and Snap. Mr. M always called him that because he said he was "quick as a snap." It was true, he'd run across the stage, and you'd barely even see him move. Each of the team stopped, spaced the length of the stage, and stared into the audience, lit the batons, and pitched them into the air. They flipped upside down standing on their hands; as they did so, and the lit torches fell, each person caught them with their foot, and twirled the wand around. The fire lit up the room, creating a blurry haze as eyes focused on the blaze.

Seconds later, they pitched them into the waiting crowd.

Before the show started, Mac and Little John had saturated the covered floor, and the bottoms of the chairs with Benzene. We hadn't used gasoline because it would smell, but we had plenty of Benzene on hand for the rides.

The tent lit up like an inferno. Fire and smoke filled the small hut so quickly, I gagged on the fumes. Monsters were running around screaming like wild men. Except they weren't men, they weren't even a known species. The cries weren't even human. I can't explain it, but it was the cry of a great thing. Kinda like a wild boar and a giant man all mixed up in one.

Mr. Macabre ran back stage and handed me a small gun. "Can you use it?" I nodded. "Good."

I ran to the tent, and peeked through the hole outside. It had cleared at bit, and I saw a complete mess on the other side. And now for the first time, as gunfire rang in the darkness, I allowed myself to believe that we would die here, alone, in Sun, without anyone to morn us. In fact, I figured that no one would probably ever find our bodies. Here, in this modest little park, in the middle of nowhere, we would remain forever.

I thought we would die, but not because things were going bad, but because they weren't going as bad as I thought they would. Everyone knew as soon as you thought you had something licked, that's when the bad things happened.

I saw Pin through the peek hole. He was fighting a man who looked as if he could have gone a round with Arnold Schwarzenegger. The thing glared at him as if he could sense his fear and was excited by it. But Pin had the best of him. He had sharpened his swords on that stage that night for a reason, and this was it. The man's blade sliced into the monster's flesh with precision, and the huge thing fell to the ground, holding the wound in his throat.

Just watching him use those things was a wonder. He darted out into the crowd and began slashing them one by one. Blood splashing his face and clothes, but he didn't seem to care. Pin was decapitating, disemboweling, stomping on his victims, with the cunning of a warrior. His blade twirled and sliced through the air faster than I would have thought humanly possible.

Beside him, other carnies, Mac and Little John, had come in at the sound of the commotion, and had also killed a substantial number of those things; the bloody corpses lay dead at their feet. These men, these people I had lived with all my life, seemed to be reveling in the fight, as though they enjoyed it.

And though I wouldn't admit it, I actually enjoyed it, too. I liked the idea of hurting these things. After all, hadn't they been hurting people all this time?

But the monsters were holding their own, I realized as I saw Doc Mayor's body lying dead on the floor. I gasped and held my mouth so that a scream wouldn't escape. I had known him all my life. If I had had a father, I would have wished it were him. He had a bullet hole in his stomach, and blood seeped from his half-opened mouth. His eyes were wide, and I would have sworn he was staring at me, accusingly. He thought the same thing I did: it was all my fault.

I should be out there, helping. I didn't know a lot about fighting, but I knew a lot about survival and that would be enough to get me through. If not, then I would die along with my friends out there. I ran through the curtain, and I heard Pin calling my name behind me. But I didn't stop, I ran head first into the room.

It was chaos in there. A shot rang over my head and went through the wall of the tent behind me. Suddenly someone shouted, "Look out, Stormy!" I turned to see one of the things aim at me and shoot. I jumped, but it was only from fear. His gun clicked, as he was out of ammo. I slowly took aim at him, and watched as he snarled and started straight for me. I shot it, and it fell to my feet, coughing.

I made my way over to the Doc and cradled his head in my lap. I thought about everything that had happened, what I had done, as I began to choke on smoke. Suddenly, I couldn't breathe, and my eyes would not focus anymore. I was losing consciousness.

I had one thought: *maybe, if I was lucky, I would wake up dead.*

I WOKE up in the back of the Winnebago. It bounced as it sped away from town. Our convoy of cars, trucks, and Winnebagos left Sun at midnight on Tuesday morning. But no one was out to see it. The normal people would come out later that morning to find a mess. They wouldn't know it, but their lives had been spared. Even if there were more of those things running around in that city, it would take them a long time to get back to where they were. And if they did...well, that would be someone else's problem.

Sometimes I wonder if I made it all up—all of it. Have you thought about it? I have. I mean, who sees monsters inside people and then destroys a whole town? That isn't normal. Or what if that touch from that woman triggered some kind of seizure or something, making me see things that weren't there. I was the catalyst. Then we destroyed a town.

Perhaps I have infected the carnival, making us all monsters.

PICKMAN'S DAUGHTER

J. C. KOCH

Harriet Pickman had never really felt like the other Changelings. For one thing, she still looked completely human. For another, her father visited her regularly. Well, as regularly as a ghoul in service to the Elder Gods could, which was still more often than any of the other Changelings at the Asylum could claim.

The Asylum was where Harriet had lived her entire life, just like the rest of the Changelings. Some of them had been at the Asylum for hundreds of years, a few even thousands—going out, doing the Elder Gods' work, then returning to their home and their companions with stories to tell of great battles fought and humans slain or enslaved.

All the Changelings were trained in the Mythos and all had the *Necronomicon* memorized. They were all ready to go out and do the good work of the Elder Gods. They were a well-trained group of zealots.

All except Harriet.

Oh, she was keen to be of service, she supposed. But really, it was hard to get excited about the Great Plan. Mostly because it sounded really boring and a long way off, and Harriet figured there had to be more interesting things to do on the human plane of existence than try to wake up Cthulhu and the rest of the Elder Gods to come have a human buffet.

Her father had been an artist of some repute before her mother had died in childbirth. The story was always told in a way that sounded like those running the Asylum had saved Harriet from dying along with her mother, but she suspected they'd had a hand in her mother's demise. After all, it was their way and she saw no reason why she or her father would have rated special treatment in this case.

But her father had come with her to the Realm and, because his art had lauded those in the Realm and was considered to be in service to the Elder Gods, he'd made a bargain: he'd given himself to the Elder Gods, but Harriet had to remain fully human, allowed to grow up and come of age, then be allowed to make her own decisions about whether or not she'd stay with those in the Realm or return to Earth.

This was agreed to because, as Old Y'Laack who ran the Asylum liked to say, "Per the Catholics, have a child until it's three and it's yours for life. And we have our children for far longer than that."

Of course, hearing this all her life had made Harriet rather determined to not acquiesce. At least, not without good reason.

However, Harriet wasn't stupid. She didn't share any of her rebellious thoughts aloud. No, on paper and in word and, so far, deed, she was a model Changeling; a credit to the Asylum's teachings and set to take her place in the Realm as soon as she came of age and was assigned to her rank and file.

Which, for Harriet, was tomorrow.

She was sixteen in human years. But time in the Realm moved far more slowly than on the human plane. She'd been born almost a hundred years ago by Earth's standards. And both birth dates, so to speak, had happened on the same day last week.

Her father had come to help her celebrate and given her a lovely gift—an ornate golden necklace with a large locket as its pendant. The locket held six pictures, rather than the usual two, and Harriet was touched by her father's thoughtfulness. He truly was a wonderful parent and Harriet felt lucky to have him. She vowed to never take the necklace off, which pleased her father greatly.

But now it was time for her to take her place and go out to do the Realm's Work.

PHOENIX, Arizona didn't have much of an underground, but that hadn't stopped the Realm from expanding there—back alleys, slums, and dark deserts could be just as harrowing as any subway or ancient sewer system. But it did take a lot more work to convert here, so it was definitely going to be a challenge.

It was, frankly, an honor to have been given any post in the American Southwest. Harriet did her best to feel honored. But there was so much sunlight and sand and concrete that at least part of her wondered if someone had read her less than faithful thoughts over the years and was punishing her with this assignment.

Most newly graduated weren't sent out alone, and Harriet was no exception. She was happy with her senior partner, though, and hoped this indicated that her less than devout attitude hadn't been spotted. Bevozoar was a hulking brute, with bloodshot and almost totally red eyes in a dog-like face with a flat nose, pointed ears, bony claws, scales over most of his body, and half-hooved feet. Also, he was really familiar. "Did my father paint you, a long time ago?"

Bevozoar smiled. "He did. I'm pleased you recognized me from that—it was a long time ago when I modeled for him."

"What are you doing out here? I thought you were assigned to Boston."

"I was, then. As the Realm has expanded, we who are more

experienced have moved to help those with less experience work in the more difficult areas." He smiled, showing all his sharp, pointed teeth. "And your father asked me to watch out for you, as a favor. How could I say no?"

Harriet laughed. "I'm glad. So, what are we going to do first?"

Bevozoar shrugged. "We're going to tour this city, our way. Then you're going to enroll in high school as a foreign exchange student. Truth in advertising and all that."

"Excuse me? I've been schooled."

"True enough. But you'll be surprised at how easy it is to really do the Elder Gods' work in that situation. You'll like the Astells—they're a Faithful Family who take in Changelings regularly, so we don't have to hide what we are with them, they know the proper forms of worship, and, best of all, they're going to leave us mostly alone."

"You'll be with me there?"

Bevozoar nodded, then shifted into a large, vicious-looking dog. "Call me Fido."

"Seriously?"

"It's easy to remember."

"It's trite."

He barked a laugh. "What would you prefer?"

"Bevo? Zoar?"

"I'll take Bevo."

"Good boy."

He snorted. "Remember who's training whom."

Bevozoar was able to transport them as if they were the wind, meaning it was easy to tour the city and its surroundings.

Phoenix didn't impress her much. It was fine—young, as cities went, crowded enough, loaded with cemeteries—but its streets rarely had alleys, twists, turns, or dead ends, which were wonderful for hunting. And the cemeteries here just weren't old enough to have a strong presence from the Realm.

There were a lot of old people scattered all over. Bevozoar showed her their enclaves. "Leave them alone. Most of them are too set to convert, and there's better eating elsewhere."

Harriet realized something was missing—the majority of these elderly were alone, no younger humans visiting them, asking for their advice, caring for them. "They don't revere their elders here?"

"They do very little here that you'll recognize from the Realm."

There was also a large homeless population, meaning Bevozoar had no issues feeding, which he had to do a lot.

Because she was fully human still, Harriet didn't indulge in eating humans, other than for holidays and special celebrations. Besides, she was picky about what she ate. They didn't eat unclean things in the Realm, and she saw no reason to start now.

"It seems unkind to take the ones who are so...helpless," she said, more to herself than Bevozoar.

He burped. "It's less unkind than letting them live in this squalor, to be alone with the thoughts the Elder Gods have put into their minds that they can't articulate. For them to be alone and unloved, uncared for. I eat them, their souls go to the Great Gods, May They Sleep Well and Dream of Horrors. It's a quick death, too." Bevozoar always bit the heads off first.

"Not everyone is as kind as you."

He shrugged and turned back into a dog. "No humans are, that's true."

BECAUSE SHE'D BEEN a good student at the Asylum, Harriet was prepared for the weird clothing, so even though she'd never had to wear a tight tank top, a mini-skirt, or high heels before

—other than in practice sessions—she did what she had to do, because that was what the Asylum had trained her for.

"You look perfect," Mother Astell said proudly. "The boys won't be able to take their eyes off you."

"Or the girls, if they're of that persuasion," Father Astell added.

"Great," Harriet said. "Is that how you all do conversions here? Via sexual attraction?"

They both shrugged. "Whatever works," Mother Astell said.

Father Astell drove her to school, Bevozoar in the back seat, panting up a storm. "Have a good day and do the Elder Gods' work."

"Will do," Harriet said as she patted Bevozoar's head and got out of the car.

She'd been trained in observation, so she noted that all the other kids were watching her. She stood up straight, tossed her hair back, and headed for the main entrance. She remembered to turn around and wave to Father Astell, who was still there, car at the curb, likely waiting for her to get inside.

"Parents are so lame, aren't they?" a girl said to her as she turned around. The girl looked about Harriet's age, and had the expression and attitude she'd learned to identify—Mean Girl. Perfect.

Harriet shrugged. "They're my host family. I think that's why they worry."

The girl's eyes lit up. "You're our new exchange student?" Harriet nodded. "Fab. I'm Marcella." She linked her arm through Harriet's. "What's your name?"

"Harriet."

Marcella raised her eyebrow. "Great. Harry, I'm going to introduce you around."

Humans enjoyed nicknames, so Harriet didn't argue with the nickname assignment. It indicated that Marcella wanted to be friends, or at least make everyone else think they were friends.

True to her word, Marcella introduced her to what felt like a quarter of the school. Marcella pointedly avoided the other three-quarters of the students, meaning Harriet was only meeting the "cool kids."

The first bell rang, and they parted for separate classes, Marcella promising to find her at lunch.

Harriet was enrolled in all Honors classes. She already spoke fifty Earth languages and had passed what humans would consider college level courses before she was ten. Her teachers were fine, but most weren't enthused about their work like those at the Asylum. Most seemed to have to spend more time making the students stop being disruptive and cruel to each other more than anything else.

All her classes were awful, but the horrors of American History were the stuff of legend. The Asylum prided itself on telling the whole truth about history, but the history teacher was blithely telling lies, half-truths, and whitewashed versions of events. Harriet managed to not start shouting corrections, but only by doodling in her notebook.

Lunch was better. Marcella found her, and she ate with a group of cheerleaders, who all insisted that Harriet try out for the squad. They were joined by some boys who were identified as football players. Per all her teachings, this made the boys prime meat. Harriet honestly couldn't see why, but she'd been faking interest all day anyway, so continued to do so now. But at least the lies these kids were telling her and each other weren't about huge events that had shaped their world.

Lunch over far too soon, it was time for afternoon classes, which were, unsurprisingly, as bad as the morning ones had been. But her Art Appreciation class was an insult—her father's works weren't even mentioned, let alone shown. When she asked about them, the teacher's reaction was completely unexpected.

"That man was insane and a menace," Mr. Roberts said angrily. "He murdered his pregnant wife and disappeared a hundred years ago. No decent museum would ever show his works, and even the museums that focus on the macabre would hesitate and likely choose a less infamous artist." He looked at his desk, where he had his attendance roster. "Are you a relative of some kind?"

The teachings had been quite clear—never tell humans the truth. "No, it's just that we have the same name, so I've looked up his art."

Mr. Roberts looked up at her with narrowed eyes. "I see. What did you think of it?"

Frankly, Harriet thought her father was an amazing artist and that he'd captured those from the Realm perfectly, as if his paintings had been photographs. But, she merely shrugged. "They were okay, if you like that sort of thing."

Mr. Roberts sniffed. "Let's go back to real artists now." He started blathering on about Michelangelo, and Harriet stopped listening.

"Roberts is an asshole," the boy behind her, whose name she was pretty sure was Joey, whispered. "He doesn't like anything *avante garde*."

This was, so far, the smartest thing any human had said to her, and Harriet was somewhat impressed. Marcella hadn't introduced her to Joey, meaning he wasn't a cool kid.

She looked behind her. Nope, he wasn't likely to be an athlete. He looked like what she'd been told a nerd, geek, or brain looked like—glasses with intelligent eyes behind them, uncool haircut, not dressed as well as the cool kids, lacking a lot of self-confidence, probably routinely beaten up by the bigger boys and dismissed by most of the girls.

"Where I come from, we embrace the *avante garde*."

He smiled. "Where you come from must be so cool."

"IF you don't mind," Mr. Roberts said, and Harriet turned around. "Thank you. Let's get back to paying attention. You two can flirt later."

This earned some titters from the class, and disparaging

snorts from the few cool kids in here, which confirmed Harriet's suspicions about Joey.

At the end of the day and per Marcella's urgings, Harriet went with her to cheerleading practice. The coach was convinced to let Harriet give it a try. Since the training at the Asylum ensured that all graduates were physically fit to the level of their race, Harriet was what humans would consider an Olympic athlete.

She did the routine as described once and performed it perfectly on the first try. The coach managed to close her mouth, then nodded enthusiastically. "You're on the squad, Harry."

The other girls cheered. It was nice. Though Harriet could pick up that they were all jealous, even Marcella. Which seemed odd since Marcella had been the one to drag Harriet to this in the first place. But the reactions weren't unexpected. Humans were identified in the Realm as being small-minded and jealous at all times.

A uniform was produced, with a skirt even shorter than the one Harriet was wearing, and a tank top tighter than the one she had on. As expected, cheerleading was going to be athletic and possibly even fun, but it was for the benefit of those watching, so they could look at the nubile girls and think what Harriet was pretty sure were going to be impure thoughts.

Now, the thing about the Elder Gods was that their idea of impure thoughts differed greatly from what humans considered impure. Sex was just something that needed to be done to create more of whatever the Elder Gods would need—servants, food, slaves, fodder. Impure thoughts were those that strayed from serving the Elder Gods. Harriet had had many impure thoughts over the years.

But human impure thoughts had been explained. Certain Changelings, of which Harriet was one, possessed great charisma. Those with it were expected to lure humans to the Elder Gods via whatever means necessary, including sex if that's what seemed likely to work best. However, that was up to the Changeling themselves. If you didn't want to have sex, then you didn't, plain and simple.

She noted several of the football players watching and Harriet was fairly sure they were watching her. Well, this was good, because that meant things were truly going according to plan. Maybe she'd actually like being a missionary.

Practice ended and Mother Astell was there to pick her up. Harriet had been given a cell phone, of course, but she didn't need to use it to reach the Astells. The Faithful assigned to a Changeling always knew when that Changeling needed them. Besides, Bevozoar was in the car.

"First day go well?" Mother Astell asked while Bevozoar put his head out the window and barked at anyone who was nearby.

"I made friends with the top Mean Girl, am on the cheerleading squad, had several boys thinking impure thoughts, made what might be a friend of an uncool kid, and I despise my Art History teacher and I believe he feels the same way about me."

"An excellent start! After dinner, we'll celebrate with ice cream."

THE WEEK WENT BY. Classes remained boring, Mr. Roberts got nastier toward her daily, boys were starting to spend a lot of time talking to her, cheerleading was indeed fun, and she'd spent some time getting to know Joey. Friday night was given to football and Harriet got to cheer for real. Her school won, which made everyone happy for a brief period of time.

As with the rest of her human experience, football wasn't all that exciting and winning seemed pointless, but she'd faked it and hugged several of the players, which seemed like the right thing to do.

She'd been taught that humans liked things that helped them not to think, and this had proven true so far, with football being only the current example. She'd been rather proud that the games created by the Realm—*Angry Birds*, *Candy Crush*, *Bejeweled*, and all those stupid building games—were hugely popular with everyone she ran across. Even Joey played them.

Saturday was spent in reverence for the Elder Gods. In honor of her first Reverence Day with them, the Astells provided a sacrifice, which Harriet found touching, since it meant they'd had to rob a grave. Mother Astell's corpse stew was quite good, and Harriet's praise for it seemed to truly make her happy.

Sundays were spent going to as many church services as everyone could fit in—lots, since the Astells were a large family and they coordinated with other Faithful in order to ensure that as many services as possible were covered each week. Everyone took notes about who at these various services seemed uninterested in being there. After the third service she attended, Harriet started noting who seemed reverent and excited to be there, because it was a much shorter list and she believed in saving time where she could.

THE NEXT SEVERAL weeks went on in this same fashion. It was always a relief to get back to school on Mondays, after all those churches loaded with people who didn't really want to be there.

At first, Harriet had felt a kinship with them—she still wasn't sure if she wanted to do all she could do for the Elder Gods, after all. But after a while, she began to pay attention to what these people did after church and all through the week.

Bevozoar enjoyed this, since it got them both out of the house, and he got to lurk in a large number of houses and scare the pets, which made him incredibly happy. He even turned a few of the dogs and cats towards the Elder Gods, so his time wasn't wasted.

Harriet felt like hers was, though, even though she was becoming excellent at entering homes, lurking in them, and leaving undetected. But almost none of the people who went to these churches followed the teachings they professed to care about.

Even those she could sort of call friends were like this. Even Joey. She knew—she'd attended all their churches and lurked in all their houses.

"They're all hypocrites?" she asked Bevozoar while they took a break and hung out in an alley behind a popular bar. Bevozoar enjoyed terrifying the various drunks and it smelled like home to Harriet. Plus, it was a safe place for her to practice shifting, which she so far had not mastered. Bevozoar thought she might be too human to manage it, which was more disappointing to her than she'd have thought it would be a month ago.

"Many. Not all. Look at it this way—it's less difficult a decision to eat a hypocrite." He cocked his head at her. "You're still human but, even if you never learn to shift, you're not like them. Remember that."

HARRIET WAS at her locker with Marcella and some of the other cheerleaders. The others were talking about boys while Harriet considered whether it would be worth it to request some imps to hide in various lockers to perform destruction and leave sigils that would drive those who viewed them mad, or if anyone would even notice if they did, when Joey came up to her.

"Excuse me, Harry, I was wondering if I could talk to you. Privately. For a minute."

"Sure."

Joey led her around the corner. He seemed embarrassed. He looked down and shuffled his feet. "Uh...I wanted to...well, Homecoming is coming..."

"Yes?" The cheerleaders had explained the significance of Homecoming. The game wasn't an issue. The dance the next day, however, was, since it fell on a Low Holy Day that was one where all the Faithful were expected to remain inside and perform sacrifices to the Elder Gods.

"I was wondering if you'd go to the Homecoming dance with me," Joey blurted out. He looked hopeful and expectant and cute.

"Oh. Oh! Well...I'd like to..." Joey's expression turned to happy and triumphant, "...but I can't," she finished sadly.

Joey's expression went dark. "Oh. Going with a football player, I guess?"

"Actually, no."

"Oh, you're like that and going with one of the other girls."

"No again. It's because—"

"Because you're not actually nice," Joey snarled. "You're really a bitch and you've been leading me on."

"Excuse me? I thought we were friends. And you haven't let me finish—"

"Oh, I don't need you to finish. I know all about the 'friend zone' thing. Figures." Joey put his face near hers and he didn't look cute at all anymore. "You'll be sorry," he hissed. "I'll show you what it means to toy with my affections." With that, he spun on his heel and ran away.

"Uh, lunatic much?" Marcella said from behind her.

"You heard?"

"Couldn't miss it. Wouldn't have missed it anyway, but couldn't because Mister Entitled to a Hot Chick there wasn't really quiet." Marcella put her arm around Harriet's shoulders. "Harry, there's reasons I've tried to keep you away from the unwashed masses. Joey is Exhibit A."

"I don't understand how he went from being my friend to being my enemy in what seems like a second."

Marcella sighed. "That's just how some people are."

THE LOW SACRAMENTS WERE OVER, and the family was relaxing. Father Astell turned on the TV for the first time all day. So they got to hear the breaking news report for the first time. Then they heard it again, checked the other channels, just to be sure, turned off the TV, and looked at each other.

"You know it's Joey, right?" Harriet asked.

They others nodded. "He's not one of us," Bevozoar said. "I confirmed that when you first met him."

"That means he's not doing the Elder Gods' work," Father Astell added.

"What will you do about it?" Mother Astell asked.

Harriet didn't answer. Instead, she looked at the locket her father had given her. The first frames held a picture of her mother and father and one of her father holding Harriet as a baby.

Unfolding the locket revealed four more frames. The first of these held a drawing of a woman being hanged for being a witch. This was her five-times-great-grandmother, who'd been hanged by Cotton Mather himself. The drawing was small, but even so, her father had captured the disdain and lack of fear she knew her greats-grandmother had felt.

The second held a miniature of her father's most famous painting, "Ghoul Feeding." He'd really captured Louis well—even in miniature you could tell who this was and how much he was enjoying his meal—and it was no wonder this was her father's most well-known work.

The third was a sketch her father had done for her when she'd had a rough patch—Cthulhu sleeping. As always, just looking at it calmed her. The Elder Gods might have a boring plan, but at least they had a plan. The Faithful knew and believed in it. Until Great Cthulhu awoke, that plan was in the hands of those in the Realm, to carry out as they saw fit.

The last frame held a card that said *Remember whose daughter you are.*

Harriet closed the locket and looked at Bevozoar. "I know what I have to do."

HARRIET AND BEVOZOAR flew like the wind to the high school. They landed inside the gym, in the hallway near the bathrooms. "Dog or the real me?" he asked.

"Dog. For now. You'll know when I want the real you."

They walked slowly, taking everything in. The gym had been decorated for the dance—Harriet had helped do that, along with the rest of the squad, even though she wasn't attending. But the decorations were mostly down.

Liquids of various kinds were spilled all over the floor and on the walls. A small fire had started near the equipment room. It would grow bigger if it wasn't put out. But that wasn't what Harriet was here for.

As the news reports had said, there was a gunman with hostages. Several people, kids and teachers, were already dead, Mr. Roberts among them. But the cheerleaders were still alive—up on the stage, being screamed at and threatened by Joey.

"Where is she?" he shrieked. "Why isn't she here?"

"It's a religious holiday for my kind," Harriet replied as Joey spun around, waving a large semiautomatic rifle.

He aimed the gun at her. "I told you you'd be sorry!" He turned the gun towards Bevozoar. "But your stupid dog dies first!"

Bevozoar shifted into his true self. Joey screamed and shot at him. He used the whole magazine. Bevozoar waited until the smoke cleared. Then he yawned, reached out, and grabbed Joey. "What do you want to do with this?"

She shrugged. "Whatever you want."

Bevozoar shrugged and bit Joey's head off.

Everyone went into more of a panic. The screaming was incredible, and Harriet was pretty sure she was going to get a headache from it. "We just saved you," she said, though no one heard her since she wasn't shouting.

She could read their minds now, their panic was so strong. They hated Bevozoar for what he looked like. But they hated her for what had happened. They all, every one of them, male and female, blamed her for what Joey had done. All of them wished that she'd been here at the start, so Joey could have killed her right away and left the rest of them alone. They hated her, for not being there, for not being dead, for bringing a terrifying monster with her.

For not being afraid.

She felt it now. The fervor that she'd never felt before. The realization that Joey was typical—that all of them were typical —that these people were so far beneath her kind that they could never be anything other than a buffet for the Elder Gods.

The realization, the fervor, gave her power. She felt herself shifting. She went large, her head brushed the ceiling and her shoulders brushed the walls. Her fingers became tentacles, as strong as steel but supple and under her control.

She used those tentacles to rip the floor up and the ground open. It only took her moments. She kept on digging, until she found what she was looking for—the pathway to the Realm.

Harriet cleared the path down, then shoved everyone in. She reached out and grabbed the policemen and firemen, the reporters and passersby, parents and family members who'd come, anyone and anything within the school's grounds.

Then she pulled it all—the people, the buildings, the cars —into the Realm. Her offering to the Elder Gods. The proof of whose daughter she was.

Bevozoar waited until she shifted back into herself. They stared into the chasm for a few moments, until they saw their brethren come and take the offering. Then he took her back to the Astells' home. The news reports now said that a terrible earthquake or pipe explosion or something like that had taken the high school down into the depths.

"Well done," Father Astell said proudly. "No other Changeling has ever done such work, let alone so quickly."

"And with no trace," Mother Astell added. "You are amazing."

"My father was an artist, and so am I." She turned to Bevozoar. "Where do we go next?"

He smiled widely. "Wherever you want, Pickman's Daughter. Wherever you want to cleanse next, we'll go."

Harriet smiled slowly. "Let's go everywhere."

US AND OURS

PREMEE MOHAMED

"**K**eep driving," Eli whispered.

"I can't. I'll..." *Kill them*, I started to say, then reconsidered. *Run over their legs* was more accurate, but the mental image made me shudder. I let the stolen Honda roll to a stop instead, my foot trembling on the brake. The creatures lined the road on both sides, close enough to tap on our windows. I hoped they didn't. My nerves were worn to a shred. Ahead, in the mist, the highway was down to one lane—tentacles and eyeballs and stalks and claws were creeping from the woods onto the damp asphalt. If we didn't get in gear, they'd block the road entirely.

"They'll move," he said.

"What are you basing that on?"

"Ray, come *on*."

Both our voices were high with adrenaline; I knew that pitch, I knew the smell on my best friend's breath, tart and chemical. I let go of the brake and stared out my window as we crept along, feeling their eyes on us—blank amber spheres, like cloudy glass, above bodies wildly segmented and twisted. Like someone had blown a house centipede up thirty feet tall and glued on a seafood buffet. The throbbing reddish-purple strips they'd laid across the road didn't flinch as we crossed them. I held my breath, waiting for retaliation.

Something slithered slowly over the roof, making slime trickle down the windshield. I hit the gas, getting up to ten – twenty – thirty-five. The shocks squeaked each time we rolled over one of the tentacles. But the monsters stayed where they were, even while the rearview mirror showed our tracks as clearly as if we'd driven over Play-Doh, black on the glistening red flesh.

"Okay," Eli gasped, and pulled up Maps on his phone, his nails jittering on the screen. "It's about a hundred miles west, and then right onto the Highway 63 ramp."

I nodded as if I'd ever driven a hundred miles before, or stolen a car, or even had my license. But I figured the usual rules didn't apply, if it was the end of the world. Even if it was just the end of the world here.

DECIDING to leave had been easy. Leaving had been hard.

It was especially hard seeing all the other houses on their empty streets, with monsters pawing stupidly at the windows and doors. Some people had retreated inside. Others had built bonfires on the main roads and were dancing around them, crying out words with too many consonants to be understood. Practically no one was trying to get out of town except us. And no one, it immediately became clear, was coming to help us— not the coast guard, not the army. Someone had put up video on YouTube and gotten five hundred comments about how fake the CGI looked.

In the night we'd heard gunshots, the roar of old shotguns and even muskets, finally the far-away booms of dynamite bought or stolen from Dewey's hardware store. That stopped us short for a minute, climbing out of Eli's basement window; should we go back? Fight?

But after we stole the Accord and got moving, fighting lost its appeal. Bodies littered the streets and lawns, some still grasped by creatures utterly untouched by human weapons. The dancing fire people stepped smoothly over unclaimed corpses, not covering them or moving them out of the way.

"Good riddance," I announced as we rolled past the school, but not too loud, in case the creatures zeroed in on us.

They were nothing like the old gods of this place, those of the hill and the green. You always knew where you stood with our local gods. Leave out your offerings—the dish of milk and bread, or oil and sage, or Oreos or a grilled cheese or whatever you had, as long as you left your best. Obey the summons if you got one. No open fires at night—we knew the rule. And sure, they stared in your windows at night a bit, but it was worth it to know that they were trying to protect us. Lost dogs returned with grass crowns. Trees that leapt to catch a falling stone before it crushed a trailer. Rifle muzzles nudged at the last second so a hungry hunter could feed his kids.

Mainly, they seemed to worry about our county in a sort of shotgun approach, and you didn't expect their gaze to fall on you for any particular reason unless you failed to pay proper respects. In which case they'd collapse your septic tank or kill your cow or drop the drive shaft out of your truck or whatever. But the respect they received was the rent we paid to live on their land, and that was the way it had always been—half-feeling them here with us, like the shadow of a blessing never quite received.

It was because of them that we didn't realize that the invasion was happening. The last sets of summons had been very strange—five or six in a sudden burst, and then the people who'd received them returning to town, which was supposed to be impossible. And suddenly the returned spread out and caught others, like one of those TV animations of a nuclear strike: the rings showing so many dead right away, so many with this kind of sickness, so many with that.

Finally, late last night, they called up something so big and old and dangerous that it woke us all from a dead sleep to go stumbling out of our houses to stare up at it. The end of the world, a world-ender. People I'd known all my life bowing at its feet, its head as high as the sky, below that, nothing but twisting tentacles, hairs, slime, bubbles of muscle and hide.

By daylight it was just monsters prowling around, but the big one was gone. And so, we decided, were we.

We drove to my house first, but couldn't convince my dad to leave. "The army'll come get us," he said, "so you just sit your ass down and don't do anything stupid, understand?"

"No one's coming," I yelled. "Nobody knows this is happening! They think it's just a gas leak. If we don't get out, they'll destroy the whole town!" And just like in a movie, something exploded a block away—a walloping crack so big it had to be a gas line going up. Pictures and knick-knacks and beer bottles toppled from every flat surface in the house. In a movie, he would have freaked out and packed a bag. But he wouldn't budge, and I went back to the car, where Eli was on the phone trying to convince his mother to leave the Reddi-Mart and come with us.

He hung up as we hit the town boundary, mumbling about his phone battery. "I think they caught it, the sickness, what-ever it was," he said. "Nobody's listening to us."

"Business as usual."

"No, I mean nobody's listening to us, *and the whole town is full of monsters.*"

THE MONSTERS finally thinned out and I pushed to sixty, still feeling unseen eyes on us. Eli reached over and turned on the headlights, which cut through the mist just enough to give me an extra ten feet of visibility. Far above, there was sun—it was almost noon—but you'd never guess it down here. Cautious

Eli, knowing not to use the hi-beams in the fog. That was just like him. He'd been the one who suggested leaving the valley to find help. "When we come back, we'll be heroes," he said, and I thought: *If. Not when.*

We weren't hero material back home, he was saying. But we could be heroes now. The world wouldn't punish him any more for being skinny and pretty and nervous; his scars might fade; his mother couldn't tell him she hated having him in the house. And I wouldn't have to defend him at school, picking up scars of my own, taunted by the other girls for my 'sissy boyfriend,' neither of which was true. No more shoves in the hallway, glue in my hair, invitations passed out behind my back for sleepovers I'd never hear about the next day.

Thinking about it made my stomach turn. Those girls were exactly the kind that would fall for the cult of the invading god: no richer or smarter or better or stronger than me, but hungry for the power and recognition you couldn't get in this town. Hungry for the kind of thing a god would promise you in exchange for joining up. They wouldn't escape. They'd revel in it. And the valley would burn.

Something huge appeared out of nowhere smack across the highway. Eli yelped as I slammed on the brakes, stopping feet in front of it. Going too fast for the conditions. Yikes. That would have been a ticket, if any cops were out.

The thing was a shiny new trailer, bits of plastic still hanging off the ladders and tank caps. Through the window, hands and faces beckoned us in. I glanced at Eli.

"I don't know," he said uneasily.

"Well, I'm going," I said. "You can guard the car, if you want."

But he trotted after me as I got out. Figured as much. The trailer door opened as we approached, hands reaching out to pull us up the steps. I balked for a second, swatting them away, then saw a half-familiar face.

"Mrs. Boon?"

"Miz!" she snapped. I let myself be pulled in and reached back to grab Eli. The door shut behind us and I felt marginally safer—it was like a perfect little house inside. It stank of cleaning products and new-car fumes.

Brenda Boon lived at the trailer park, Whateley Acres, and taught one of the lower grades at Edenderry Elementary, though she didn't have that teacher-y Mary Poppins look. She was built like me, like a lot of women around here—broad hips, big ribcage, a stubborn chin. Like a good linebacker, not a quarterback. Her dark hair was braided back, like mine, and she was chewing on an unlit cigarette. I supposed she didn't want to get smoke smell into their brand-new, maybe stolen, trailer.

"New recruits!" she said gleefully.

"Um," Eli said.

"Now this here's Miz Codie Arthur, who you know, and that's Pete DeGarmo, and this is Mr. Kabore—"

"Raydeene Willard and Eli Foster," I said, nudging Eli. "Headed out of town too, Miz Boon?"

"Nope," she said, sitting in the plush shotgun seat next to Pete, a skinny young guy with a lot of reddish facial fluff. "This land belongs to us, Ray. Well, rightly it belongs to the old gods —but they're one and the same. The land comes with the gods. And this intruder's gotta be driven off. Which is what we're doing."

"Are we?" I asked, astonished. "Can we?"

She shrugged. "Codie?"

Ms. Arthur smiled. I knew her, too; you'd see her at the farmer's market on Saturdays, selling her vegetables and flowers. No one knew what she did for a living except the market. Around major holidays we all bought her herbs, neatly packaged in ribbon and cut-paper decorations, to put out with our offerings. Only a few weeks ago I'd put one of the bundles into the dish of milk on our front step, watching as the paper picked up the liquid and began to curl protectively around the stems.

She was a tiny, dainty old lady with a gleam in her eye that seemed more intense this close up. "Of course," she said softly. "We need all hands on deck."

Against my better judgement we ditched the car and brought our bags into the trailer, plopping them down just as Pete started it up. We had to drive almost all the way to the *WELCOME TO EDENDERRY!* sign to get enough space to turn the trailer.

Eli and I crowded into the front to stare at our town, cupped in the valley's bowl of dark trees like a pool of glittering water. But the glitter wasn't streetlights. A dozen or more houses were burning, and further north where the trees thinned out, the trailer park was just starting to catch. The fog made the flames fuzzy and soft-looking; almost harmless. Tentacles and claws reared out of the grey here and there, startlingly bright.

"It's not even on the news," I said, jabbing my phone irritatedly at the window. "I keep checking."

"Good," said Ms. Arthur. "It's our business. Don't want folks flying in here and getting zapped by things they don't have a hope of understanding."

"Hope Mom got out of the Reddi-Mart," Eli said tonelessly.

"Really? I hope my Dad's still sitting in the living room."

"Ray."

"They're both fine," Ms. Arthur said; I felt her small hand steal onto my shoulder, smelling faintly of thyme. "Those of the hill and the green are fighting for them."

I didn't know what to say to that, but a lump formed in my throat, thinking of our gods, invisible and fierce and small, not like the one we knew from church, nor the winged, tentacled nightmare that had moved in. Our gods had been here since the land had been here. Long before humans, long before the town. "How did this happen?"

"I have a theory," said Mr. Kabore. I looked at him appreciatively; he was black and had an accent, maybe British, not from around here. Older but as handsome as a movie star, tall and nicely dressed in a gray suit. I could barely remember the last time I'd met someone not in jeans. Eli elbowed me to pay attention.

"Last year, a child went missing," he said. "Just outside Derby."

I nodded; Derby was a mine town about fifty miles away and was considered something of a fun trip if you had wheels, as it had a movie theater and a library and other amenities that Edenderry would never earn. Even its trailer park was bigger.

"My coworker determined that she'd been taken by a god," Kabore went on. "Not a local god. Something else. Something that had been...propagating. Quietly. Waiting for its chance. At first it wasn't clear what power it had, if any. And then..."

"And then?" I asked, my voice much fainter than I had expected.

He shrugged. "And then it took him, too. And the girl's mother. And the trailer park, and then perhaps half the people still left in Derby before they fled."

"Your coworker?" Eli asked. "What do you do, Mr. Kabore?"

"I'm an Evaluator," he said. "The name of the company's not important. We need to fly a little under the radar, if you know what I mean. Our main duties are to evaluate things that may be caused by spirits, gods, lead in the tap water, whatever. We know about gods, therefore. Maybe not yours specifically, but gods in general. Which is how I know what this is. The big bad."

He pointed down at the town, vulnerable, shimmering in the trees. "You wouldn't know him, if it's who I think. And I myself will not say his name. But he's older than this universe, him and all his kin; they live beneath our history and memories, in a space we cannot go. He has arisen a dozen times, but there were always sorcerers, witches, armies united to fight him and send him back to sleep. Now..."

"Now that's us," Ms. Boon said firmly. "Us and our kin, versus him and his."

"Hell yes," I said; the lump in my throat was gone, replaced with something fizzing and bright. "What do we do?"

"Pete?" she said.

Pete was chewing on his bottom lip, white-knuckled on the steering wheel. "We gotta go to my house."

PETE'S HOUSE was a nice bungalow with pale-blue vinyl siding and white trim, and was also, for absolutely no reason I could tell, suspended about five feet off the ground on a branch. I walked underneath it, looking up at the smooth, sealed concrete of the foundation, and touched the branch gingerly. It was about as thick as my thumb.

"Stop it, Ray!" Eli yelled.

"Oh, it's fine," Pete said, strolling over. "It's just showing off, really. A sign to your gods that I'm genuine. It's not even buried that deep, see?" He kicked it. "Come on up."

A set of steps dropped down from the front door at his gesture; I gave Ms. Arthur my arm to walk up them, and we gathered in his kitchen. He put the coffeemaker on and opened a bag of chips to pass around. The walls were papered with drawings, maps, paintings, and postcards, as thickly shingled as a butterfly's wing. A few of the drawings glowed hot in white or blue.

"There is a way," Pete was saying. "To put the Great Old One back under again, at least for a few centuries. He's strong now from the belief of his new followers. But that's what—eight, nine hundred people? We've got to move before he gets out of the valley and gets even stronger."

He dug under the coffee table in the living room and returned with more drawings, mostly black ink and very complicated, like gears but layered on top of each other, dozens and dozens of them on a single sheet.

"I'm a grad student," he said at Eli's questioning look.

"Doing fieldwork here for my PhD, occult history down at U of M. Yeah, I know there's no money in it. But in the meantime, I know how to make the ancient sigils and wards—they're much stronger than the new ones—and how to open up a Great Gate. Maybe just for a few seconds—long enough to suck the Old One back in."

"Holy smokes," I breathed, touching the topmost drawing; it wriggled away from my finger. Another one nipped at my nail, breaking off a chip of glitter polish. Rude.

"My company provides its agents some raw magic for self-defense," Mr. Kabore said. "I can't get more from the head office, though." He reached into his jacket and brought out three dark lumps, blurrily carved as if they had been made out of wax, though they rang on the kitchen table like metal. "Ms. Arthur and I both know how to use it. If we can approach him close enough...."

The silence stretched till I figured it out. "Oh, okay," I said. "Bait. I can do that." Eli went pale, all the blood washing out from beneath his tan until he was just eyebrows and glasses.

"No, honey, not you," Ms. Boon said.

"What?" I said.

Pete shook his head. "Nope. I don't have the gift like these two, but even I know: not you, Ray. They'll never fall for it. We need someone more...."

Susceptible. We turned and looked at Eli, who had started to shake. I could hear his shoes on the linoleum floor, a fast chatter. Without them saying it, I knew what they meant. He was always the quiet one, the nervous one, the emptiness inside him questing for something to make him complete. We'd always thought he had found that in me—his complete opposite. Always, ever since we were kids. But if we could all tell that he had those puzzle pieces missing inside, a god surely would. And he would sniff his way over.

"We'll be right there with you," Ms. Arthur said. "All of us."

"All of us," I echoed, prodding his ankle with my foot. What

I really wanted to do was grab his hand, but I was worried we'd both start crying. It had been a long day.

"HEY," Eli whispered.

"What?" I whispered back.

"Remember when we...when we wanted our parents to get married? Even though they never even talked?"

"Because of that stupid movie."

"Yeah. Even though everyone in town agrees that your dad is too mean to date."

"I know. Literally everybody." I shifted in the damp needles, feeling wetness creep up my jeans. Behind us, Pete and Mr. Kabore were finishing up the last pieces of the huge ward, drawn on four pieces of posterboard taped together. "And your mom is the worst."

"I know."

"Well, we were kids," I said.

He gave me a look suggesting that now, at fourteen, we weren't exactly not kids, but I ignored it.

"Eli," Ms. Boon called. "Come on. We found a good spot."

We headed through the trees to where Ms. Boon was waiting in a large clearing that they had cleared further, clipping away the long grass till flowers and moss poked through. It was cool in the shade and the fog, just the occasional patch of light on the pale green.

Eli stood in the center and cleared his throat. "It was a dumb idea. I knew that even then. I just...wanted us to be family," he said thickly, looking down at the grass, the water working its way up his gray sneakers.

I grabbed his hand and squeezed, not looking at him either, only the pale and bony fingers. "*Hey*. We're family."

"Ray," Ms. Codie called from the trees. "Get out of there. It's starting."

I squeezed one last time and scurried back to the others, not trusting myself to say anything else. All those years standing in front of him as the kids approached with their fists up, all those years with him in the stands at my volleyball games, all those years of my rashness and his forethought never quite cancelling out; all those years of bickering over baseball cards, Mario Kart scores, lost or stolen jackets; all those years we'd hidden in each other's basements, dazed from the rages of our elders. Of course we were family. What else did he think we could be?

Also, *what* was starting?

But in a second I knew—the clean scent of the damp trees was replaced with an eruption of stench, just like we'd smelled in the town, like sulphur and ozone and the black-green smell of a rotting carcass. I covered my mouth and nose, staring down at Eli from our perch high up the slope. He looked very small. And something big was coming.

Something hissed behind us—a monster, covered in eyes, not golden this time, but bright blue, with a huge, horizontal pupil crazed like a cracked windshield. It glanced at us suspiciously, then kept moving towards the clearing below, sliding on the needles and leaves, its tentacles whipping out to snatch at the trees. It brought a strange noise, a hum or a buzz, like thousands of deep voices far away. Pete had used a blue sharpie to draw a ward on the back of Eli's neck, just visible now above his sweatshirt—a ward, he'd explained, of calling. A ward of desire. That's what they were coming for.

They were coming all right—more and more, creeping through the woods. I chewed on the inside of my cheek. I felt like dead weight, just here for moral support. There was nothing we could do but watch.

Eli finally disappeared under the towering creatures, and I held my breath, waiting for him to start screaming for help. But there was only the wind and the faint, roaring voices, chanting something that became clearer each moment. Ms.

Boon stuck her thumbs in her ears, and I resisted an urge to do the same.

There. The swaying cone of praying monsters around Eli shivered and broke as if some invisible force had struck it, and the ground began to glow—a dull, dirty red, like charcoal. They all turned their eyes and antennas and fang-toothed open mouths toward the big one, the Great Old One, crunching through the trees. My heart pounded so hard I felt it might simply stop. Don't touch him, don't you dare touch him....

Mr. Kabore stepped out from behind a tree as soon as the Old One was fully inside the clearing—not rushing, not jumping, just one clean step, holding up the ward on the multicolored posterboard. The black marker lit up like a lightning strike, so that I cried out and looked away, blinking away complicated afterimages. When I could see again, both he and Ms. Arthur were at the very foot of the Old One, who had frozen, apparently in surprise, wings still.

Behind the monster something was forming—not a doorway as I had expected when they said 'gate,' or even a rip, but a...thinning; something going dark and clear, emitting a high scream of inflowing air. Leaf litter spattered against my back as I dug in against the pull of the gate. "Eli!" I shouted. "Get out of there! They don't need you!"

He spun and slid on a tentacle immediately, barely breaking his fall before crashing onto his face into the grass. The smaller monsters roared and turned on him again; Ms. Boon grabbed my wrist as I stood, nearly yanking my arm from the socket. But I twisted to break her grip and slid down, feeling my shoes fill with needles and grit, reaching for my pocketknife. I was pretty sure I couldn't stab them to death, if guns and dynamite couldn't hurt them, but I'd be damned if I'd go down without a fight.

Eli was still thrashing in the damp grass, too disoriented from fear to even get to his feet; any other time, it would have been funny. I ran between two monsters, their bulging shells disgustingly cold to the touch, like supermarket meat, and pulled him upright.

"Is it working?" he yelled over the wind.

"I think so! Come on!"

But the monsters were closing ranks again, blocking out the scant sun; with a light, cold shock I realized that we were trapped. The wall of their bodies shifted and squeaked as they moved towards us, but they hadn't left any gaps. Worse yet, just above their wriggling antennae and waving claws, I could still see the Great Old One, still hear the buzz of his magic over-powering ours. Mr. Kabore screamed, his voice thin and imme-diately blown away. What had he said? *'That's it'* or *'That's all'*? Were they done, or out of magic?

The question answered itself a second later, as the Old One shook himself, once, sharply, as if waking up, and leaned towards us, erasing sky, trees, sound. His mouth gaped as big as a house, filled not with teeth, but with a trillion wriggling things with eyes of their own, eager and bright.

The wards had failed. Pete had drawn them wrong. Or there just hadn't been enough magic to make them go. It didn't matter anyway. I looked away, numb, not wanting to see the end. Big difference between the end of the world and the end of your life, it turned out. Not even enough time to say a real goodbye to my dad, to Eli, to Edenderry, to my gods...

...to...to those of the...

"Close your eyes!" I shouted to Eli and kicked the back of his knees so that he folded like a deckchair. I knelt next to him and put both hands on the cool grass, feeling the moss fluff up between my grasping fingers. The air smelled cleaner down here, sweet and alive, like the woods I knew. I squeezed my eyes shut.

You of the hill and the green, I know you, I prayed, squeezing the ground in my fists. *And you know me. I was born here, I've lived here all my life. I've paid you the respects you requested, if not as much as you deserved. In bone-cold, in drenching rain, there was*

always the dish on the step, always the darkness at night. Whatever
we had, we gave. Now I have nothing. But please help us. You cannot
let these gods stay on your land. Our land. Please.

Please.

But when I opened my eyes, there was nothing but the
encroaching darkness of the Old One's wriggling mouth, looming, ever closer. I looped my arm through Eli's, snapping the
last button off my jean jacket.

Wait. No. Not nothing.

A breeze, fast and fragrant, musk, sap, sweat, blood, spores,
the stagnant bottom of the creek, the tartness of rotting oaks.
And then the cry and roar of the small gods of the land,
rumbling below us as if tunneling from impossible depths.
White light shone up as we stumbled to our feet and ran
straight for the massed monsters, knowing now that a gap
would open.

We squirted through it, barely, and kept going, up the hill
towards Ms. Boon and the others, panting, leaping fresh rifts in
the soft ground. Something huge and dark and transparent, lit
from within like the night sky, flowed down the hill towards us.
I stood my ground as it found us and stopped, flapping in the
breeze like a damp sheet, studying us without eyes. After a
moment, it began to melt, shrink, reform itself into a huge stag,
too many points to count, each topped with a tiny star that
gleamed in the mist. I could see Pete gesturing frantically
through its translucent body, but couldn't hear him.

"Oh, Ray," Eli said softly.

"I know," I said, and pulled my arm from his. *You give your*
best. Whatever that is.

I took my torn jacket off and let it fall, brushing Eli's frantic
hands away as if he were a moth. *Whatever that turns out to be.*

Belief wasn't enough. Prayer wasn't enough. It wasn't
enough for the Great Old One, and it wasn't enough for those
of the hills either. *Whatever you've got.*

The antlers were so sharp that I barely felt them part the

skin of my throat, only the impact, like being hit by a car. The ground rose and slammed into my back, my teeth clicking together. Blood flooded over my shirt, across my face and into my ears, and the last thing I saw was sunshine, clear and true, through the tops of the swaying trees.

"RAY? Ray? Come on, Raydeene, up you get."

A noise by my ear, something weirdly familiar but unplaceable—no, the crack and hiss of a can opening. I opened my eyes and struggled to sit up, feeling someone's hand in the small of my back. The world focused slowly—Ms. Boon, holding out a can of Coke, and behind her Eli and Pete, their faces splotched red and pink as if they'd been crying. Mr. Kabore was holding me up, his nice grey suit scorched and torn. Ms. Arthur, sitting placidly on a stump, was opening another can of Coke and handing it to Eli. It was even more silent than the normal quiet of the woods. No wind, no birds, no bugs.

"What happened?" I croaked, taking the Coke. It was warm, but tasted like heaven.

"We won," Mr. Kabore said, squeezing my shoulder. "You missed it. Your little gods rose from the ground like flames, and pushed the invader through the gate."

"As soon as he was gone, the ward killed off his minions," Pete said excitedly. "Man, that was a powerful one, it used up almost a whole—"

"Pete."

"Sorry."

Mr. Kabore turned back to me. "But none of it would have worked if you had not made an offering to them. In gratitude, after the land was cleansed, they made a repayment."

"So not a sacrifice," I said. "A loan."

"Perhaps."

"Yes, okay," I said. "Dang. Sorry I missed it. Sorry not sorry. At all."

THEY DROPPED us back at our stolen Accord, unlocked and untouched, with the trail of slime on top of it flaking off in the sun. "You have quite a story to tell," Ms. Arthur said, standing on the top step of the RV.

"I guess so," I said. "If anyone believes it."

"My dear, if anyone could be brought to believe anything, it would be after today," she said. "But I hope you won't speak of it to outsiders. It's local business, you know."

I nodded. The term had taken on a kind of sacrosanct weight over the last few days. I thought they'd probably come up with something, if people came around asking nosy questions. A gas leak, neurotoxic effects, mass hallucinations. And it wasn't even a full lie, really—at least one of the big mains had gone up. The town had burned for quite ordinary reasons, aside from all the magical ones.

She kissed me, shook Eli's hand, and shut the trailer door. We waved as they made about an eighty-seven point turn and sailed off down the highway, brake lights blinking once, like a last farewell.

I jingled the Accord's keys in my hand. It had been parked in front of a burning house swarmed with monsters, a dozen entranced people posturing and prancing in front of it. They wouldn't want it back, would they?

"Well," Eli said.

"Well." I sighed. "Back to help clean up, I guess."

"Yeah."

We tossed our bags onto the back seat and got in. It was warm and stuffy; I started up the engine to get the AC going. I touched my neck for the millionth time since I'd woken up in the woods. Nothing, not even a scar. I looked over at Eli.

"Or," he said.

I grinned, waiting.

"Or, we could have a few adventures first."

"Listen to you," I said, reversing around, away from the town. "I must be a pretty bad influence."

"Must be."

I knew we'd be back one day—probably soon. But for now, there was the empty highway, and half a tank of gas, and trees and sun and light and gods and hope.

THE ART OF DREAMING

JOSH VOGT

Harper wanted to wake up and know it had all been a dream. But she needed to fall asleep first for that to happen.

Sighing, Harper checked over her room to make sure everything looked ready. Her Wonder Woman alarm clock was unplugged, and nothing else remained in sight or powered on that could make any noise or light to disturb her. She'd duct-taped a couple pillows against her window and even tucked her powered-down laptop into the desk.

Harper started to feel hopeful as she changed into her Star Wars PJs. She tugged her long, blonde hair out of its ponytail and ran a mental inventory of the precautions she'd taken.

Tomorrow was Saturday. No school, and her friends knew she spent most of the day working on her painting. They wouldn't bother her until Sunday, when they'd planned to visit the Denver Art Museum to check out the new Latin American jewelry exhibit. She'd even asked her parents for permission to sleep in as long as possible. They'd looked surprised at the direct request. After all, what else would a fifteen-year-old girl do on a weekend?

Perfect. Time to start dreaming my way out of community college.

She grabbed her phone from the bedstand. After double-checking its alarms were muted, she pulled up Smart Thermometer, an app that used the phone's temperature sensors to measure the room's ambient heat. Sixty-three degrees. Well within the sleep comfort zone.

Then she hit the icon of the app she'd downloaded just that morning. A floral, bluish-green pattern filled the screen. Calligraphic text faded into view.

Dreamscape Journeys.

A play/pause bar appeared at the bottom, like a simple music player. The track title read: *Lucid Dreams Induction via Binaural Beats. 8 Hour Sleep Cycle.*

Harper frowned, still dubious.

Glen better be right about this.

She hit the light switch and used the phone screen to guide herself to bed. Once perfectly comfortable, head on pillow, blanket snug, Harper breathed deep and tried not to worry. If anything, this just wouldn't work, and she'd be back where she started, trying to brute force her paintings into something worth looking at.

She activated the track and set the phone back on the bedstand. As the screen dimmed, gentle music floated through the room—a mix of chimes, light fluting, and harmonic humming.

Pretty. But is this really going to help?

Harper began going through exercises that were supposed to enhance lucid dreaming. Deep breathing. Mental reinforcement that she would remember her dreams. Shedding any distractions from the day or concerns about the next.

Glen, her lucid dreaming forum buddy, had said that for the app to work best, she needed to visualize her desired experience. To focus on the dream's potential and let those thoughts guide her subconscious as she fell asleep.

Harper tried to boil all her thoughts and fears and worries and hopes down into something she could fit into a dream. A waking dream that she could bring back to the real world and use as inspiration for her art.

I want something beautiful.

No. Too simple. Too normal.

I...want something unbelievable. Indescribable. Totally unique. Like nothing anyone has ever seen.

This swirled through her mind, winding around like a velvet ribbon until it tangled and tugged all other thoughts away, leaving her afloat in a void.

As she drifted, another sound tickled her ears, just below the humming. Whispering? She'd thought it'd just be music. She resisted the urge to make sure the app was working right, holding herself in the border between waking and sleeping.

The elusive words lingered on the edge of comprehension. They teased her, as if beckoning her to follow them. Drawing her down somewhere deep. Promising her all sorts of secrets....

Harper blinked as light blossomed through her closed eyelids. One of her parents must have opened the bedroom door to check on her. Annoyed beyond belief, she opened her eyes and sat up, mouth open to—

And woke to another world.

Harper sat on a bed of gray-green moss in the middle of a forest, with trees so tall she couldn't see the tops through the mist coiling overhead. Sporadic beams of sunlight broke through the unseen canopy, shining a strange, glimmering yellow.

She exhaled, and her breath huffed with an odd, metallic echo. Pulse racing, she rose, movements slow as if the air was thick enough to swim through. Turning a circle revealed a path through the thorny-barked trees, and she walked that way on noiseless feet.

As she progressed, her excitement escalated until she thought she might shake apart. Branches with blood-red leaves tugged at her as she passed, but she finally came to the forest's edge. Beyond stretched a landscape stitched together from a hundred different vistas, and she could see impossibly far across it all.

To her left, silver rivers snaked through black canyons until they fed into an ocean without waves. Ahead, icy mountains jutted like giant teeth. At their base rose the spires of...a city? Harper cocked her head, trying to interpret the city's convoluted architecture. It warped in upon itself.

No wind stirred. In the distance, the noise of trumpeting and whistling played a chaotic chorus.

Harper grinned and pressed a hand to one cheek.

Oh. My. God. I'm dreaming. And I'm totally aware of it!

"I did it," she cried. Then she clapped hands over her mouth as her voice shot into the distance.

A black form winged overhead, and giggling laughter trailed in its wake. Harper's gaze snapped up and locked onto the enormous moon. Nothing like Earth's moon. Ten times as big, one half utterly smooth with the other half carved up by ragged craters. Several sets of concentric rings marked other areas, intersected by lines that could've been roads or channels. Cities on the moon?

She tried to soak it all in and lock it in her mind.

"I will remember this," she said. "I'll remember it all."

"Remember what?" came a soft voice.

Yelping, Harper spun, still feeling slightly slower than normal. An animal perched on a rock a few feet away, half-hidden by a low branch. Knowing she was perfectly safe within her dream, Harper crouched to get a better look.

"Hello," she said. "Did you just talk to me?"

The creature slunk into full view, revealing a black-and-orange furred body that looked like a cross between a cat and a monkey. Its long tail twitched, as did the thin tendrils surrounding its pink nose. Just out of reach, it sat back on its haunches and blinked luminescent, green eyes.

"I did," it said. "Are you lost, kitten? Do you need a guide?"

It held out a tiny claw. After a moment's hesitation, Harper reached back. Just as her fingers touched, one talon tugged. It nicked her forefinger and sharp pain made Harper gasp and fall back. The fall didn't end, and she tumbled ever backward into a void, flailing, soundlessly screaming until—

She jerked awake in her dark room. The app music played all around her, and she fumbled for her phone. The screen had locked. She swiped the code. Yet as the screen brightened, shedding light, her fingertip left a few dark smears on it.

Frowning, Harper hopped out of bed and turned on the light. She studied her left forefinger, where the tiniest cut trickled blood. Harper sucked on this as she pondered how it could've happened.

Weird. I must've scratched myself while sleeping, and that somehow made me dream about it.

Thinking about the dream sent images racing through her brain. Cities and oceans and mountains and trees and the moon...

I've gotta journal this!

She got her laptop out and hit the browser bookmark for theartofdreaming.com. She'd been searching online for ways to improve her art when she'd stumbled across the site and got snagged by random curiosity. Hours later, she'd come up for air, absolutely fascinated.

The concept captivated her. Being awake and aware inside a dreamscape? Being in control of a whole world...a whole reality? She loved reading people's vivid dream descriptions, and how many talked about the way lucid dreaming enhanced their real lives—giving them deeper senses of purpose, healing them emotionally and mentally, inspiring them to try unique experiences. The site hosted a huge gallery of uploaded images where people had sketched or painted creatures and scenes from their dreams.

That last part particularly intrigued her. She'd been

wanting new inspiration all this time. A way to elevate her painting talent and advance her plans to become a famous artist.

For years, she'd dreamed of attending the Art Institute of Colorado, which she saw as a stepping stone to greatness. Yet she knew her family would never be able to afford the tuition unless she won a scholarship or other source of financial help. She'd researched every contest and grant available, but her heart had plummeted when she saw the compositions that had won in past years. Her paintings just didn't compare.

She needed to develop a style so breathtakingly unique that her work would blow everything else away. Lucid dreaming seemed to offer a potential—if unorthodox—solution.

Harper logged into the site under her WanderingGrrl username and went to the dream journal subforum. Her fingers danced over the keyboard as she recorded her dream in a new post. She kept having to pause to dab up the occasional spot of blood from her forefinger, and she finally resorted to keeping that finger raised until the cut clotted.

Right as she submitted the post, an alert icon flashed.

MoonB3ast has posted an update.

Surprised, she popped up the site's private message window and pinged the other user.

WanderingGrrl: *Heya, Glen. You're up, too?*

He replied seconds later.

MoonB3ast: *Heya, whatsherface.*

Harper rolled her eyes. When they'd started private chatting, he'd quickly shared his real first name, but she'd never reciprocated, heeding her parent's constant warnings about giving out too much personal info online.

MoonB3ast: *I was just recording a dream I had tonight before it faded.*

Harper grinned.

WanderingGrrl: *Me too!*

MoonB3ast: *So the app worked?*

WanderingGrrl: *Musta! I just posted my journal entry. It was totally unbelievable.*

A forum link appeared in the messenger.

MoonB3ast: *Here's mine.*

Harper shot him the direct link to her post and then went to read his. Less than a minute later, she returned to the chat.

WanderingGrrl: *Uh, is it just me or are our dreams sounding almost identical? A giant moon? A forest with red leaves? Ice mountains and a weird city?*

MoonB3ast: *I noticed.*

WanderingGrrl: *How's that possible?*

He went unresponsive for a minute. She worried he'd disconnected, but his user status still showed him logged in.

WanderingGrrl: *Did I do something wrong?*

MoonB3ast: *No. This is way more advanced than lucid dreaming.*

WanderingGrrl: *What is?*

MoonB3ast: *Dream sharing. Only a few people can do it. We must've been experiencing the same dreamscape at the same time!*

Harper pulled back for a moment, stunned.

WanderingGrrl: *Is that even possible?*

MoonB3ast: *Obviously. How else do you explain this?*

WanderingGrrl: *Yah, but aren't dreams supposed to be private?*

MoonB3ast: *There are all sorts of theories about it. Like that all humans have a shared subconsciousness, or that every dream is just a fragment of one bigger dream that we only catch pieces of. Maybe using the same app tuned us in to the same part of that Big Dream.*

WanderingGrrl: *That's heavy. But kinda cool.*

MoonB3ast: *Right? You wanna experiment more? Prove we shared a dream?*

WanderingGrrl: *Tonight?*

MoonB3ast: *You mean this morning? Lol. How about tomorrow night? We can try to find each other in the dream. If we don't*

connect, we can both post a journal and see if our dreams were
similar again.

Harper gnawed on her fingertip, barely noticing that she'd
opened the cut again. This was weird...but also awesome in a
strange way. Glen had said only a few people could do this sort
of thing. If she was one of them, maybe it meant she'd end up
being exceptional in her art, too.

WanderingGrrl: *K. Deal! How do we find each other, though?*

MoonB3ast: *You saw the twisted city, right? I saw roads*
leading to it, with occasional crossroads. There was one with a
bunch of large stones surrounding it. Try walking there and I'll do the
same.

They chatted excitedly a few minutes longer before true
exhaustion lured Harper back to bed. She didn't remember
falling asleep, yet she woke just before noon with a surge of
energy.

AFTER SCARFING DOWN A QUICK LUNCH, she set up her easel, got
out her paint supplies, and attacked the blank canvas with a
vengeance. She focused on the dream, trying to capture the
essence of the strange place she'd experienced. But the scenes
all blurred together in her mind.

She reread her journal post, but it was as if a stranger wrote
it. The harder she tried, the less it felt like her painting did the
dream any justice. Harper kept at it until her mother forced her
to come down for dinner. Afterward, she went back to her
room and studied her efforts.

The painting she'd made was certainly different than her
normal style—surreal, with swirls and blotches of blues and
reds and greens and yellows. Still, she had to admit it was
something new. Maybe the more she lucid dreamed, the better
she'd get at expressing it.

A huge yawn escaped, and she realized that even half a day

of painting had wiped her. But this also perked her mood up, as she figured it'd help her fall asleep faster.

She gave her parents an early goodnight and went through her prep routine. Once tucked in bed and swathed in darkness, she activated the Dreamscape Journeys app and let it float her away on an incomprehensible wave of music and whispers.

It seemed like moments this time before she opened her eyes to the dreamworld. She stood where she'd been last, on the edge of the crimson forest, the moon looming above. Nothing seemed to have changed, though she did a quick search for the cat-creature and was relieved at its absence.

Now to find Glen. If he's even here.

The forest path continued on until it became a wide, dusty road leading toward the spired city, which stood an unfathomable distance away. Harper headed that direction, eyes wide as she searched for her friend while taking in more details.

The sky appeared simultaneously dark and light, filled with stars far brighter and closer than she'd ever seen. Alien auroras shimmered with colors that made her feel slightly nauseous until they winked away. Over where the rivers wound, Harper spotted an object moving along one of them, and barely made out a set of sails.

A ship? Does that mean people are on it? Other dreamers?

She wandered on, losing any sense of time until she found herself approaching an intersection of three roads. Where they crossed, a ring of nine monolithic stones stood, each at least twenty feet high, cylindrical, and perfectly smooth. Harper studied them in awe.

This must be where Glen meant.

She searched for any sign that he'd beaten her there but saw nothing. She sat against the base of one stone and waited. Without any means of measuring time, she had no idea how long she stayed there. Did time work differently in dreams? Faster? Slower?

She explored the crossroads and strange stones, but found

nothing but dirt, rubble, and scraps of polished metal. At last, when she figured it'd been at least an hour, she began to worry that she would wake up before Glen arrived. If he ever did. Maybe the dream similarities had just been a weird coincidence. Still, what if she woke and he arrived later?

Maybe I should leave a message. But what? Write 'WG Wuz Here' in the dirt?

She stared down the road that led off to the city, imagining what secrets and wonders it held. What if she traveled there? Maybe if she saw it up close she'd be able to paint it bet—

"Wandering Girl?"

Harper instinctively lunged for cover. Her shoulder struck the side of the nearest stone column, bruising and spinning her down into the copper-colored dust, that rose in a cloud about it. She coughed and pushed up as a shadowed figure approached through the dust.

She pressed her back against the stone as the person resolved into a tall, wiry, man in a gold-white robe. The robe hid most of his body, wrapped tight around his thin limbs, but left pale hands bared. He wore a coiling headdress with a yellow veil strung across his mouth and nose. Wide gray eyes peered down at her.

She blinked. "G-glen?"

A hint of a smile shifted behind the veil and he spread overly long fingers. "We meet at last."

"Uh...why do you look like that?"

He bowed gracefully. "It's a dream avatar. You can make yourself look like anything you want in a dreamscape. Like you do in video games."

Harper looked down at herself, having wandered the dreamscape in her PJs. She visualized being properly dressed, but her clothing didn't budge.

"I can't do it."

His chuckle rippled over her. "You just don't have enough practice. But I can teach you."

He offered a hand. After a moment, she took it. His skin was cool and soft as he helped her up.

"Teach me here?" she asked as she dusted herself off.

"Of course. In just a few hours of dreaming, we could spend days exploring and learning. Time moves more slowly here." He winked. "Most of the time."

"I was just wondering about that."

"See? I've already taught you something. We can keep meeting as often as you like for lessons." His bright gray eyes pierced her. "But the important question is: what do you want to learn?"

"Me?"

"Few people pursue lucid dreaming without wanting something from it. Some want an escape. Some want deeper meaning to life. Others want to learn. And you ask a lot of questions." He bobbed his head as if in self-congratulation. "I've helped you answer the most important one: how does one lucid dream? So, what's your next big question?"

Harper scrunched her face up in thought. Then she pointed at the city. "How do we get there?"

His head tilted at an odd angle. "Ah. I should've figured you'd be drawn there. I always guessed that you had a creative soul."

"Creative?"

"Oh, yes. A city like that could only have been built by minds inspired by the extraordinary. Artists that could see the impossible and make it real. And so, it calls to you. If we went there, I doubt you'd ever want to leave." He paused a moment before chuckling. "Want a visit?"

Harper narrowed her eyes at the city, seeing it as her next challenge, the next obstacle to overcome in achieving her goals. "You betcha."

The dreamworld trembled. Harper stumbled a step, but Glen didn't waver.

She hugged herself. "Oh, no. I think I'm waking up."

He nodded sadly, still staring into the distance. "That's another thing I can teach you. To stay here as long as you want. But next time, we'll both be right here and can start off where we left." His voice grew distant as the dreamworld went gray. "One last thing. When you journal this, leave out our meeting. I think it's best we don't let others on the site know about this until we have a bit more proof of shared dreaming. We wouldn't want to get ourselves banned for supposed trolling, would we?"

Harper woke in darkness but stayed that way for several minutes. She peered into the black, envisioning the city that beckoned to her.

"I'm gonna get there, no matter what," she whispered.

THE NEXT NIGHT, she met Glen at the crossroads and they began journeying to the city. Her steps were light as she kept up with his long strides. As promised, he began telling her how to control her presence and keep herself there longer, plus visualization techniques to eventually be able to change her dreaming form. Though, he warned some techniques could take years to learn.

When awake, she began spending whole weekends painting, ignoring invites to the art museum, parties, and movie nights. When her supplies ran out, she spent everything she'd saved from her allowance to buy more and even began using old canvases, painting over previous works—including a piece she'd been working on as a gift for her parent's upcoming anniversary.

She was getting better. Her paintings showed more vivid details, more concrete visualizations of the dreamworld's abstract elements.

Each night that they could coordinate, she met Glen in the dreamscape where they explored and talked and moved down the road. She marveled at his knowledge of the place, as if he'd been there his whole life. He'd even given some locations odd names, calling the city Celephais, and talking about places like Kadath, Inganok, and Ilarnek. Each night drew them further along toward the strange city, though it seemed to never come closer.

They passed through dead forests and crossed giant bridges of bronze. They walked through fields of constant heatless flame and rainstorms where the droplets flew upward. Everything she saw fed her sense of wonder; it also made her feel torn between spending more time painting or more time dreaming.

Then, as one session drew to a close, Glen held a long-fingered hand up. "I think tomorrow night will be special, WG," he said.

Harper smirked. Despite their sharing a dream, she'd still hesitated to surrender her real name. He'd never pressed the matter, and at least "WG" was better than being called "whatsherface."

"Why's that?" she asked.

He pointed ahead. "Because we should reach Celephais then."

She followed his finger and started in surprise. The city dominated the horizon enough to conceal the mountains once visible behind it.

When did that happen? Come on, Harper, you can't get distracted if you want to learn anything here.

She made fists. "Awesome. This is gonna totally change everything for me."

"I don't doubt it will," Glen said, sounding amused.

THE NEXT DAY—HARPER had to check her phone to find out it was Friday, as she'd been losing track of weeks—both dragged on and whipped by. She doodled in a sketchpad during all her classes, filling page after page with mazes of black spires and towers, impossibly bent, upside down, with streets below leading nowhere or looping in on themselves. She filled the skies with shapeless orbs, winged figures, and floating geometric shapes.

Once home, she fidgeted through dinner and rushed through homework so she'd have a couple extra hours in the dreamscape. As she began prepping the room, a knock on the door preceded her father peeking in.

"Hey, snookums," he said, the childish nickname she couldn't convince him to drop. "You've been sleeping an awful lot, lately. Everything all right? You feeling okay?"

"I'm fine, Dad." She beamed a smile. "It's just...all the painting. The practice." She pointed to where she'd stored some finished canvases by her closet. For some reason, she'd faced them to the wall, feeling oddly hesitant to let anyone see her evolving style.

He smiled softly. "I understand. Your mother and I were just concerned that you're pushing yourself too much."

"My art means everything to me," she said. "I'm just trying to get better. Don't worry. I'll take a break soon. I've got an important project to finish. It's...." She glanced aside. "It's a surprise."

He chuckled. "Well, I'm proud of you for chasing your dreams. Just don't forget. There's more to life than work."

She stared at the door after he shut it.

He doesn't understand. Nobody understands. This is my whole life.

Minutes later, those thoughts floated away with her awareness of the waking world. She opened her eyes to the dreamscape. Glen stood before her in his usual attire, so close that he blocked out everything behind him.

She blinked up at him. "Waiting for me?"

"Only a little while," he said. "I arrived early to prepare a surprise in celebration of the end of your journey." He stepped aside.

Harper gasped. The city was mere yards away, its ebony wall and spires rearing like mountains themselves. Every surface was covered with carvings. Some were fascinating in how they endlessly spiraled in on themselves while others made her wince and glance aside as if she'd stared into the sun. A main road led into the city, quickly branching off into a maze of endless twists and turns.

She looked to Glen. "What kind of surprise?"

He gestured behind her. "A welcoming party."

Harper turned and then froze. A gaggle of creatures crowded the road leading back the way she and Glen had come. Several looked humanoid, but with huge wings, oily black skin, and no features where their faces should've been. Another group was made of enormous, muscular beasts with matted fur and arms that split at the elbows to end in four clawed hands. As Harper stared, one of the beast's head split vertically down the middle, revealing a slavering maw filled with sharp teeth.

A few pale, squat monsters lurked behind these, hunched bodies looking like giant toads while a mass of writhing tentacles sprouted from their necks and dozens of the cat-like animals scampered about the feet of the amassed creatures.

"Who..." She cleared her throat. "Who's this? More dreamers?"

"Oh, no," Glen said. "These are all natives of the Dreamlands."

"Natives?" she echoed. "Dreamlands?"

"The true name of this realm," he said. "Your new home."

Harper backed away from Glen. "What're you talking about? This isn't funny."

His chuckle gained an oily quality. "Actually, I find it quite amusing." He looked to the creatures and waved her way as if presenting a gift. "Give her a proper welcome."

As one, the creatures loped, crawled, and winged Harper's way. With a scream, Harper turned and bolted for the only escape available—into the depths of Celephais. Hoots, laughter, and roars echoed behind. The city's black streets swallowed her within seconds. Her feet slapped over engraved roads, with the only louder noise being her panicked huffing.

Harper took turns blindly, desperate to lose the chasing monsters. The ground quaked as the four-armed beasts thundered after her. Black forms scared overhead. She glanced back at the cat creatures, that swarmed over each other in their haste. Behind these, the tentacle-faced brutes plodded along, knuckling forward like gorillas.

Glen was nowhere to be seen, but Harper imagined his laughter chasing her as well.

How could he do this? Why would he do this? Is he insane?

She took another turn and found herself standing in a wide courtyard. Empty doorways and windows ringed the space, and a dead fountain stood at the center. The figure carved in the middle of the fountain appeared to be a mass of eye-covered tentacles writhing up for the sky. Just glimpsing it made Harper want to puke.

Clutching her stomach, she searched for any way out. None of the pathways made any sense, and she was already so turned around she couldn't retrace her steps if she tried.

Hoots and screeches filled the air as several of the creatures appeared out of the passage she'd just exited. Adrenaline jolted Harper back into motion, and she sprinted down a new road at random. Her normal body would've been exhausted already, but her dreaming self didn't obey the same laws of physics, and it felt like she could flee forever. Yet that wouldn't help if she had no clue of where to flee.

Shrieks and bellows resounded throughout the city. She whipped through another blur of mind-bending, eye-dizzying avenues, over a couple bridges that spanned bottomless chasms, and double-backed from dead ends. She shot through another opening—and into the same courtyard she'd found a minute before. Panting, Harper studied the twisted fountain out of the corner of her eyes. The exact same place, or just similar? She couldn't tell.

What's it matter? I'm still being chased!

Distant thumping and roaring drew closer by the second. Harper ground fists into her temples, trying to force an idea into being.

If I can't outrun them, then I can escape by waking up.

Harper opened her eyes. "Okay. Time to wake up." The courtyard remained the same, without so much as a flicker of light or shift of the surroundings. Harper drew on all her will and focus, hammering against the imprisoning dreamscape. "Wake. Up. Wake up wake up wake up!"

She pinched and slapped herself over and over, but the pain simply stung and bruised. She tried all the lucid dreaming tricks for waking up, such as envisioning herself lying on her bed, holding her breath until the world went wobbly, or taking several steps forward while imagining herself walking through a doorway back to consciousness.

Nothing. As despair crept into her heart, Harper realized one awful truth.

All of Glen's teachings and talks had never covered how to wake herself up. It had always just happened without her having any real control over it.

"I'm afraid you're a bit too here for that to work."

Harper whirled at Glen's voice. He stood in a passageway, taller and thinner than ever. Harper turned in place, seeking another way out, but horrific creatures blocked them all.

Glen strode toward her, his stride impossibly fluid. Harper retreated toward the fountain. The monstrous beasts advanced to form a ring around her.

Harper tripped and fell back, bruising her hands as she caught herself. She crab-crawled back until her shoulders hit the fountain rim. Still Glen and the creatures crowded closer.

One cat critter scrambled in and leaped onto Harper's foot, sinking fangs into her big toe.

She cried out as she kicked the creature away. "This isn't real. It's just a dream!"

Glen paused and held up a hand. The other creatures all stopped just a few steps away from where she huddled.

"Dreams can be as real as anything," he said. "Sometimes even more so."

Trembling, Harper held her hands up as if she could wipe them all away like wet paint.

"Who are you?" she asked.

"A Man of Leng," he said. "To speak my true name, you'd need at least one extra tongue."

Glen? Leng? Extra tongue? That's not...not human. He's not human. He can't be.

She swallowed hard. "What are you?"

He clasped his hands. "A businessman, you might say. I represent certain parties who would be very interested in acquiring gifts such as yours."

"Gifts?" The cold of the stone seeped into her and she clenched her teeth to keep from chattering.

"Your art, of course. You want to be a painter. I know. But more than just any painter. You want to be special. To be adored for your work." His eyes glinted like silver nuggets. "That sort of status comes at a price. I know many who'd pay a high price for a talent like yours, as fledgling as it is." He nodded at the bulbous, tentacle-faced beasts lurking a few feet away. "Such as these. They always enjoy taking the finest slaves to the moon. Though, what they do with them there is entirely their business."

"No!" Harper shot to her feet. "You can't let them take me."

"No?" Glen/Leng hummed to himself. "I suppose I'm not above striking a deal with you."

Harper narrowed her eyes. "What kind of deal?"

"I let you live and remain free." A hint of a smile behind

that veil. "To a degree, at least. You keep on painting and getting better. You win contests. You get scholarships. The art institute. Art galleries across the world hung with nothing but your work. You get everything you've ever dreamed of. And more."

He flourished a hand and suddenly held a tray set with a dozen glass vials, each filled with a viscous fluid. The substances glowed in hues that Harper knew she'd never be able to put into words.

"I will even still teach you. To learn to paint with colors from beyond your simple reality." He pointed to various vials. "Colors only the mad can see. Colors only the dying can see. Colors that can turn minds inside out. Ones that would elevate your art beyond all mortal reasoning."

Harper stared, dazzled by the array of impossible colors. Could it be true? Could she really learn to paint beyond the known spectrum?

"You've lied to me all along," she said, anger burning away a smidge of her terror. "Why should I believe you now?"

"Lied?" He splayed his other hand across his chest. "I haven't lied. I've given you everything you wanted. I helped you lucid dream. I brought you to a realm of endless inspiration. I even guided you to this city when you asked. It was all you. So desperate and willing to go to any lengths. Well..." He wobbled his head, indicating everything around them. "This is the next stretch."

Harper stood shaken and aghast. He was right. She'd rushed into all this so blindly, so ready to do anything that she'd never really considered the consequences.

"What would it cost?" she asked.

"That you work for me." He waved off the protest on her lips. "Oh, nothing too time-consuming. I wouldn't want to distract you from your artistic flourishing. To start, you help others learn to lucid dream. Bring them here, eventually. Introduce us, and I'll take them from there.

"As for your art, you hone that talent into something spectacular. Because I believe that some of those paintings are going to be truly special. That when people gaze upon them, when they walk through your galleries, when they view your work online and anywhere else it's displayed..." another liquid chuckle, "they will be absolutely transported."

His gaze locked on hers. "That's my offer. Accept it and live. Reject it and... well, I can't promise you'll die, but you might wish you had."

Harper gazed around at all the hideous creatures. Leng's power must be holding them back. Maybe that meant he could really do everything he promised. Give her the ability to become an unparalleled artist, enjoying fame and fortune. Living her dream.

"How...how would it work?" She shivered. *Am I really considering this? Do I have a choice?*

She did, she realized. She could fight to the death. She could let herself be taken. Or she could strike this deal and find a way to break free from it later. What if she outsmarted him? Figured out how his magic worked and used it against him? Secretly recruited other dreamers to fight against him here in the Dreamlands? To do all that, though, she needed to stay as free and alive as possible.

Leng shifted closer. "I need one simple thing to seal our contract."

"What's that?"

He bent over so his face came within inches of hers. She forced herself to not flinch.

"Your name. Your real one."

"Why?" she whispered.

"It will let me know where you are and what you're doing at all times. To summon you whenever I need your skill, and to whisper more teachings in your ear whenever you are ready to accept them. What do you say?"

His hand rose with the tray of impossible colors shining

like alien gems. Harper fixed on it. She reached for the nearest vial. Something twisted inside her, a knot of certainty tightening, knowing that this was what she needed to achieve everything she'd ever dreamed of being and doing.

She grasped a vial, the colors within making her think of a dying star.

"Harper. My name is Harper."

VISIONS OF THE DREAM WITCH

LUCY A. SNYDER

Quietly cursing our luck, I helped my cousin Jake limp down the muddy, rutted road. I wished we were back in New Orleans instead of the ass end of swamp country. But Jake and I got a little too curious about late-night shenanigans in a boarded-up warehouse near his father Rudy's auction house. We'd handled occult items during our three summers working there, so we both knew esoteric magic was real. But we never believed in the Outer Gods until we watched those damn fool cult members summon the Dream Witch Yidhra and her pack of enslaved shoggoths.

Beauty and her beasts. We did what we could with crowbars and gasoline. Yidhra vanished as the warehouse burned. She's truly something to behold, but you don't want to look her in the eye unless you want her inside your head. And you don't want to be bitten by a shoggoth unless you want to slowly, painfully turn into one.

By the time we set foot on that soggy back road, it had been thirty-six hours since one of the monsters munched Jake's shoulder. The ER docs stitched him up and gave him an antibiotics shot. But his arm swelled and started breaking out in ugly dark boils that stank of brimstone. I called Beau LeRoux, a local professor who often bid on esoteric items we auctioned, hoping he might know what to do. LeRoux said there was only one person in the whole state who might be able to do something for Jake: Madame Caplette.

My cousin's whole arm puffed up like an andouille sausage and turned black with those horrible boils. The bones in his hand were soft, rubbery. Worse, the swelling spread from his shoulder to his neck. He'd lost his voice and had a tough time breathing. The corruption moved down his spine, and he could barely walk. I could tell it hurt like absolute hell.

"She's gonna be able to help you, I know it," I told him.

He grunted and gave me a half-hearted thumbs-up. We trekked on with him leaning heavily on my shoulder.

Jake was the closest thing I had to a brother. We're nearly the same age. His parents took me to raise after my mom OD'd when I was just six. Adulterated heroin, back before it was cool. Dad was already serving a life sentence for dealing coke. Uncle Rudy's too softhearted to tell many hard truths to a little kid, but he never made any bones about what took my parents from me. Hate's a strong word, but that's how I feel about the turds who peddle poison. Jake loved my mom, too, and so we'd both been vigilant about watching for dealers in the neighborhood. We were certain that the cultists were selling meth, but we kinda lost our focus on that after Yidhra showed up.

I was glad he took after his mama and was a thin, wiry kid; if he'd been a linebacker type like Uncle Rudy, I couldn't have gotten him down the road. But woe betide any cocky dude who thought skinny meant weak; Jake boxed until he learned about chronic traumatic encephalopathy. He had a left hook like a lightning bolt. I prayed he'd be able to keep his arm.

The road wound through a copse of oaks furred with Spanish moss and lichens to a sprawling blue ranch house with a red barn out back. A huge magnolia tree bloomed in the front yard, the white blossoms humming with bees. The front door was open behind a closed screen.

An African statue of a man decorated entirely with cowry shells stood beside the galvanized steel mailbox of different shades of white, yellow, and brown. He held out a small bronze bowl that contained an assortment of blue glass beads; whether they were offers from or to visitors I couldn't tell. I left them alone.

A knock-kneed girl of nine or ten in a purple jumper and bright pink Chuck Taylors came running around the side of the house, then slid to a dead stop when she saw us. "Gran-maaa-AAAA!" she hollered, pelting into the house, curly black pigtails bouncing. "There's people heeeere!"

A moment later, a stooped old woman came out of the house, squinting at us from behind thick old-fashioned bifocals. She leaned heavily on a staff of gnarled black wood. A cowry bracelet hung from her bony wrist.

"Who are you kids, and what do you want?" Her voice conveyed strength that seemed impossible given her apparent physical frailty.

"I'm Pepper Mouton, and this is Jake Garza," I called back. "Beau LeRoux said he'd call about us?"

She stepped forward, looking over the tops of her spectacles at Jake's arm. "Lord have mercy. Get that boy into the house."

Once we got Jake settled on her couch, the old witch pulled a footstool over and began to examine my cousin's boils.

"Shoggoth?" she asked.

I nodded. "He got bit almost two days ago."

She rubbed her chin thoughtfully. "I can heal him, I reckon. But I'm a mite short of heart-juice for the potion. It's one more night to the new moon...it has to be taken when there's nothing but starlight. Monique can take you there, but you have to do the harvest. I'm too old to go running around in the bayou after that critter."

"What critter?" I asked.

"Sap Daddy. The beast come here with the Spaniards four

hunnert years ago; they let it go in the swamp when it got too big to keep as a pet. And there it stayed, eating gators and getting bigger and bigger. When it died, something in the swamp kept it alive. It's more plant than animal now, but that don't make it no less dangerous. Sap from its heart and some other bits and bobs are just the thing we need here."

"Can you keep Jake from getting any worse until we go out hunting?"

She nodded. "I 'spect I can."

MADAME CAPLETTE TOOK me to a back workroom that had been outfitted in mismatched kitchen counters and cabinets with open shelving above. The old woman stood upon her tiptoes and pulled down a cardboard box that she set on the Formica work surface.

"This here is what you'll need for the collectin'." She opened the box and pulled out a copper-clad glass jug with a black rubber stopper and a galvanized steel funnel. Both looked like they had come from some backwoods moonshine still.

"And this is for the cuttin'." She unrolled a burlap bundle as long as my shinbone to reveal an African ceremonial knife. It had an elongated, leaf-shaped iron blade with a dark hardwood hilt and matching scabbard. The weapon looked positively ancient, and I could feel a strange vibration from it.

"Should I fill the whole jug?" I asked.

She nodded and pulled an old blue nylon gym bag that had to date from the 1970s down from another shelf. "As close to full as you can get, but don't take more'n that, and don't waste none. Sap Daddy is a genuine gold-egg goose for us, and we need him healthy. Well, healthy as a thing like him can possibly be, I s'pose."

"Yes ma'am."

"All you got to do is get him to settle down and cut one of the little heart-vines." She gave the bag's white shoulder strap a couple of yanks; apparently satisfied that it would hold, she started loading up the equipment. "But he don't always come along easy. Monique is good with witch-song, but she's real young. If the beast gets rambunctious, mind she don't get hurt. And don't you go dropping this here knife over the side of the boat, or I'll make you go diving to find it again, you hear?"

"Yes ma'am. How do we find him?"

"Use the old pole boat I got in the shed out back—motor noise scares him off—and take it up the stream that runs behind my property. Monique's real good at finding him, so don't worry none about that. Just hang onto your boots and get the jug full up and bring it back here, lickety-split."

THE NEXT NIGHT I dragged the old flat-bottomed skiff to the shallow water just after eleven p.m. and tied it to the old tree stump that served as a mooring. There was no breeze to speak of. A piney haze in the air dimmed the stars. Without any moonlight, the stream bank seemed oppressively dark.

"So, once we find this thing, how do we catch it?" I asked Monique as we carefully stepped into the boat with our gear.

"I sing to him, and he gets still," she replied, setting her waterproof, hand-crank LED lantern on the wooden seat beside her.

"For real?" I put the old blue gym bag down in the cargo area, checked my shotgun, and stowed it along the inner hull. Madame Caplette had warned me that we might encounter some fairly large gators.

"For real." She dipped her paddle in the water.

I pushed off the bank with the long white fiberglass pole. "Bollywood tunes, or lullabies, or what?"

The girl rolled her eyes. "It likes old Spanish Christmas

songs like *'Venid pastores.'* I guess they used to sing that stuff to him back in the old days."

"So, no Lady Gaga?"

Monique gave me a sidelong squint that would've made Clint Eastwood proud. "Uh, *no.*"

"That's good. 'Bad Romance' isn't really in my range."

"You're weird," she said.

"You have no idea," I replied.

The girl fell silent, and I kept pushing us along. The only sound was the faint swish of the water and the frogs calling to each other in the cattails. A few fireflies flitted to and fro, blinking come-hithers.

A woman laughed right behind me. I nearly dropped the pole in surprise. The boat rocked as I whirled around. The frogs went silent, startled by the sudden slap and splash of the hull. Nobody was there.

"What's the matter?" Monique frowned at me.

"Did you hear that?" I held my breath, trying to listen, scanning the weeds and dark water. Still nothing.

"Hear what?" she asked.

"That laugh."

"Uh, no..." The girl was staring at me as if she wasn't sure if I was messing with her or not.

"Seriously, you didn't hear that?"

"No, ma'am."

I swore under my breath and pushed the boat off again. "Never mind. Just my nerves, I guess."

Problem was, I didn't think I'd been all that nervous. Not enough to start hearing things, anyway. Jake's life depended on this. Pressure? Sure. But this was something a 9-year-old could do. Had done several times, apparently. How bad could it be?

"Oh, there's plenty that could go bad tonight." Yidhra's voice. Directly behind me.

I cussed and turned again, holding the pole like a spear. My heart was thudding. "Where the hell are you?"

Her head broke the surface a few yards behind the boat, just beyond my pole's reach. She smiled. "I'm right here. Or am I?"

"What do you mean?" My voice shook.

"Maybe I'm not here at all." Yidhra smoothly breaststroked forward, graceful as a naiad, still keeping her distance. Her long black hair fanned out in the water behind her. "Maybe I'm just a hallucination. Maybe you caught a virus that's eating away at your brain, and you're going crazy."

"Uh, ma'am, who are you talking to?" Monique sounded worried.

I swallowed, my throat suddenly dry.

"Or maybe I'm here, and your songbird just can't see me," Yidhra continued. "And she won't see me even when I cut her skinny little throat."

"Leave her alone." I gripped the pole with my left hand and bent down to pick up my Mossberg with my right. I trained the shotgun on Yidhra, who just laughed at me.

"What's going on?" Monique sounded genuinely scared. "Is —is someone out there?"

I looked back at the girl. Her brown eyes were huge, and her cheeks were wet with frightened tears.

"Don't worry." I tried to sound calm and confident. "There's a problem, but it's my problem, all right? Just get us to Sap Daddy."

Monique nodded and wiped her face. "Okay."

"I might say some stuff to my friend in the water," I continued. "Just...just ignore it. Okay?"

The request sounded stupid the moment I made it, but Monique simply nodded again, all her eye-rolling sassiness gone. One good thing about kids who've been raised around witchcraft is that while they might be annoyingly cavalier about some stuff, they know to take it seriously when real monsters come calling. Or at least they'll go with real monsters as plausible, and not immediately assume that the person in the boat with you has just transformed into a hallucinating, gun-waving lunatic.

"A lunatic without a moon to howl at." Yidhra laughed again. "How ironic. How sad."

I set my shotgun down and poled us away from her fast as I could, my shoulders straining with my effort, but the death goddess easily kept pace with the boat.

"Shove off," I said.

"You're just heartbroken over your cousin, aren't you?" Her voice was husky with fake sympathy. "Here you are, trying so hard to save him, and every minute that ticks off the clock is a minute he's closer to death. He's suffering so much, Pepper, so much more than you know. And you've put his future in the hands of a little girl and an old witch. Do you really think they can save him?"

"Do you have a point?" I spat.

"I think it would be a mercy to put him out of his misery," she replied. "And take his soul for safekeeping."

"Go to hell."

"Perhaps I should put the old woman down. Perhaps I'm at her house, right this very minute, and before you can get your little boat turned around I'll have her scattered all over her garden. You can watch Jake die horribly tomorrow."

My heart pounded so hard that my vision shook. I stared at Yidhra, who was floating on her back, just her face and naked breasts clear of the water. "Why would you do that?"

She shrugged. "Because I can. Because you and your cousin disrupted my plans. I'm merely returning the favor."

"If you hurt Jake or Madame Caplette," I growled, "I won't rest until I've destroyed you. I will see you burn."

Yidhra laughed uproariously at that, splashing merrily. I focused on poling the boat as quickly as I could while Yidhra began to detail all the grotesque ways she would kill my loved ones, and their loved ones. I wished I had a pair of earplugs, but I knew she'd wormed her way into my brain. Not even a jet engine would drown out her voice.

We reached the mouth of the stream. It opened into the dark maze of a bald cypress swamp. The tree limbs dripped with Spanish moss. The water here was stagnant, the surface thick with duckweed and drifting mats of ragged algae. I could smell rotting vegetation and the rankness of reptile dung, either from gators or something much bigger.

"...in Tepes' time, a good impaler could hammer in a stake without destroying any major organs," Yidhra said, "and a young, healthy victim could suffer for two or even three days before he died. But I've heard that with modern piercing techniques and saline and antibiotics you can keep your playmate aware and in agony for nearly twice as long. I think I'll try that with your Uncle Rudy—he's not that young, but he seems pretty strong, don't you think?"

A terrible image rose in my mind, a psychic sucker punch: my uncle hanging screaming from a huge wooden spike that someone had rammed up under his ribcage and out through his shoulder. My senses spun with vertigo, and I fell to my knees in the boat. Fortunately, I didn't lose my pole. Or my dinner.

"What's the matter?" Monique looked even more scared than before.

"Just got dizzy." I blinked to try to clear my vision and got to my feet. "Where do we go from here?"

"That way." She pointed out into the darkness. "I can feel him."

I kept on poling the boat through the debris and cypresses as Yidhra's descriptions grew even more horrifying and vivid. Sometimes the water around us turned into a lake of blood and dismembered bodies. Vegetal rot turned to a charnel house stench. Sometimes the Spanish moss transformed into festoons of steaming entrails. The trees became a thousand crooked gallows decorated with the corpses of the condemned. Sometimes the entire landscape around me looked like a Hieronymus Bosch nightmare.

"I'm...having a hard time seeing straight," I finally told Monique. "Make sure I'm going the right way, okay? If it seems like I'm going to wreck the boat, say something. Please."

The girl gazed at me, and I flinched. It looked like someone had scraped her face off with a length of razor wire.

"Are you okay?" The part of my head that was buying Yidhra's illusion marveled at how well Monique could speak without any lips.

I shook my head. "It's my problem, not yours. Just don't let me wreck us."

A little while later, she inhaled sharply.

"What is it?" I couldn't glimpse anything but the landscape of carnage.

"It's him. He's here, I know it."

"Where?" I strained to see past the bloody veil.

"I dunno, I can't—"

The girl shrieked as something big and strong rammed the bottom of our boat, knocking it sideways. Suddenly, I was plunging into the warm, sticky gore. I went under completely for a moment, fighting against what felt like a dozen dead hands grasping my arms and clothes, but I managed to surface, spitting foul gore from my mouth.

Monique was still screeching in panic. The girl definitely had a sturdy set of lungs.

"It'll be okay!" I hollered up at her, part of me wondering if I was telling her a terrible lie. I still couldn't see the beast, but I could feel the vibrations of something huge pulling itself across the muddy swamp bottom. "You know what to do...sing to it!"

I heard her take a deep breath. I figured she'd just start screaming again—hell, if I'd been in her situation when I was nine they could have strapped me to the roof of a fire truck and used me as a siren. What came out was a beautiful soprano note, a little shaky at first, but it got stronger and stronger and became a sound of such transcendent clarity you could compare it to the purest stream in the mountains above Shangri-la or the gleam of Caladbolg's steel or the glitter of the Hope Diamond and all those other things would seem mundane and unimpressive. Monique had the kind of voice that could make the most cynical, hard-minded atheist instantly believe in a benevolent higher power, believe in *anything*.

She held the note a little longer, then took another breath and began to sing an old Spanish Christmas song. I didn't understand the lyrics, but the words didn't matter. The power was all in her voice, and as Monique's music flowed over me, Yidhra's horrible vision evaporated like fog in sunshine. The gore around me became innocuous swamp water, and what had seemed to be zombie hands grabbing at my legs was just a tangle of common riverweeds.

I looked up and found myself staring up into a set of toothed jaws the size of Madame Caplette's Volkswagen. I'd have been petrified if the sight of the monster wasn't such a welcome relief from Yidhra's visions. It was the skeleton of a dragon reanimated by the swamp. Creaking green vines were muscle and sinew linking the ancient bones. Moss bearded the dragon's jaw and huge scarlet rose mallow flowers bloomed in caches of muddy debris on its back and sides. I could see between its ribs, and where the dragon's flesh heart should have been was a knot of dark, shiny vines that pulsed with a faint blue glow.

Monique stood ramrod straight in the boat, giving the song everything she had. I caught her eye and she pointed at the gear bag with a get on with it expression.

I splashed back to the boat for the bag, slung it across my back, and climbed the beast's slippery vines to reach the heart. The heart was blocked by some stray vegetation; I cut as little of it away as possible, just enough so I could squeeze the jug and funnel into the chest cavity. I positioned the funnel beneath one thin, pulsing black vine, then slit it with the tip of the knife.

Black sap began to ooze from the core of the vine down into the funnel and the jug. The fishy odor was much more pungent in this fresh dragon molasses. My eyes watered. The vine clogged after a little while and I had to make another cut. My thigh muscles began to ache from the effort of clinging to the rib, but I hung on until the jug was full. I carefully corked the jug, slipped it and the knife and funnel back in the gym bag, and slid down to the water.

Once I was back in the boat, Monique continued caroling as I poled us away back toward the stream, avoiding the mossy wrecks of other boats that had ventured into the swamp after Sap Daddy.

"Do you think you can keep singing long enough for us to get home?" I asked. Whatever witchcraft the girl was able to weave in her music, it was doing a fabulous job of keeping Yidhra out of my head. I knew Monique couldn't keep it up forever, but I'd enjoy what peace I could get while it lasted.

Monique nodded, looking a little mischievous. She took a deep breath and started belting out "99 Bottles of Beer on the Wall."

I smiled and began to sing along with her.

MADAME CAPLETTE WAS WAITING for us on the stream bank, looking impatient. "Why you singing that, girl? I told you not to waste your skills on them silly songs!"

Looking innocent, Monique pointed at me.

I shrugged. "She's helping me out with a little problem tonight." I threw the loop of the mooring rope over the tree stump and stepped out of the boat with the gear bag. "We got the sap; you want it?"

The old witch ignored the bag and frowned up at me. "'A

little problem' my bony posterior! Bend down here so I can take a look at your eyes, girl."

I did as she asked, and she took off her spectacles and peered into my eye, holding up her kerosene lantern for a better look.

Monique hopped out of the boat and peered at my face. "Ooh, your eyes have gotten all purple! They look like grapes!"

"Well, now, when was you gonna tell me you're possessed?" Madame Caplette's sharp tone of disapproval made my innards clench.

"Well, now, since when do you care?" I shot back. "It's my problem, not yours."

"It gets to be my problem right quick if your head starts a' spinnin' while I'm in the middle of the ritual. If I get distracted, your cousin gets *dead*. Do you want that?"

I flinched, realizing I'd been an idiot. "No, ma'am. I'm sorry."

Her expression softened. "Got a notion of who's in you?"

"Yidhra." The name tasted like cigarette ash on my tongue.

"And the beast that bit your cousin, was it in thrall to her?"

"Yeah."

"And you didn't think to mention that?" She scowled. "You didn't think that all this would have been a thing I needed to know right when you brung him here?"

Heat rose in my cheeks. "No."

"Lord Almighty." She lowered her lantern and sighed at me, shaking her head. "Come on to the house. I got something that'll keep it from getting any worse. It ain't a permanent solution, but it'll work for now. Looks like I gotta rethink everything, because it ain't just Jake who needs healing."

She took me to a back bedroom where she unlocked a large mahogany jewelry chest and pulled out a necklace made of blue glass beads with a large round turquoise pendant. When she held the necklace out to me, I realized the beads and stone were carved to look like eyes.

"Wear it close to your heart," she said.

"Yes ma'am." I slipped the necklace on over my head and tucked it under my tee shirt. The moment the stone and glass touched my bare skin, I felt the same kind of cool washing-over relief that Monique's song had given me in the swamp.

I helped Madame Caplette set up a black iron cauldron on a tripod over a pine log fire in the middle of a big circle of packed earth in the back yard. We gathered fresh herbs from her garden then put the dragon molasses, plants, a jug of rum, some silver nitrate powder, and a whole lot of black pepper into the cauldron to boil.

Next, she had me and Monique dig two post holes inside the arcane circle just beyond the worst of the heat from the fire and pound sturdy wooden 6-by-6s into both of them. The posts were standard pressure-treated lumber like you'd use for a deck, but someone had screwed D-rings into the sides. I'd seen the same kind of thing in someone's bondage dungeon once.

"You're not gonna tie us up out here, are you?" I joked nervously.

The old witch looked grave. "Matter of fact, I have to. The evil in you ain't gonna let go without a fight."

I went back into the house and helped Jake stumble to the arcane circle. Monique was nervously twisting a bundle of hemp rope when I came back out. She helped me tie Jake sitting with his back to his post, and then tied me to mine.

Madame Caplette went back into the house and returned wearing a loose blue caftan. In one hand she carried an oak bucket that held a long-handled steel dipper and an owl-feathered rattle made from a dried gourd lashed to a human radius bone.

She stepped barefoot onto the dirt circle and set the bucket and cooler down just inside the circle's edge, away from the heat. For the next hour, she got down on her hands and knees inscribing various arcane symbols in the dirt with the ceremonial knife. Some she put around the cauldron's fire, others she drew around me and Jake.

Monique sat on a log near us, watching her grandmother work with rapt interest. Madame Caplette finished scratching the last symbol into the ground. Her knees and back popped audibly as she got to her feet and stretched, raising the muddy knife toward the still-dark morning sky.

I held my breath and nervously twisted my wrists in their ropes as Madame Caplette started the ritual. The old witch raised the owl-feathered rattle and the ceremonial knife. She began to chant, stomp and dance around the potion bubbling in the cauldron. A bucket of dry ice for cooling the finished potion sent an eerie low fog across the ground beyond the fire. Her motions were practiced and utterly confident. She slashed the air with the knife as if she were cutting down every last one of the forces of evil.

Jake moaned and struggled against his post. I couldn't understand much of the chant, but I caught enough to know she was calling on the whole *guédé* loa family to help us fend off Yidhra and her minions. Loas don't always have good will towards humankind. But they are of the Earth, and Yidhra pretends to be but is not. This was a clear supernatural turf war if ever there was one. Madame Caplette brought all her authority to the chant, and she wielded an ancient, powerful magic that was downright scary. Hairs rose on my arms and the back of my neck, as if a thunderstorm was gathering above us, but the sky was clear.

A shock rocketed through me as if Jake had slammed me with one of his haymaking left hooks. Suddenly there I was, back in the burning warehouse, facing Yidhra in all her terrible beauty.

"I've seen into your heart." She smiled at me. "I know exactly what you want, Pepper. It can all be yours if you give yourself to me."

She showed a vision of me holding court for socialites and

politicians in a grand old house in Lakewood. Everybody knew my name because I'd personally funded all the drug rehab programs, homeless shelters, and job programs. All the misery and poverty in the city was gone because of me. I was smart, respected, cool. Any old thing I decided to wear became that season's fashion. Pop stars like Beyoncé wanted to meet me. People asked for my autograph at parties. Our city was no longer the punchline of jokes about drunks or hurricanes. New Orleans shone as the brightest diamond in America's crown, and I was its princess.

I saw it all so clearly, and I wanted it so badly. I just had to let Yidhra devour me, heart and soul, and the dream would come true. But deep down I knew it would be an illusion that only existed inside my own head. Because if the dark goddess could do all that, why hadn't it been done?

"No," I said.

"If you refuse me, your family will suffer like none before."

She showed me visions of Jake screaming, his skin dripping off his body as the shoggoth corruption took hold and crushed his bones to mush before he became a formless, blister-eyed monstrosity. I saw Rudy flayed, his arms and legs smashed with a sledgehammer. I saw his wife Lori chopped to pieces in our basement. I saw myself doing all these terrible things to my aunt and uncle. The goddess would take hold of me and force me to torture them if I refused her. I'd end up locked away in some asylum, mad and savage and hated until I finally died.

I grabbed Yidhra by her long, beautiful hair and dragged her with me into the heart of the warehouse fire. She screamed and clawed at my face as we both burned, our skin blistering and blackening. The agony of it took the air from my lungs, but I had to protect my family. I had to. The pain of immolation was worse than anything I'd ever imagined, but I held the shrieking goddess in the flames. My will was stronger than flesh and bone.

I came back to the real world, gagging as Madame Caplette poured the hot, bitter, tarry potion down my throat.

"You got to swallow it!" she ordered.

I did as she told me. My clothes were soaked through with sweat, and my wrists and arms ached, raw from my fighting against the ropes all night. The eye-stone necklace still hung solid and cool around my neck. Dawn was breaking through the trees, and the early morning sky was lit in delicate reds and purples.

My cousin sat slumped over, still bound to his post. He was breathing. I wasn't sure, but it seemed like the swelling in his arm had gone down.

"Jake," I called. "You still with us?"

He slowly raised his head. "That was a real messed-up dream I just had." His voice was hoarse, but strong.

"I think y'all are both on the mend," said Madame Caplette.

"You know she's gonna come back, right?" Jake stared at me, his eyes clear and unafraid. "She got a taste of both our souls, and she ain't gonna give up so easy."

"Well, she can't be more persistent than any of the effin' narco gangs who keep coming into our neighborhood, can she?" I replied. "If she wants another ass-kicking, by gods we'll give her one."

Jake smiled. "That we will, cuz. That we will."

THE TALL ONES

STEPHEN ROSS

I ate a lime. I had a paper bag full of them. Some people chain-smoked cigarettes or chewed gum. I ate limes; a doctor had recommended I do so, and I had done so since I was ten.

"We're almost there, Nicolas," my aunt said.

Aunt Augusta was a lousy driver. Five hours on the road, and every ten minutes she'd announce our impending arrival. We headed south, following the eastern shoreline of Lake Michigan, with a destination of Redgrave.

Redgrave. I'd never heard of the place until that day. It was Aunt Augusta's hometown—a small village on the shore of Lake Michigan. I didn't know, as we drove into it that afternoon, that I was going to lose my mind there. I didn't know I was going to hear about the Tall Ones, and I didn't know I was going to meet a girl (I think).

I didn't ordinarily meet girls.

"You need a girlfriend, Nicolas," my aunt would say, at least once a week, whenever she thought I looked glum. I was sixteen. What I needed was privacy. I was a man of science. I intended to go to university and study quantum physics. I didn't need a girlfriend.

The first thing I learned on arriving in Redgrave was that there was barely any cell phone coverage; I had been hotspotting my phone for my laptops internet connection. There was maybe enough signal in town for a short text message.

"It's the holidays," said a woman who looked exactly like my aunt. "It happens every first week of July. The internet and the mobility telephones slow down. It's probably on account of all the holidaymakers who've come into town."

Mobility telephones?

The woman, Agatha, looked exactly like my aunt, because she was my aunt's twin sister; she owned a little hotel in the middle of town.

Let me describe my aunt—you can cut-n-paste the description for her sister. Five and a half feet tall, seventy years old, thin, dressed in more colors than you could imagine, head of messy blonde hair that looked like a family of birds lived there.

Aunt Augusta really wasn't my aunt. My parents had both left each other on the same night: my tenth birthday. They each independently packed up a suitcase and walked out—one out the front door, one out the back door—never to be seen again, each of them assuming the other would take care of me. I was left with an old house, a birthday cake, and a brand-new blue bicycle. Aunt Augusta was the kindly old lady who lived across the street; as I had no next of kin, she signed some papers and became my legal guardian.

"What brings you to Redgrave?" asked Agatha.

"I'm going to swim in the lake," Aunt Augusta said.

"You don't want to do that," said Agatha. "You don't want to swim in the water."

My aunt screwed up her face in disgust. "Not that again."

We'd been on the road for three weeks. My aunt had this bucket list of taking a swim in each of the Great Lakes, and Michigan was the last one. Come hell or high water, or low tide, she was going to complete her list.

"Why shouldn't she swim in the lake?" I asked.

"People disappear," said Agatha.

"What do you mean?"

"Sometimes, people go out for a swim in the water at Redgrave, and they don't come back. The Tall Ones get them."

"The Tall Ones?"

Aunt Augusta had heard enough. She grunted. "I don't believe in the Tall Ones. I never have, and I never will. It's just a myth. It's superstitious nonsense."

She looked at me. "A dozen or so people have gone missing in the lake over the years. Any rational person will tell you they were simply inexperienced swimmers who got caught up in the lake's unpredictable currents."

She looked back at her sister and barked with authority. "I am not an inexperienced swimmer!"

That was the end of the discussion.

Agatha showed us up to our rooms. Mine was on the third floor. There was a view of the lake. Agatha explained there was no in-house Wi-Fi, but there was a network socket on the wall behind the television set, and the bandwidth was complimentary.

She left.

Finally, I was alone.

I sat on the edge of the bed in my tiny room; my suitcase on the floor, my laptop on the bed. At least I had a room; I had had to sleep in the car at Lake Erie. And there was indeed a socket on the wall to plug in a network cable.

I ate my last lime.

I didn't have a network cable.

AUNT AUGUSTA'S sister didn't have any cables. She suggested I try the convenience store down at the waterfront. A walk sounded like a nice idea. I had spent three minutes in my room, and the organic spirals and swirls of the ancient wallpaper already bored me.

I walked two blocks to the lake's edge. There was a pier and a dozen boats for hire moored to it. There were few people about, hardly a holiday horde. Redgrave was little more than a handful of gift shops and a handful of hotels; a scenic pullover for travelers headed elsewhere, anywhere.

The lake water was oddly still. The late afternoon sun didn't reflect off it. There was no sparkle. I didn't believe in superstition, or myths, or Tall Ones—whatever they were meant to be—but I wouldn't have swum in the lake, either. Purely for scientific reasons. I knew my way around chemistry, and there was something strange about the water off the shore of Redgrave. Something weird about the way it lapped at the old blackened wooden poles of the pier. In the late afternoon light, it looked more like soup than lake water. There appeared to be a texture to it, a thickness.

Or maybe I needed new glasses.

The convenience store stood across the street from the pier, and I walked over to it.

A pair of suspicious eyes watched me come. There were two amateur hoods leaning against a brick wall near the store's entrance; locals, no older than me, smoking cigarettes.

The one with no hair gave me a dirty look, as though he desperately wanted me to behold his coolness, the cut of his leather jacket, the magnificence of his shaved head, but then, was far too cool to actually want me to look. He sneered as though he'd fight me for even daring to glance at him. Idiot.

The convenience store was sufficiently convenient. I found a network cable and headed to a small fruit section at the rear. Then a girl with a shopping trolley nearly drove over me.

"Sorry," she said, steering her trolley around me. It was loaded with bag upon bag of salt, and a couple of random grocery items. She wheeled it past.

She was about my height, with long dark hair. She was

maybe a year older, and her clothes looked colorful and old-fashioned, like she had gotten dressed sometime in the last century, maybe the 1980s; I knew nothing about clothes, to be sure.

I was going to say, *That's a lot of salt.* But I didn't talk to girls.

She glanced at me.

She had green eyes. Vivid.

I don't think I had ever seen a girl with green eyes. But, I couldn't remember the color of any girl's eyes. Maybe I just hadn't ever been looking?

Then she was gone.

I filled a small bag with limes. I took it, along with the network cable, to the checkout.

I was served by a large, unshaved man with droopy eyes and adult tattoos. He was a bulky fellow with a voice as deep as a tunnel. He could have moonlighted as a grizzly bear.

I paid and left.

"Let's get naked, green eyes."

The two local hoods were following the girl with green eyes along the sidewalk. She was carrying six full grocery bags.

The no-hair one was working a theme. "Yo, green eyes. Let's get naked together."

"Yo, *head*," I called out. "Not even your bathroom mirror wants to see you take your clothes off. Leave her alone."

I had no idea how those words formed and came out of my mouth, but they did. The two hoods and the girl stopped to look back at me. I don't know why, but I walked in their direction. Who did I think I was? I had absolutely no idea. It was like some kind of chemical reaction had taken place inside my brain, and my body was dutifully following along.

Maybe I was fed up? Fed up with being hassled by morons, who loitered outside convenience stores, or in school corridors, or anywhere I wanted to go about my lawful business. And maybe I was fed up with the three weeks of traveling on a loop of the Great Lakes with my certifiably loopy aunt.

Maybe I had finally lost my temper.

The no-hair hood stepped in my direction. He probably wanted to know who I thought I was. When we got close enough to each other for introductions, he punched me in the mouth. His fist was like a boulder. I spun about on the spot and went from vertical to horizontal, slamming down onto the ground.

I opened an eye: sidewalk, gum. I heard a voice growling. It was the grizzly bear. He had come out of his store. He said something about eating the two hoods, if he ever saw them again.

They walked away.

"Are you okay?" the girl asked. She knelt alongside me. She helped me sit up and wiped my lips with her fingers, and I saw my saliva and a trace of my blood on her fingertips. She studied it with curiosity. "Your saliva is a strange color," she remarked. "It's golden."

Then she did something I wasn't expecting. She licked her fingertips. I had never seen anyone do that.

Her green eyes sparkled, as though they were catching the last rays of the afternoon sun. "You're special," she said. She looked across at the two hoods walking off together into the sunset, and there was anger in those eyes. "That wasn't the first time. Shall I do something back to them?"

"I wish you could," I laughed. I wasn't entirely sure she couldn't.

She helped me onto my feet then turned her attention to collecting up all six of her grocery bags.

I picked up my bag of limes and network cable. "Can I help?" I asked. "Do you have far to walk?"

"To the lighthouse."

I looked behind me. The lighthouse was in the other direction, down at the other end of town; a tall, shiny white structure with its light already lit for the coming evening.

She shook her head. "The old lighthouse. It's a half-mile walk, but there's a shortcut."

I took three of her grocery bags, and we walked together along the sidewalk. "You have a lot of salt in these bags," I said.

"You have a lot of saliva," she replied. "More than other people, I think."

"I have a condition. Hyper-salivation." I didn't know how she knew; it wasn't as though I was noticeably dribbling. "What do you need with all the salt?"

"It's a long story."

I didn't ask.

"We're not from around here," she said.

"Neither am I."

"Every summer, my uncle brings me to Redgrave. We've been coming here since before I can remember anything."

"This is my first time."

We turned off the main street and took a detour down an alley. At the end of it lay the beginnings of the woodlands that encroached on the town. We went in, and she led me along an overgrown pathway through the woods. I quickly became aware that there was silence; no birds. I could hear nothing except for the sound of our shoes on the loose gravel of the pathway.

"Thank you for what you did back in town," she said. "It means a lot."

I shrugged in a casual manner. I don't think I had ever done that before.

"My name is Lucia."

"I'm Nicolas."

The old lighthouse was another five minutes walking, during which time I discovered we didn't have much in common. Lucia hadn't read any of the books I'd read. She wasn't a gamer. She'd never heard of Carl Sagan, but she knew what quantum physics was, and she could name every one of Jupiter's moons, which made me very happy.

The lighthouse stood fifty yards back from the lake and was surrounded by a thicket of trees and overgrown bushes. It was a towering brick and concrete structure made black with an entanglement of creeping vines and dirt. Only the very top of the tower, above the trees, showed any sign of its exterior having once been white. The glass windows of the lantern room at its peak were mostly smashed and shattered, and above that thrust a rusted lightening rod into the sky. I couldn't entirely make it out, but there looked to be some kind of antenna attached to the lightening rod; it hung loose and moved on the breeze. I couldn't guess its purpose.

The door to the lighthouse was open and, as we walked up to it, I became aware of the throbbing sound of an engine, and of hammering; the noise was coming from inside.

"My uncle is rather old and rather odd," Lucia said. "It's best to ignore anything he might say."

We went inside.

The engine was the lighthouse's power generator; a great cumbersome chunk of 19th century engineering that filled the ground floor of the building and vibrated the earth with its pulsing. It wasn't alone. The room overflowed with machinery; it was a kaleidoscope of old and new technology. There were old pipes and gauges, and steam rising, and wiring and cables, and computer towers, and a bank of twenty computer monitors —each flickering with screensavers I hadn't seen since I was in kindergarten.

Lucia's uncle was halfway up a ladder, leaning over the generator, hammering a metal pipe.

"What is this?" I whispered to Lucia.

"It's my uncle's machine."

The man stopped hammering. He turned to look at us, with his head turning in a way that didn't seem possible for a head to do, as though his head could move independently of his body. It was probably a trick of the room's dim light.

His two dark eyes stared at Lucia and then at me, where they stayed staring.

"This is Nicolas," Lucia said. "He helped me carry the grocery bags from town."

The man came down off his ladder. He dropped his hammer and came over for a closer inspection.

"Nicolas, this is my Uncle Otto."

I held out my hand.

Uncle Otto didn't take it. He sniffed the air. He looked like he had gotten dressed sometime in the last century, or maybe in the century before that. His machine burped. A new cloud of steam rose from it and the bank of computer monitors came to life. Across each screen flashed a continual stream of web pages, each lasting barely a second before being replaced by the next.

"What does your machine do?" I asked.

Uncle Otto grinned. His teeth were filthy.

Up close, his head didn't look right. There were odd proportions, his eyes were out of alignment, and there were bumps where there shouldn't have been bumps. His body didn't look right, either. It was like it was bursting to break out of its containment, like an overripe piece of fruit the moment before it split its skin.

"It's going to open a door," he said. His eyes were wide. His mouth contorted into a maniacal grin.

I didn't know if the man was speaking metaphorically, or whether he meant it would literally open a door. "What kind of door?"

"A door to the interesting things," he said. "Do you know what the interesting things are?"

"No."

The grin became more intense. "When I break the door open, you'll get to meet them."

"We need to take these bags up to the kitchen," Lucia announced. She didn't seem entirely happy her uncle was planning to open a door to interesting things. She led me over to a staircase that hugged the curve of the lighthouse's inner wall and spiraled up, and we climbed its rusted metal steps.

A kitchen lay on the next floor up. There was an old stove in the corner. There was an old wooden table and a couple of chairs. The room was made of wood, and large chunks of it were rotting. The room's sole window was smashed, and decades of weather and wildlife had freely rained in. It was my guess the lighthouse was at least 150 years old. Everything was decrepit. No wonder they had built a new one.

We put the grocery bags on the table. Lucia took out one of the bags of salt. She opened it.

"Your uncle is indeed rather odd," I remarked.

"It's his machine," she said. "He's been working on it for a long time."

"Every summer?"

"Yes."

She took a handful of salt and ate it.

I had never seen anyone do that.

She pointed upwards. "Want to see the lake from up at the top?"

Scenery wasn't really my thing, but it was the first time I had ever been inside a lighthouse. "Sure." I left my bag of limes and the network cable on the table.

The spiral staircase continued up. There was another floor above the kitchen: a bedroom. There were two bunks and an old dresser. Broken window. Decay. It didn't look like anyone had slept in the room for a long time.

I followed Lucia up the staircase. The walls came closer the further up we went, as the lighthouse tapered to its top where we climbed up into the lantern room.

The lantern room was a glassed-in housing for the lamp and its lens—the magnifying glass that concentrated the lamp light and made it visible over great distances. It was a room of shattered glass, and there was a steady breeze through it.

We climbed out onto the catwalk that ran a ring around the lantern room, and I got a closer look up at the antenna that had been attached to the tower's lightning rod. It was held on with duct tape and looked to have been made of broken cell phone tower components. A thick cable ran from it and down the side of the lighthouse.

Lucia and I gazed out at the lake.

The lake water appeared dark, and the disappearing sun falling behind the horizon didn't reflect off any part of it. Lake Michigan was supposed to be blue. Through my eyes, it looked like a dark, muddy green soup.

"We are young," Lucia said. "This is our time. This is our world."

I couldn't have agreed with her more. I glanced. She watched me.

"You're different than the others," she said.

I shrugged; for the second time that day. I had no idea how to do this kind of thing, but I knew I desperately wanted to kiss her.

She knew it as well. She put her hand over my mouth. "I'm different, too."

"I don't care."

She took her hand away. She looked at her fingers and my saliva on it. She licked her hand. Her eyes sparkled once more.

I leaned toward her, to kiss her.

"I think you can help me," she said. "Do you want to?"

"Of course. Help you do what?"

My cell phone rang.

I slunk back. I guessed I was high enough up in the air to receive a signal. I yanked the thing out of my pocket and answered it.

"Nicolas?" It was Agatha, Aunt Augusta's sister.

"What?"

"Your aunt has gone missing. In the lake."

I sighed. "I'm coming back to town, now." I put the phone

back in my pocket. The most amazing moment of my life had come to an end. "I have to go.'

I knew Lucia wasn't happy. She didn't say anything. She turned away, hiding her eyes from me, and looked out over the lake.

I left her on the catwalk and made my way back down the stairs.

Uncle Otto was seated at the table in the kitchen; he glanced at me as I entered. He held a spoon. On the table before him was a soup bowl. It was full of salt. He proceeded to shovel a great spoonful of the stuff into his mouth.

I retrieved my bag of limes and network cable and left. There was something very odd about these people.

I RAN BACK TO TOWN; it was late twilight. I could barely navigate my way along the pathway through the darkening woods. I tripped twice.

It was nighttime at the pier. There was a crowd gathered. There was a police wagon and a deputy asking questions. A fishing boat was loaded up for a search: several men, flashlights, a couple of rifles, a spear gun, binoculars, life preserver. The boat was cast off, and it slowly moved out into the darkness.

My aunt's sister was at the pier. I went to her, and she explained what had happened. Aunt Augusta had decided to take her lake swim that late afternoon as the sun was setting; she didn't want to waste any time in completing her list. She dived into the lake, swam out two hundred yards, and then vanished.

"I told her not to go into the lake," Agatha said. "But away she went and did it. And look what happened."

"There's evil in that water," someone said. The crowd at the pier had gravitated around us, all wide-eyed and fearful.

"The Tall Ones got her," someone else murmured.

There was hushed agreement.

"What are these Tall Ones?" I asked.

Silence.

"What are they?" I demanded to know.

The crowd solemnly dispersed. Nobody wanted to tell me. Even the deputy sheriff looked sheepish.

Agatha stared at me as though she had caught me performing an unspeakable act on her living room rug. "It is best not to talk of them," she said in a whisper. "It brings no good luck to do so."

My head hurt.

My aunt's sister and all those who lived in town were overwhelmed by some type of medieval superstition and hysteria. It was the 21st century outside of Redgrave. It was the *11th* in it.

I was a man of science. Of learning. Of reason. There had to be some explanation for the disappearances in the lake. Maybe it had to do with the currents. Redgrave jutted out into the lake sharply, like a very large rock lying along a smooth shoreline; it was not for nothing the town needed a lighthouse. Maybe the combination of rocky outcrop and the water currents around it were the explanation?

I returned to my room at the hotel. I unraveled the network cable and plugged my laptop into the internet. I was determined to look up some facts; some proven, reliable, scientific information.

I searched. The internet connection was painfully slow. *Pain...fully*.

I learned. Lake Michigan's currents were quick and often dangerous—rip and longshore currents. There had been numerous drownings over the years, with most bodies being recovered. I found nothing specifically about the currents at Redgrave.

However. More than 200 people had disappeared in the lake at Redgrave since 1888—when the town's newspaper first went into print and started keeping records—disappeared and never seen again.

How was this not a thing? How had I never heard about these vanishings before?

I found a dusty website that talked about the Redgrave legend: *The Tall Ones*. The website was older than I was; green on black text, blink tags, visitor counter in the tens of millions. According to the legend, hundreds of years ago, there was no town at Redgrave, but the land still jutted out into the lake, and on this outcrop there lived monsters; or so said the stories that had been handed down from generation to generation by the Indian tribes that had lived in the surrounding region at the time.

The Indians feared these monsters, which they called the Tall Ones. The Tall Ones could not be stopped by arrow, tomahawk, or fire. The Tall Ones were unnatural. And if caught by one, your fate was to be eaten.

However. There came one day, the son of a chief. As a young man, he was sent from the tribe to seek knowledge, to find a way to destroy these monsters.

This young man journeyed to the North, East, and West, and then into the South, and into Mesoamerica, where he met the Aztecs, from whom he learned a great knowledge of spells and magic. It was from them he learned the Water Spell.

Anything can become water. Put a lime into it and, with time, the lime will decay. It will lose its form and become part of the water itself, where it will remain trapped forever. The Water Spell took away the need for time; the Aztecs knew how to make the decay immediate.

The young man returned to his tribe.

It was widely known that the Tall Ones had a weakness: Salt. It was their drug and they feasted upon it. So, a great harvest of salt was made by the tribe, producing it from the ashes of burnt plants. Once enough salt had been extracted, a canoe was laden with it, and the young man took it out onto the lake.

The monsters followed.

A slobbering great herd of them waded into the water and headed out after the canoe. And, once in the water, the young man cast the spell. The legend said the sky cracked open that day, and the waters of the lake boiled, and the Tall Ones screamed. They were decayed. Then they were no more. They were of the lake.

The rocky outcrop of land where the monsters had once lived was given the name of the Water Spell, which, over the years, became corrupted by the white settlers to Redgrave.

I took a lime out of the bag and began to eat it.

Salt.

Monsters.

Redgrave.

My head spun.

It hit me; I hadn't really been paying attention. Uncle Otto had built some kind of a machine. It was going to open a door. It was going to open the lake and let the interesting things out. Uncle Otto was going to free the Tall Ones.

I was certain of this.

I knew I had to stop him.

There was a mirror on the wall in my room. I stared at myself in it. What was happening to me? I was a man of science, and there I was succumbing to the madness that had been handed down from generation to generation of townspeople.

I closed my eyes.

All I really wanted to think about was Lucia, and the odd, gelatinous touch of her hand on my lips.

MAYBE I HAD BECOME INSANE. I left the actuality of my room and an internet connection to head back to the old lighthouse.

I didn't know Lucia's shortcut through the woods, and least of all in the night. I went back along the shoreline, with its empty dunes lit only by moonlight. The water of the lake seemed to be swelling, as though a great, turbulent force was within it. As I drew closer to the lighthouse, I could hear a thunderous sound through the woods.

There were cables.

There was a thick string of shiny black cables running into the lake, into the water; too many to count, bundled together in a wad as thick as a log. I followed them from the shore, and they snaked their way through the woods to the lighthouse. They flowed out of its door. The thunderous noise was the machine inside.

At the lighthouse, I could see Uncle Otto up at the top of it; out on the catwalk outside the lantern room, with his hands gripping the railing, his mouth open like a bucket, his mad eyes cast out to the lake.

I went in.

The cables fed out of his machine, and the machine was fit to explode. Clouds of smoke billowed. Large, loose chunks of the machine's metal body vibrated in a blur. The smell of the diesel powering the generator was overwhelming.

The banks of computer monitors mounted above flickered too rapidly to see or understand their content. One at the end did not. It flickered at a fraction of the pace of the others, and on it I could see it was a flow of internet content: feedback forums, user messages, comment threads. I recognized the tone at once; a familiar sea of negativity and anger.

I took a closer look at Uncle Otto's machine. I knew my way around computer parts, and some of its components I knew well: routers, modems, hubs, switches, and a bank of RAM on a string of connected motherboards, more than I had ever seen in one place.

It was no wonder that there was next to no internet or Wi-Fi in Redgrave. It seemed plain to me. Uncle Otto was downloading the internet; specifically, anything negative or full of anger and hatred. He was doing so on an industrial scale. It was probably gigabyte upon gigabyte of data per second. All of it was being fed into a chain of technology I didn't recognize or understand. Out of that came the black cables that went out and fed into the lake.

At that moment, a hand grabbed my shoulder and spun me around. Uncle Otto thrust his face within an inch of mine. His eyes glowed with the red of fire, and his breath was a gust of foul air and salt.

I struggled to free myself from his grip. If it weren't for his hands being so slippery and wet, I would never have gotten away from him. I ran from the lighthouse and into the woods. When I realized he hadn't followed, I knew I had to return. I had to wreck his machine.

At that moment, I came face to face with Lucia. She had been running from the other direction.

"I've been to the lighthouse," I said.

"I went into the town," she answered. "I was looking for you."

"Is your uncle downloading the internet into the lake?"

"Yes." Her green eyes stared into mine, and mine into hers. I don't think I had ever looked into anyone's eyes that seriously. And there was, at that moment, complicity between us; an unspoken connection and understanding. A binding.

"He's using the negativity of the world as a power source," she said.

We returned to the lighthouse. The uncle was now nowhere to be seen. The fat log of cables pouring out through the door now glowed red with heat. The thunder of the machine inside was deafening. The lighthouse itself shuddered.

"My uncle has harnessed human anger," Lucia shouted. "He wants to—"

"I know," I shouted over her. I stood at the foot of the staircase of madness.

"I have to stop him," I shouted. "I have to stop his machine." I ran inside. I looked for something I could smash it with: a hammer, a pole, a weight.

Lucia followed. She spun me around. "Do you trust me?" she shouted.

"Yes."

"I want his machine to work."

I stared at her.

She grabbed my shoulders. She shook me. "Do you trust me?" she shouted with desperation.

My instincts said no. My heart screamed. "Yes," I shouted.

Lucia pulled me to her and kissed me. Open mouth. Saliva and salt. Her lips hard against mine. I didn't know how regular kisses with girls went, but this one felt like she was sucking the saliva from me with the strength of a vacuum cleaner.

She broke from the kiss and stood back. Her green eyes shone brilliantly, and her face glowed a greenish color I had never seen before. She ran to the machine and grabbed it with both hands. She screamed as she gripped it with an ear-piercing cry.

All at once, the machine attained perfection. It became silent. Its ground-shaking vibrations stopped. The cables that had glowed red now became white. For no more than a handful of heartbeats, the machine worked at full capacity and then, one by one, like a string of firecrackers, the computer monitors exploded, blowing out great shards of glass and smoke.

"To the lake," Lucia shouted, letting go.

We ran to the lake, following the log of white-hot cables.

Uncle Otto was at the water's edge. "It's working," he shouted. "After all these years, I found a way!"

The water at his feet began to part, as though it were a door, and beyond it, inside, tall, hideous creatures were beginning to form, taking their shape from billions upon billions of particles coming together out of the lake water.

What had I done? What had I helped to do?

"We are free," Uncle Otto shouted into the hole in the water, his hands cast in the air in victory.

Suddenly, the overripe piece of fruit that he was burst his skin, shredding his clothes and making a mess of flesh about him on the beach. From the shape of an ill-formed man, he sprang up into a towering creature.

He was not just freeing the Tall Ones, he was one.

Then Lucia pushed him in.

The tall creature the man had become fell, screaming, into the gaping mouth of the water.

Lucia spat a fire hose burst of green fluid across the cables. They were immediately burnt and severed by it. The internet ceased being downloaded into the lake. Before our eyes, the open door in the lake shut. The half-resurrected creatures within, screaming, were returned once again to their primordial soup of the lake water. Uncle Otto went with them.

There was a thundering explosion behind us. I turned back to see the lighthouse ablaze, with its top exploded, and meteor-like shards of flaming debris raining down from the sky.

"That is the last of them," Lucia said. "The old ones are now all gone."

"The Tall Ones?"

She nodded. "My uncle was the only one of them who wasn't in the water when the others were taken. He was caring for me. I was only newly born to the world."

We stood together at the edge of the lake, staring at its waters as it began to calm and, for the first time, in the light of the moon, I saw a hint of blue.

Lucia then shed her clothes and skin and changed into her

true form. She must have been over ten feet tall. "It is the time of the young," she said.

"Yes," I answered.

She took my hand in her tentacle.

Aunt Augusta was right. I did need a girlfriend. I may have been a man of science, but some things were plainly beyond science.

And I supposed I would get used to the salt.

JUST IMAGINE

TIM WAGGONER

Trinity Moon sat at a table in CaffeNation, laptop open before her, phone lying on the table next to it, backpack at her feet. Her email program was on the screen, and she stared at the most recent message, written in all caps.

WE SELECTED YOU FOR THIS. DO NOT BETRAY US.

She sipped her caramel-flavored coffee drink and read the message again, as if somehow it would make more sense this time. The sender was identified only by a long string of what seemed like random numbers, and the subject line was blank.

It's just spam, she told herself. *Or some kind of joke.*

Still, there was something sinister about the two sentences —especially the threat implied by the second one—that creeped her out. Although she knew it was stupid, she looked around to see if anyone was watching her. Not that it would be much of a surprise if someone was. Trinity was used to people looking at her when she was out, especially older folks who didn't quite know what to make of her two-toned hair—bright red on the left side, bright green on the right—her anime-character T-shirts, black sweater, black skirt, and knee-high black boots. People around her own age—fifteen—didn't give her a second look, and she figured if she'd lived in a city instead of boring Ash Creek, Ohio, her hair and clothes would be almost conservative. But she didn't, and she often drew glances that ranged from *She looks awesome!* to *What's wrong with that freak?* but she'd gotten used to them

The place was almost full, with maybe a dozen customers beside her and three baristas behind the counter. There was the usual mix—students like her who'd stopped in after school to get their homework done, mothers who'd brought their young children in for a treat, business people who'd stepped out of the office for a change of scenery, along with a caffeine-boost, while they worked. There were some older people, too, men and women in their sixties and seventies. Retirees who'd come here to spend a couple hours of their day sipping coffee and complaining about how millennials were ruining the world. These folks would often sneak sideways glances at her while they talked, as if she were a perfect example of today's lazy, social-media-obsessed youth. They'd probably roll their eyes if they heard her name—*Thanks, Mom and Dad*—but she wondered what they'd say if they knew she was a straight-A honors student who planned to graduate high school early and go into pre-med.

No one was looking at her now, not even the older people. They were all too busy doing their own thing. Talking, drinking, eating, working, reading, listening to music. Nothing even slightly sinister about any of them.

Trinity was stressed and exhausted. Despite her parents' objections, she'd taken too many AP classes this semester, and the workload was kicking her butt. She was doing homework from the time school let out until she went to bed; staying up later and later to get more work done. At this point, she was getting an average of four hours of sleep a night, if that. No wonder she was feeling a little paranoid, especially after getting that weird email.

She turned back to her computer screen, intending to delete the message, but before she could do so, the world outside the coffee shop went dark. Completely, totally, and utterly. It was like somehow the windows had been painted black in the time it took her to blink. The front entrance was made of glass, and one wall of the shop had a large picture window in it. Several tables were positioned next to the window, and they were all occupied. But those customers appeared not to notice the sudden change. They continued texting, talking on their phones, chatting with each other, and not one of them so much as glanced at the inky darkness outside.

Trinity felt a sudden flush of warmth spread through her body. This always happened to her when she was scared. Some people felt lightheaded, some nauseated. She felt hot, as if her interior thermostat had been raised to boiling level. She turned to the counter to see if the baristas had noticed the darkness, but the three of them continued working, oblivious.

She was the only one who saw it. Either she was seeing something no one else could...or she was seeing something that wasn't there. Neither prospect was particularly appealing. She concentrated on taking slow, even breaths, attempting to forestall her burgeoning panic. She was prone to anxiety—their family doctor had told her that intelligent people were especially susceptible to it—but instead of prescribing pills, she'd referred Trinity to a therapist who'd taught her techniques for dealing with anxiety. Deep breathing was one of them. After a couple of minutes, she felt better—a little, anyway. She was still warm, but she didn't feel like she was burning up anymore.

The entire time she'd been deep breathing she'd avoided looking at the windows, but now she did. She hoped that she'd find they'd returned to normal, that the relaxation exercise had cleared her mind as well as calmed her, that whatever had happened in her brain was only a temporary glitch and was fixed now. But the world outside the window was still pitch-black.

Was she having a breakdown of some kind? Her parents

were always cautioning her not to work so hard, to take some time to relax. *You're not a machine*, her dad once told her. *You keep going the way you're going, and you'll end up physically and mentally wrung out. When that happens, it's hard to keep up your defenses. And it's important to keep them up. Vital. It can be a hard world, Trinity. You have to stay tough.*

A little overly dramatic, she'd thought, but she understood the message. She spent almost all her waking hours doing some kind of work, and when she finished, she watched online videos about various medical procedures. She knew that getting into a good medical school would be hard, and she was determined to do everything she could to make herself a competitive candidate. But at what cost? What good were straight A's at school when you started hallucinating?

She reached for her phone, intending to call someone, anyone, for help or at least reassurance that she wasn't going crazy. But who *could* she call? Ashley, her best friend, had cross-country practice this afternoon, and both of Trinity's parents were at work. She didn't want to bother them, but they'd always stressed that they wanted her to call if she needed them, no matter how minor or even crazy the reason might seem to her. So, she called. Neither of her parents answered. She left more or less the same message for them.

"It's me. I stopped at CaffeNation after school to do homework and, well, this is going to sound kind of weird, but I got this strange email and then it turned dark outside. Not like nighttime but pitch black. I'm not sure what's happening, and I'm getting a little freaked out. Call me when you can, okay?"

Edmund and Kathryn Moon were creativity consultants who ran their own business called *Just Imagine*. They often met with clients, and when they did, they gave them their full attention. Trinity knew they'd call her back as soon as they got her message, but until then, she was on her own

She put her phone back on the table. Now what? If she was so smart, she should be able to handle this on her own, right?

She had a problem that needed solving, which meant it was kind of like a test. And she knew how to *crush* tests. She remembered the weird email then. It was still displayed on her computer screen, and she read it once more.

WE SELECTED YOU FOR THIS. DO NOT BETRAY US.

Was it a coincidence that she'd received the message just before the windows had gone black? She started to feel hot again, and she made herself breathe deeply for several moments until she grew calm once more.

Forget the email for now. First things first. She needed to verify that the world outside the coffee shop had gone dark. She rose from her seat and walked toward the picture widow. She had to maneuver around other tables and customers to do so, but none of them paid her any attention. It was as if they didn't see her, as if she wasn't really there.

To get up to the window, she would need to squeeze between two customers sitting at different tables, their backs to each other, so close there was only twelve inches between them, maybe less.

The two customers were women. One was in her twenties, with glasses and long brown hair, talking animatedly with a friend her own age who looked a lot like her, except she wasn't wearing glasses. Trinity wondered if they were sisters. The woman at the other table was older, in her forties or fifties. She was stout, with short black hair and a nose piercing that seemed out of place on someone her age. She sat alone, watching video on a tablet computer. It looked like some kind of TV show, but Trinity didn't recognize it.

"Excuse me," she said as she slipped between the two women, but neither responded or even looked at her.

She felt cold emanating from the glass as she drew near. It was early October, but it had felt more like spring when she'd walked here from school. Nevertheless, the cold coming off the glass was more suitable to winter, and not a normal winter, either, but a harsh one, the kind with howling winds and temperatures well below zero. But the two women she'd squeezed between appeared not to notice the cold, even though neither of them was dressed for it. Trinity was reluctant to touch the glass, but she needed to confirm the reality of what she was experiencing. She reached out with her right hand—which only trembled a little—and slowly, hesitantly touched her fingers to the glass.

She immediately jerked her hand back with a hissing breath. The glass was so cold that touching it *hurt*. She looked at her fingertips and saw they were red, as if they'd been burned. She tapped each finger to her thumb and discovered all her digits were numb, and there was an ache deep in the bones, as if the cold had seeped through her fingertips and was slowly spreading throughout her hand. She wrapped her hand around her waist and pressed the other arm against it, hoping to warm it with her body. Then, standing in the arctic cold that radiated from the glass, she observed the blackness.

She saw no lights—no streetlights, no vehicle headlights. It didn't look as if sudden cloud cover had plunged the coffee shop into shade or the skies had darkened because of an approaching storm. Now that she was close to it, she could see that the darkness wasn't uniform. It was darker in some places than others, and shapes seemed to roil and swirl within it. The shapes were unlike anything she'd seen before, sometimes angular and geometric, sometimes amorphous and free-flowing. The shapes didn't resemble anything living—at least, not anything Trinity was familiar with—but she couldn't escape the feeling that there was something out there watching her. Many somethings. The idea terrified her, and she looked away from the window.

Trinity didn't like the dark. When she was little, she was absolutely terrified of it. She was convinced there were monsters in her closet and under her bed, and more than anything they wanted to be released from their prisons so they could get at her. Sometimes, she thought she could hear them whispering.

Let us in... Let us in...

Whenever this happened, she'd duck beneath the covers and put her pillow over her head in an attempt to shut out the voices. But it never helped, for the voices seemed to be coming from within her own mind.

She told her mother about the monsters, but she'd said they were nothing to worry about.

"They're just your imagination playing tricks on you. You're very smart and creative, sweetie, which means you've got a bigger imagination than most people. Most of the time that's a blessing, but other times, not so much. But even if monsters are real, they can't hurt you if you don't let them in."

"In where?" Trinity had asked.

"Just in. Remember that, okay?"

"I will, Mommy."

Trinity hadn't been entirely sure what her mother meant, but she understood the gist of it. Her imagination created the monsters, which meant that—if she tried hard enough—she could uncreate them.

That night, when she felt the monsters' presence, when she heard their whispers, she concentrated on making them go away. It took several nights, but eventually she didn't feel the monsters' presence anymore, and their voices were silent. From that point on, if she occasionally sensed that she wasn't alone in her room, if she heard a whisper so soft and quiet she wasn't sure she'd heard it at all, she didn't worry about it. It was just her mind up to its old tricks.

Was her mind playing tricks on her now? She hoped so, for the alternative was too terrifying to contemplate.

She turned to the middle-aged woman watching video on her tablet. "Pardon me," Trinity said. She was surprised by how calm she sounded, when inside all she wanted to do was scream.

The woman didn't react at first, and Trinity had a sudden fear that the woman couldn't see or hear her, that maybe, somehow, she wasn't really here at all. But then the woman looked up from her tablet, an expression of annoyance on her face.

"Yes?"

She sounded almost angry, and Trinity was suddenly unsure what to say. The woman continued to look at her, almost glaring actually, and Trinity opened her mouth to speak. But then she glanced at the tablet and saw that the screen displayed an image of herself standing at the coffee shop's entrance, staring at the darkness beyond, hand on the bar of the door, ready to open it.

Trinity was unable to take her gaze from the tablet. "I, uh...Do you see it? Outside, I mean." She knew she wasn't making much sense, but it was the best she was capable of at that moment.

The woman turned to glance out the window, then faced Trinity once more. "See what?" the woman asked.

Trinity wanted to shout, *The great big black Nothing outside!* But when she looked at the woman, her words died in her throat. The woman's eyes were now a glossy black, as if a pair of highly polished stones had been shoved into the sockets. Trinity gaped at the woman's eyes, her mouth opening and closing as she tried to make herself say something. All she could come up with was a mumbled, "Never mind."

Trinity quickly turned away and headed for her table. She glanced back over her shoulder and saw the woman had returned to watching the video on her tablet. Trinity wondered what she saw there: a scene of Trinity opening the coffee shop's door? Or did she see something else, something normal?

Trinity thought about the door as she returned to her table. No one had entered CaffeNation since the darkness appeared, and while the coffee shop wasn't all that busy in the afternoons, usually there was a steady stream of customers coming in to grab a coffee or muffin to go. But the door hadn't opened, not once. That was strange, but the next thought Trinity had was far more disturbing. What would happen if someone did open the door, whether to come in or leave? Would the darkness remain outside, or would it rush in like a flood of frigid black water, filling the building, surrounding them, rushing down their throats to fill their lungs and swell their bellies?

She felt panic welling up inside her. She told herself that she was being ridiculous, that darkness wasn't a thing in and of itself. It was simply the absence of light. It had no form, no weight, no mass. She thought then of the shifting, roiling movement she'd seen in the darkness outside the window, and she was no longer confident that this darkness followed the scientific laws she knew. She wasn't sure it followed any rules at all.

Her phone chirped, announcing that she'd received a text. She picked it up and looked at the screen, hoping the message was from either her mom or dad, but it wasn't. It was a single word in all caps.

OPEN.

She felt a chill that had nothing to do with the cold outside. She dropped her phone on the table, eager to be rid of it, as if it were a poisonous thing that might bite her.

Open *what*?

The door, of course. What else could it be?

It wants in, she thought. *No, they want in*. The things in the darkness, the ones responsible for the swirling shapes she'd seen outside. It wasn't the dark you needed to fear, she realized. It was what the dark concealed.

She glanced at her computer screen, then down at her phone, and she mentally put the two messages together.

WE SELECTED YOU FOR THIS. DO NOT BETRAY US.

OPEN.

She thought of the scene displayed on the black-eyed woman's tablet, video of her holding the door handle, preparing to open it. The message was clear. Whatever was happening, whether it was real, imaginary, or somewhere in between, something wanted her to open the door. Something outside wanted in. Just like when she was a child sitting in her bed in the dark, alone and frightened, hearing voices whispering, *Let us in.... Let us in....*

She sat at the table, picked up her phone, and replied to the text in all caps.

NO.

She sent the message and waited to see if whoever—or whatever—had written her would reply. Instead of her phone chirping, her laptop dinged. Another email. She opened it.

YES. WE CHOSE YOU. YOUYOUYOUYOUYOU!!!

Why me? The answer came to her right away, and it came to her in her mother's words.

You're smart and creative, sweetie, which means you've got a bigger imagination than most people.

Big enough to open a door that maybe wasn't a physical door, one that kept the things outside—things that dwelled in the dark and the cold—from coming in where there was light and warmth and life?

Her phone chirped. The new text said: SMART, YES, VERY. NOW OPEN!

So the things—the *Outsiders*—wanted in, but they couldn't break through the barrier between the Dark and the real world. Not without help from someone on the other side. They could sense things from the Dark, could search for minds capable of helping them, minds of children who could be touched by them. Influenced. Trinity wondered how many children who thought they saw monsters in the dark really sensed the Outsiders touching their minds. Who knows? Maybe every closet monster and monster under the bed was really an Outsider that desperately wanted to be granted entrance into the real world.

Those children learned to shut out the Outsiders' voices as

they grew up. But if they became overly tired and stressed-out —as she had—maybe their psychic defenses weakened, giving the Outsiders an opportunity to influence them again. She had no intellectual reason to believe any of this, but it *felt* right.

She wondered if she'd fallen asleep at her laptop in the coffee shop, allowing the Outsiders to infiltrate her mind. Or was she awake, but in some kind of in-between place, halfway between the real world and the Dark? Either way, whatever happened in this place would affect the real world. If she opened the door, the Outsiders would enter, and once they were loose in the world they'd...do what? She wasn't sure, but whatever they wanted, it couldn't be good. She had to make sure that didn't happen, but she had no idea how to do it. She—

She had a sudden sensation that she was being watched. She looked around the coffee shop and saw that everyone—the customers, the baristas—had stopped what they were doing and were now looking at her. Like the woman at the window, their eyes were solid, glossy obsidian. They opened their mouths and spoke a single word in unison.

"Open."

These weren't the Outsiders, but they were speaking for them as avatars. Creatures with only the appearance of life and with no real minds to speak of, else they would've been able to open the door for their masters.

"No," Trinity said. Her voice was soft but firm.

A pause, and then everyone stood at the same time, moving with eerie mechanical precision. They then started walking toward her.

"Open," they said once more, and then they began repeating the word. *"Open, open, open, open, open, open...."*

They were trying to scare her, she knew that, but the knowledge didn't make her feel any less frightened. What would they do when they reached her? They wouldn't kill her. The Outsiders needed her to open the door.

But they can hurt you, she thought. *Hurt you bad.*

She experienced a nearly overwhelming urge to run to the door, fling it open, rush outside, and escape the black-eyed things coming for her. But she knew this was exactly what the Outsiders wanted. They didn't care why she opened the door, just so long as she did. The door was the key to everything, not only to the Outsiders' victory but also to their defeat. Could she lock it? No, that wouldn't work. The avatars would force her to unlock it and open it. But she couldn't open the door if it wasn't there anymore, could she?

The coffee shop had become a place of the mind—of *imagination*—and hers was strong. Maybe strong enough to do what needed to be done.

She stood, grabbed hold of her chair, and ran toward the door. The avatars shouted "No!" and increased their speed, running now. Out of the corner of her eye, she saw violent swirls in the darkness outside the windows—the Outsiders, upset by what she was attempting to do.

If the door had been a real one, breaking it would allow the Outsiders to come in. But this door was a symbol of the passageway between worlds, a creation of mental energy. If she could imagine hard enough, put all her will and determination into the strike, she could *unmake* the door and destroy the passageway, maybe forever.

She sensed avatars crowding behind her, felt fingers grabbing the fabric of her sweater. She was within a few feet of the door and the infinite blackness that lay behind it. She could feel the cold radiating from the glass, and for an instant she doubted herself, feared the Outsiders had tricked her into doing this, that she would be releasing them from their ancient prison if she continued. But she pushed those doubts aside and flung the chair toward the glass door, sending with it the full force of her considerable will.

The chair struck the door and the glass shattered. At the same time, the avatars let out a collective moan of pain. Trinity turned and saw cracks appear in their skin, fissures that spread and widened with impossible speed. One moment they were standing there looking at her with ebon eyes, and the next they collapsed in showers of glass fragments which clattered to the tiled floor.

Trinity was alone. The door was gone, replaced by a wall. The windows, too.

What happens now? She wondered if she was doomed to be trapped in this nowhere place for the rest of her life. There was no way out now, she'd seen to that. What could she—

The floor beneath her feet began to shudder, and she looked down to see cracks spiderwebbing across its surface. The cracks sped through the floor, up the walls, and onto the ceiling. Trinity threw herself beneath a table as CaffeNation exploded into a million-million shards, and the universe fell all around her.

TRINITY LOOKED up with a start and took a quick glance around.

CaffeNation was once more intact. Baristas behind the counter, customers sitting at tables, windows and door back in place, and outside...a pleasant sunny day. She checked her computer and phone, but there was no sign of the message the Outsiders had sent. Maybe what had happened was a dream or maybe it was something else. Whatever, she was just glad it was over.

The door opened then, and she turned toward it, half expecting to see a mass of darkness flooding toward her. But it was her mom and dad. They hurried over to her, faces filled with worry. Obviously, they'd gotten her message.

Her parents were both in their early forties. Her dad had black hair and a black goatee. He wore glasses and a blue suit when working, which made him look very professional, but he favored silly ties. The one he wore today had pictures of goldfish on it. Her mother's hair was dyed maroon—a more conservative color than Trinity's—and she wore colorful patterned blouses with black slacks for her business attire. Today's blouse was gray with images of black-eyed Susans on the fabric.

"Are you okay?" her mother asked.

Her dad looked around. "Are they gone?"

"I'm fine," Trinity said. But then she realized what her father had said. "*They*? You know about them? The...," she lowered her voice, "Outsiders?"

Her parents exchanged a glance before nodding.

"We didn't tell you because we didn't want to scare you," Mom said in the same lowered voice.

"And we hoped this day would never come for you," Dad said.

"We've been worried about you lately. You've been working so hard...we feared your mental defenses might be weakened."

"But we told ourselves you'd be fine. You resisted the Outsiders when you were little, and they never bothered you again. We thought maybe they never would."

Mom sighed. "Obviously, we were wrong."

As bizarre as dealing with the Outsiders had been, she was finding this even harder to believe. Her parents not only knew about the Outsiders, it sounded like they'd known about them for a long time, at least as long as she'd been alive.

"When did you first learn about them?"

"When we were teenagers ourselves," Mom said. "That's how your father and I met, actually. We were around your age and were at a skating rink when the Outsiders tried to use both of us to get in."

"No one was aware of them besides us," Dad said. "We worked together to keep them out, and—"

"We've been together ever since," Mom finished.

"But you handled the Outsiders all on your own," Dad said. "We're so very proud of you—and relieved that you're safe."

"There are others like us, more than you'd think," Mom

said. "Smart, creative people whose minds can function like doorways between worlds."

"If you know how to open them," Dad added.

"And it's up to us to make sure no one uses us as a way into our world."

"Like the Outsiders?" Trinity asked.

"Yes," Mom said. "And there are others."

"Are they as bad as the Outsiders?" When neither her Mom or Dad answered, Trinity asked, "Worse?"

Her parents exchanged looks, but then they faced her and smiled.

"We'll tell you all about it," Dad said. "Later."

Mom agreed. "Maybe over a cup of coffee."

Trinity prepared to leave with her parents. She threw away the rest of her drink, then closed her laptop, slid it into her backpack, then stood. She shouldered the pack, picked up her phone and started toward the door, her parents preceding her. But just as she was about to go through, her phone chirped. She checked the display and saw two words, all caps.

NEXT TIME.

She smiled grimly as she texted back.

I'LL BE READY.

HOLDING BACK

LISA MORTON

"I hold stuff back."

That was one of the first things Lucio ever said to me, as I sat across the table from him in the cafeteria during the lunch break. I thought I knew what he meant when he said it.

I was so wrong.

LUCIO MCKINLEY SHOWED up when I was in eighth grade. I didn't notice him right away, and I'm not sure anyone else did either. He was one of those kids who's quiet, not too smart and not too not-smart, doesn't hang with any particular crowd. He had long straight dark hair and wore a lot of black, so you might have thought he was a Goth, except he didn't have any tattoos or piercings or shirts with obscure band logos. He never looked anyone in the eye, volunteered for anything, or raised a hand in class.

In fact, like most everyone else at our school I might never have noticed him if it hadn't been for Jase Cooley.

Jase Cooley was the semi-official school bully. Every school's got one: the junior douchebag who has nothing going for him except a mean streak and a propensity to attract a following of smaller douchebags who will happily do his bidding. Somewhere over the spring break, "Cool J" had decided he liked me. O joyous day. I managed to avoid him during the weeks of freedom, but when school started up again encounters in classrooms and hallways were inevitable.

At first, they were just irritating, but as he realized I had zero interest in him his intent changed to the bully's need to dominate. He posted innuendos on my social media that got him banned. He texted me things he probably thought were really hot, like photos of him shirtless; I thought he looked like Jabba the Hutt without the tail.

Finally, one day he and his gang of three got me barricaded into a corner in the school library, right there in the aisle between psychology and sports books. While his flunkies kept a lookout, he pressed up against me, leaving me no room to maneuver around him.

"Go out with me," he said, shoving his ugly face close.

I turned mine aside. "There are around five hundred other girls in this school," I told him, looking down at a shelf of Sigmund Freud titles. "You can find somebody else."

"But I like *you*." He pressed up closer. I tried not to gag.

Beyond gagging, I was getting anxious, like "I'm having a panic attack" anxious. It was late in the afternoon; I'd come into the library (little used these days) to research a paper on the Civil War. If I called out for help, would anyone hear me? If they heard...would they help? Or would the minions turn them away so the boss could get on with his business?

"C'mon, just give me a chance," Jase said, as he lowered his face down to mine. "I've got big plans for May."

I would normally have thought that was incredibly weird, but right then I was more focused on the fact that he seemed to be trying to kiss me. I'd only been kissed once before by a non-relative, not even a non-relative I thought was cute (a kid named Lionel, during a field trip last year), and it hadn't been what I was expecting. No sparks had flown, or fireworks exploded. If anything, I just felt a vague unease. I'd avoided Lionel ever since.

But I really did not want to kiss Jase Cooley. Not here, not now, not ever. The thought of him made me ill on multiple levels. I tried to edge away, but he put an arm against the wall, blocking my exit. This was getting less acceptable by the second.

"Don't make me beg," he said, but the way he snarled the last word made "beg" sound more like "angry."

My heart hammered for the wrong reasons. I felt like I might cry—

"Leave her alone."

I couldn't place the voice, but relief flooded through me. I managed to stand on tiptoes to look past Jase, and there stood Lucio McKinley. Jase's pals stood behind Lucio, looking sheepish; whatever he'd said to them, it'd been effective.

Jase turned slowly to look back, releasing me in the process. "What did you say?"

Lucio turned his dark eyes on me. "You okay?"

"Barely," I said, squeezing past Jase. He made a half-hearted attempt to grab me but missed. I moved well past Lucio and the minions, but stopped to look back.

Jase strode down the aisle, his big meaty paws already clenched into fists. Lucio just stood there, calm, poised. Jase reached him, pulled back an arm for a swing – and in that instant, Lucio just raised one arm, long and firm, palm up. Jase thudded to a stop against the hand, tried to press on past the hand, tried to pull Lucio's arm away, but Lucio was immovable, a guardian statue.

Lucio called back over one shoulder, "He didn't hurt you, did he, Allie?"

"No." My throat was too dry to manage anything else. I cleared my throat, stifled a laugh when I saw Jase take a clumsy swing that failed to come anywhere near Lucio. Pretending to back off, Jase half-turned away, then charged Lucio, leading with his shoulder.

Lucio was amazing. He stepped aside, put out a foot, and when Jase went down Lucio was on him instantly, one knee digging painfully into Jase's back. Jase huffed and squirmed, but couldn't get up.

"Are we done here?" Lucio asked.

Jase winced once, then said, "Yeah, sure."

Lucio let him up. The minions gave Lucio a wide berth as he approached me. "You should probably go," he said.

I nodded, gathered up my books and stuffed them into my backpack before following Lucio out. Once we were outside the library, I said, "Thank you."

"Don't mention it."

Lucio walked away.

I stood for a few seconds, feeling useless and puzzled. Who saves someone from the school bully and then just takes off without a second thought?

Lucio McKinley, that's who.

THE NEXT DAY, when I saw Lucio eating lunch alone (like always), I excused myself from my friend Jenna (who I had been eating with, like always) and went to sit across from Lucio. He barely looked up as my tray hit the table.

"So about yesterday..."

Lucio was gobbling pizza. He took his next bite without looking up at me. "Don't worry about it. It's just what I do."

I punched my juice box with the straw and asked, "What you do?"

He nodded before adding, "I hold stuff back."

"Oh. You mean like...feelings?"

Lucio shook his head, swallowed another bite of pizza, said, "No. I mean like...bad things like Cooley."

"Bad *things*?"

He shrugged and nodded at the same time, kind of saying *Yeah, Cooley's a 'thing,' but don't ask me how I know that.*

We ate together every day after that.

Slowly, he started to relax around me, even meet my eyes from time to time. I found out his mom had been Italian, and he'd been named after her grandfather. That same grandfather had raised him after both parents had died in a car crash, and his grandmother had died ten years ago of pneumonia. His favorite kind of music was classical, favorite composer Prokofiev. He liked poetry, cats, and dark chocolate, not necessarily in that order.

My friend Jenna got mad at me for dumping her at lunch, so in an ongoing act of revenge porn she started eating with Jase Cooley. When Lucio saw that the first time, his face flushed with anger. "If you still talk to your friend, you should warn her away from him."

"No point in that—the whole school knows about that dumbass already."

"No, they don't."

Something about his tone—just the sheer *force* of it—made me look at my new friend closely. He was staring at Cooley, his thick brows knotting together.

"Lucio," I asked softly, leaning forward so I could almost whisper, "do you know something about Jase Cooley that I don't?"

For a few seconds Lucio ignored me, then he looked away and mumbled, "Forget about him."

As much as Lucio revealed stuff to me, I think I revealed more to him. I told him stuff I'd never told anyone, not even Jenna (before she replaced me with the school bully, that is). He heard about how I'd never really felt like I fit in anywhere, how I was happiest being alone, how I didn't have any idea what I'd do with my life after high school. He was a good listener; he'd nod, ask questions, but he never frowned or looked away, I never felt like he was judging me.

It didn't take long for me to feel really close to Lucio, but weirdly enough—given that teens are supposed to have raging hormones—I wasn't attracted to him, and I didn't think he was to me. We felt more like siblings; we were both only children, and although I'd never wanted a brother, I could imagine that being around Lucio would've been like having one.

I was thankful to have Lucio as a new friend because things were getting weird at school. Not the usual kids engaging in weirdness, but weird like a horror movie. One of Cooley's side-kicks, a skinny, dull-eyed boy named Jack Moss, started screaming for no reason in Chemistry one day and had to be carted off. There were rumors that a butchered dog had been found in the Principal's office one morning.

And then there was the thing with the mirror.

I was late one day getting ready after P.E., alone in the girls' bathroom, trying to get my hair to make some kind of sense when I heard a sort of whispering sound. I turned around to look, but nobody else was in there. When I looked into the mirror again, the light in the mirror had somehow dimmed, even though the overhead fluorescents hadn't changed. Feeling the hairs on my arm rise, I saw the mirror slowly cloud over, as if fog was filling the room behind me. I had the sense that *something* was in that fog, something that would be reaching out, maybe even reaching through the mirror....

I didn't wait to find out. I grabbed my stuff and got out of there.

I couldn't wait to see Lucio after school and tell him what had happened. We'd started hanging out after school at each other's houses. My mom didn't know what to make of Lucio, and I had to keep assuring her that we were "just friends." Lucio's grandfather also eyed me with suspicion, but there was something different about it; he'd scowl at me and then give Lucio these warning looks. I asked Lucio about it on my third trip to his house, and he just did one of his characteristic shrugs. "Grandpa's a little wack."

When I told Lucio what I'd experienced in the bathroom, he didn't snicker or say "Wow." Instead he frowned and said, "That's not good."

"Lucio, do you know what's going on?"

"I..." He looked me right in the eye, with an expression I'd never seen. He was torn about something. But then he dropped his gaze and shrugged. "It's weird, is all."

ONE WEDNESDAY, I ran into this girl Tisha near my locker. In the past, she'd occasionally hung out with Jenna and me, although I didn't really like her much—if she'd been any more shallow, she'd be a single drop of water.

She was opening her locker, three away from mine, when she spotted me. She glanced around, leaned close and half-whispered, "Did you hear about the big party at Jase Cooley's house this Friday?"

"No."

She half-smiled and moved even closer. "His parents are off somewhere for a vacation, so he's throwing this huge bash. Jenna's helping him set it all up."

When I looked a little dumbstruck, Tisha cocked one eyebrow. "That's weird that you didn't know. I thought you and Jenna were besties."

I lied. "Sure, I knew. Guess I'll see you there," I said, before turning to walk away, numb.

As soon as I was away from Tisha, I pulled out my phone and texted Jenna. She answered right away, confirming that she'd been at Jase's house all week helping "set up something SICK in the backyard. Oh, btw, your invited Fri night!!!!"

Two hours later, we were in Lucio's room, with its full bookcases and something classical playing, trying to figure out some math equations. I'd waited until we were away from school to tell him. "Guess what I heard today? Jase Cooley's throwing a big party on Friday, and Jenna's been helping him set it up in the backyard."

Lucio's brow creased, and he took a few seconds before asking, "Do you know what this Friday is?"

I thought about it, but came up empty. "The day after tomorrow?"

"May Eve."

"May *what*?"

"Beltane."

My friend said that word with such intensity that I felt guilty for not knowing it. He must have seen my look and figured it out, because he added, "In the old pagan calendar there were two days of power, spaced exactly six months apart. One was Samhain—Halloween to us—and the other was Beltane. The celebration started when the sun went down on April 30th, and it was a night when all kinds of bad shit was in play."

"Bad shit? Like...what?"

"Like the stuff you told me you saw in the bathroom mirror at school. And like..." Lucio trailed off, turning away.

I took a guess. "Like Jase Cooley?"

Lucio's eyes fixed on me with fresh appreciation. "Yeah. Like Cooley." He hesitated for a few seconds before getting up from where we were sitting. "C'mon. There's something I think I need to show you."

We left Lucio's bedroom and walked down the hall to a closed door. I'd passed it plenty of times, mildly curious about what was behind it, but just figured it was a spare bedroom or storage or something.

Lucio opened the door and pushed it back. Beyond was an empty room with one curtained window. A closet was inset into one pale cream-colored wall. The floor was a neutral shade of carpet. The whole room was, in other words, completely unspectacular.

But Lucio had a little gleam in his eye, so I felt as if there was something I was supposed to see here. I looked again, but nothing.

He asked, "Empty, right?"

I nodded.

Lucio stepped into the room and then waited. "Close your eyes and walk forward."

Feeling slightly silly, I did as instructed. I took two steps forward before Lucio's hand stopped me. "Okay. You can open 'em now."

I did—and my breath caught in my throat.

The room was completely different. For one thing it was dark, no window. The light came from computer screens—three of them—atop a desk that curved around two walls of the room. The screens all seemed to show people doing things, as if seen by security camera: on one screen, I saw one of Jase Cooley's buds, Johnny Gonzalez, in a kitchen eating a sandwich; another showed Jack Moss, the kid that had gone crazy, wearing pajamas and sitting in some sort of institutional-looking room, staring slack-jawed at a TV mounted high in one corner. I got the impression that he was drugged to the gills.

Jase Cooley was on the last screen. He was in what I imagined must have been his bedroom, playing a violent video game on a console.

Beyond the monitors were low cases full of books, one big freestanding cabinet like you'd keep guns in, and scraps of paper with scribbled notes. "Lucio, what is this? And how did you do it?"

"Allie," Lucio said, sounding as serious as I'd ever heard him, "you trust me, right?"

"You know I do."

"Because what I'm going to tell you...well, you'll probably

think at first that it's crazy, but it's not. It's all real, and it's all happening now."

"Okay."

Lucio gestured at a desk chair. "Why don't you sit there."

I did. Lucio sat in another chair, rolled up closer to me, and said, "Before humans were even a gleam in evolution's eye, the world had other masters. Today, we'd call them monsters. They didn't look much like humans. They were huge and very powerful, which is why they're called the Great Old Ones. The earth belonged to them for millions of years, until something happened and they fell into this sort of hibernation."

Lucio paused, looking at me. I wanted to say, "Is this a story you're writing?" or "Isn't it a little late for April Fools?" but he'd never been a practical joker. He was dead serious, so I said, "Hibernation...so...they're still here?"

"Some of them are. Others just left and went to parallel dimensions. But here's the thing: the ones who are still here *will reawaken*. And when they do, it'll be adios for all of us."

"Lucio, how do you know all this?"

He drew himself up straight, with pride. "Because I'm part of a group dedicated to making sure they don't succeed. My mom and dad did it—in fact, they died doing it."

"They didn't die in a car crash?"

"No. They died fighting a group of people who were dedicated to calling the Great Old Ones."

If Lucio were telling the truth—and all I could say for certain was that he believed all this—I couldn't imagine why anyone would want to wake up monsters who were going to kill us all. But then I thought about people who were obsessed with stuff like the Rapture, or even zombie movies, and I realized there were people who would welcome the end of the world. People like...

"Jase Cooley," I blurted out, looking up at Lucio to see if I was right.

He smiled, nodding. "Yes. We found out a while back that

sometimes bullies are more than just bullies. Their pathetic need for power and control can make them seek out alliances with forces who they think can give them what they want. They don't even realize that their own death is usually included in the deal."

"You came to our school because of Jase Cooley, didn't you?"

He nodded. "Yes. He got hooked up with some of the Great Old Ones' followers last year."

"So, this party..."

Lucio turned and glanced at the array of screens. "It's got to be a ritual to call them. Beltane would be the best day of the year to hold one. My guess is that he's going to try an invocation, create a portal between dimensions for the Great Old Ones to cross through, and then try to make a deal with them to let him live."

"I don't get it: if you know Jase Cooley is going to try this awful thing, why not just get rid of him now?"

"We protect the human race—all of it, even the bad ones. Besides, we've got other ways of working. See Cooley there?"

I followed Lucio's gaze to the image of Cooley in his room playing the wild first-person-shooter game. "Yeah, but...how are we seeing this?"

Lucio waved a hand across the bank of monitors. "We've managed to combine technology with some old magic. We have a spell, not a camera, in Cooley's room. In fact, that game he's playing is imbued with spells. It's keeping him distracted. If it works the way it's supposed to, he'll forget all about the preparations he'd need to make to enact a major invocation in two days."

Something was wrong; something pinged off the back of my brain. I thought back to the last couple of days, finally remembered the conversation with Tisha: "Jenna's helping him set it all up."

I asked Lucio, "Have you been watching that video of Cooley all week?"

"Yeah. Why?"

The video image that was supposed to be Cooley showed mostly of the back of his head as he followed the action in the videogame. It looked like his big shoulders, his light brown, short hair, but it could have been someone else. "You're sure that's him?"

Lucio blinked in surprise. "Why?"

"Because Jenna told me they've been working in his back-yard all week."

Lucio frowned and looked back to the monitor. He started to reach out a hand, but stopped when the image of Jase Cooley stopped playing the game, dropping his hands. He turned his head, slowly, until he was looking right at us.

Except it wasn't Jase Cooley. In fact, it wasn't anything human. Where a face should have been was a bumpy, slimy, grayish mass, with dozens of eyes inset. No mouth, no nose, no ears...just lots and lots of eyes, all looking right at us. It raised its arms, except they weren't arms any more—they were pseudopods, semi-translucent and growing longer as they came towards us—

They pushed through the screen.

Lucio and I both cried out and danced back as the length-ening appendages shot into space between us. I stumbled over my chair, but sidestepped a third pseudopod that appeared out of the screen. Lucio was yelling something in a language I couldn't identify, leaping from side to side to avoid the things reaching for him. He finally dove under them for the screen, got a hand behind it, and tore out a power cord. The screen went dead, and in that instant the pseudopods vanished. We looked at each other wide-eyed and panting for a few seconds before Lucio asked, "Do you believe me now?"

After our heartbeats returned to calmer rates, Lucio picked his chair back up, plopped down into it, and started thinking.

"Damn," he muttered, "they've been ahead of us all along...that thing was a shoggoth. It's like the foot soldier for the Old Ones. The fact that it was able to come at us like that means that forces are building." At that point he turned to me. "Has your friend sent you any pictures of what they've been working on?"

"No, but I'll bet I can get her to do it."

Five minutes later, we were examining a photo of a raised platform in the middle of a backyard of dying, withered plants. On the platform was a big folding table draped with a gray cloth. The sides of the platform and the cloth had drawings of tentacle-headed horrors crudely scrawled on them. Jenna said she was going to climb on it at midnight and they had a whole little scene they'd rehearsed together that was "super dramatic!!!!"

"It's an altar," Lucio said, after looking at the photo. "Exactly what I figured. They're going to try to sacrifice your friend on it."

"What?" I might have had a falling out with Jenna, but I didn't want her to die, especially not as an offering to something with calamari for a head.

Lucio explained. "It takes a lot to open the way for a Great Old One. They'd have to offer a human sacrifice."

I thought back to that day in the library, when Jase had said something about "big plans for May," and I shivered as I realized that I might have been that sacrifice.

I asked, "So what do we do now?"

"*You* don't do anything, except go home, avoid Cooley, and stay away from that party. I prepare."

"How?"

He got up and crossed to the tall cabinet against the wall. He opened it, reached in, and drew out the biggest book I'd ever seen—it must have weighed as much as a bowling ball. It was obviously old, bound in leather with metal clasps, and it had all kinds of more recent pages shoved into it. Lucio dropped it onto the desk with a thud. "I study this. It's all the knowledge my parents had, and their parents before them, and so on. Every generation adds to it as we learn things."

I joined him and ran my fingers over the binding, which was embossed with all kinds of geometrical shapes. "Wow. It's beautiful."

He nodded and then looked up at me. "Allie, I need to get to work. I think I can still stop this, but only if I'm prepared."

"Do you have to do this alone? Can't anyone help?"

"I'll have help. My grandfather...well, I should tell you that he's not really my grandfather. He's an Elder. They're like good versions of the Great Old Ones, and they help us to hold them back. My real grandfather died before I was born."

"Oh." It made about as much sense as anything else I'd heard today.

Lucio walked me back to his room, where I gathered up my stuff to go. Before I left, he said, "Allie, stay away from the party on Friday, okay?"

I'd like to think he knew I wouldn't be able to do that, that he just felt obligated to say it. I told him I would, but I think we both knew that was a lie.

Lucio went back to the room with the monitors. As I made my way to the front door, I encountered his "grandfather" in the living room, and I couldn't stifle another shiver. The way he looked at me...for a second, I thought I could see something incredibly old and alien there, something that didn't think like me at all, but was ultimately benevolent.

I didn't like imagining a non-benevolent version of that.

LUCIO DIDN'T SHOW up at school on Thursday or Friday, but Jase Cooley did. He strutted through the hallways like a king, with his two remaining minions and Jenna trailing behind him. At one point, he caught my eye and winked at me. I thought I might vomit.

The worst part was not being able to tell anyone, even Jenna, who thought this was all just fun and games. Who'd believe any of this? If I hadn't seen gelatinous arms reaching through a computer monitor for me, I might have thought Lucio was just—well, very peculiar. But I *had* seen that, and it meant that I'd learned very abruptly that the world wasn't what I thought it was. It was really a place where bullies friended ancient monsters to destroy the world.

Fortunately, it was also a place where heroes like Lucio McKinley held them back.

ON FRIDAY MORNING, I woke up to two texts. The one from Jenna said, "Your coming tonight, right??!!!"

The one from Lucio read, "I got this. You're staying home tonight, right?"

The school felt strange that day, like the way air felt before a storm moved in, or how spring made your nose tickle.

I didn't see Lucio or Jase. Jenna was there, but I avoided her.

That night at 9 p.m., I left my home. I'd told my mom I was going to a party at Jenna's. She said it was okay.

Cooley lived maybe four blocks from me. By the time I'd walked half the distance, I could already hear the music and the sound of voices. I knew his neighbors must love that. I also knew he thought his neighbors would be dead by Saturday.

There must've been a hundred kids at the party. They spilled out of the backyard onto the front lawn and the sidewalks. As I pushed my way through, they were in groups talking, dancing, drinking, smoking, flirting. A few said "hi." Most didn't notice me.

In the back, a deejay bobbed behind a table that held a laptop, a turntable, and huge speakers. More tables were set up with sodas and cups and potato chips.

Then there was the altar. It squatted in the middle of the

backyard. Cooley had put up sawhorse barriers around it and stationed his two flunkies there to act as security. They scowled, trying to look tough. I wondered if they had the slightest idea what was about to go down.

I didn't see Jase, Jenna, or Lucio. I tried to blend into the crowd, to engage in meaningless chatter with friends while I sipped flat soda from a plastic cup and tried not to think about anything.

Time passed too slowly. I thought I might explode from nerves.

Finally, 11:45 arrived. The music stopped. The chatter died down as everyone waited to see what was going on.

Jase and Jenna came out of the house. Jenna was dressed in some white robe that left one shoulder bare. She was also obviously drunk, barely able to stay upright, giggling, as she let Cooley lead her through the party.

Cooley also had on a robe, but his was green and covered with symbols. Unlike the cheap altar cloth, the robe was hand embroidered and looked rich, authentically old.

He held Jenna by one hand and carried a large bag in the other. The crowd applauded as he led Jenna through their midst, past the guards and the sawhorses, up onto the altar.

As she lay down on it, I almost ran forward. I wanted to tell her to wake up, get off there before it was too late, but I knew it would just get me hauled out of the party. I forced myself to stay quiet and watch as Cooley took up position at one end of the altar, above Jenna's head, and opened the bag to withdraw a book, not as old or as big as the one Lucio had, but nevertheless impressive.

He opened the book to a marked passage, held up one arm for silence, and began reading in some language that sounded like he was speaking in tongues.

Some of the kids around me whispered in perplexity; others applauded, thinking this was some party skit. But a few others, who weren't already drunk or stoned or too preoccupied with looking cool, could sense a change in the very air, an oppressive feeling of forces in motion. Cooley felt it, as he paused once and looked up, expectantly, before resuming his reading with more speed.

Where was Lucio? This was going down now. Whatever he had prepared, he'd better set it in motion pretty quick.

Cooley kept reading. At 11:55, he shifted the book to his left hand, used his right to reach down into the bag, and came up with a huge, very sharp-looking knife. This wasn't some kitchen knife, even one of the big ones; it had a carved hilt, and the blade looked thick and well-used.

He lifted it over Jenna.

She giggled.

He kept reading.

Above him, the air began to glow. I thought I could see dozens of eyes taking shape there.

Cooley saw it, too. He raised the knife higher.

A voice, impossibly loud, boomed out from the crowd of onlookers, a voice speaking in that same strange, rolling tongue that Cooley was using.

Lucio!

Cooley stopped reading as he looked for the source of the shout, but immediately returned to the book as his minions moved forward. The crowd parted like the Red Sea and there stood Lucio, alone, one arm raised in the same way that he'd held Cooley back in the library.

Lucio was glimmering. Not glowing with the sort of sickly green that was swirling in the air overhead, but with a shimmery gold that sparked at the edges. He wore his usual black jeans and t-shirt, but there were symbols etched onto his face, and he wore a pendant that was so bright it hurt to look at it.

He strode forward confidently as the two flunkies ran at him—and bounced back as if he was surrounded by a shield. They fell to the grass and he walked by them.

It was 11:59.

He walked up to the altar, where Cooley was still reading, but Cooley's attention was divided now and he stumbled on the words. He glanced at his watch, saw the time, and tossed the book aside carelessly so he could grip the knife in both hands. Overhead, something was taking shape, something the size of a trailer truck, studded with eyes and those groping, jelly-like arms. People were screaming, running, pushing each other to get away.

No one paid attention to Jase Cooley as he raised the knife over my friend.

One person noticed: Lucio. Still shouting in that weird language, he leapt up to the platform and caught Cooley's knife hand as it came down. They struggled for a few seconds.

A snake-like arm wrapped around Cooley's throat. He forgot the knife; Lucio caught it as it fell. Without wasting a second, he used the blade to hack at the thing strangling Cooley.

He was trying to save his enemy.

Lucio severed the arm just as several wrapped around him. One had his wrist, two had his legs. He was pulled up, struggling and squirming.

I screamed and rushed forward, acting on pure instinct. I couldn't just stand by silently and watch Lucio die. I jumped up on the platform, reaching up—

But Lucio was already too far. I could hear him still shouting as he was pulled higher and higher, into the glowing green mass of eyes and arms.

Then it all winked out. In an eyeblink, it was all gone—the swirling cloud, the charge in the air...and my friend.

I wasn't sure what had just happened, but I knew that whatever it was, Cooley had failed. He stood there gaping upward, his mouth hanging open. I shoved him, and he fell backward, landing on his ass on the ground. I jumped down next to him and said, "If I ever see you again, you'll regret it."

From the look on his face, I knew he believed it.

I guess neither of us quite realized I was crying as I said it.

I WENT HOME AFTER THAT. But I didn't sleep that night.

In the morning, I went to Lucio's house. His "grandfather" met me at the door.

"Do you know what happened last night?" I asked.

He nodded.

"Did you make it stop?"

"Yes," he said, in a voice that buzzed inhumanly at the end of syllables. "But I couldn't save Lucio."

I asked to see the special room, the one I now realized was guarded by magic to hide it. When I went in, all the monitors were dark...but the book he'd shown me was still there, the one that he'd said held all the knowledge.

I picked it up and turned to the Elder. "May I take this?"

He understood what I was really asking. "It is a very heavy responsibility."

"Will you help me as you did Lucio?"

"Yes."

I'd like to think that Lucio is still alive, carrying on his fight on the other side of that glowing green cloud. He still had the knife, after all, and I think the pendant he wore gave him more powers. Maybe, after I've studied the book long enough, I'll be able to find him, to save him as he saved all of us.

In the meantime, I'll be here.

I'll be the one guarding against the darkness and the Old Ones that want our world. I'll be the one holding back.

THE MOUTH OF THE MERRIMACK

DOUGLAS WYNNE

S hane Rundell rode his bike to the job that night, pumping the pedals in short bursts, then coasting long stretches of Water Street, winding past the Joppa flats and over the bridge to Plum Island. He knew the house, though he'd never been there before—knew it as soon as Mr. Williamson described it over the chatter of students funneling out of AP History. It was a modest colonial facing the ocean at the mouth of the Merrimack, distinguished from the crowd of cedar shingle beach shacks by its pink clapboard siding, octagonal cupola, and iron widow's walk.

Shane had noticed the house on kayaking trips he'd taken around the island, though it had never been his destination until today. And he'd never seen it quite like this—set against the gray trim of a cloudbank as the sky drained of color, an aquamarine glow shifting behind the leaded glass panes of the cupola, as if someone had left a lava lamp cooking up there. Mr. Williamson didn't strike Shane as the lava lamp type—less than ever when he answered the door in a tuxedo.

The effect was startling. In the classroom, the history teacher was partial to rumpled plaid shirts and corduroys, but there was no denying that he cleaned up nicely; the sharp attire lending an air of sophistication to a freshly trimmed salt-and-pepper beard. It was Shane's first time babysitting for the Williamsons, and the tux added an aspect of the surreal to the brief tour Mr. Williamson gave him while his wife did her hair and makeup.

"Jonah, say hello to Shane. Shane is one of my students. He's going to be your babysitter tonight while Mama and I have our date."

"I'm not a baby," Jonah said without looking up from the sketchpad in his lap. He sat at the center of a glossy pine plank floor, hunched over his art, colored pencils scattered like kindling around him.

The teacher cracked an asymmetrical smile at Shane as if to say, *See what you're in for?*

And because a single correction to his statement wasn't enough, a female voice carried down the hall, curled with teasing melodic admonishment. "It's not a date night, darling. You're getting a medal."

"You are?" Shane tucked his head back as if blown on the wind of the man's achievement.

"It's nothing. They're giving me a jewel—a *pin*—for service to the Masonic lodge. I'm not the only one receiving the honor tonight. Phoebe just wants to remind me that it doesn't get me off the hook for a *real* date this month, even though we're doing a harbor cruise with cocktails afterward." He waved a hand at the broad step at the foot of a flight of stairs. "You can set your bag down there. Kitchen's this way. Phoebe already prepared Jonah's supper. You'll find it in a casserole dish in the fridge. Just needs to be reheated. The microwave settings are right here."

Mr. Williams tapped a notepad on the gold-flecked marble slab that topped the kitchen island. "She's so organized. Opposites attract, right?"

Shane laughed, following the man through a series of

rooms that juxtaposed roughhewn beams with stylish modern embellishments.

"I'm afraid we don't have much of a home entertainment system to keep you occupied. But there's a stereo with some vinyl and plenty of books. Did you bring your homework?"

"Yeah. Got my notes for the local history paper. Figured I'd bang out a first draft. *If* Jonah lets me, of course."

"Good man. You should be able to get some work done after you tuck him in. Bedtime is eight-thirty. His toothbrush already has paste on it up in the upstairs bathroom. And if you read to him, it won't take long before he's out like a light. Lullabies work too, but that's Phoebe's department. Jonah loves music almost as much as drawing. I'm sure he'll play his recorder for you. He can't resist a fresh audience."

Mr. Williamson turned to face Shane, tucked his hands in his pockets, and rocked on the heels of his shiny black shoes, his Masonic lapel pins glinting gold in the lamplight. They'd arrived at the second-floor balcony overlooking Jonah in the living room, the top sheet of his sketchpad covered in a furious tangle of turquoise and violet. "Any questions?"

"None that I can think of. It's a beautiful house. I've always noticed it because of the widow's walk."

Mr. Williamson smiled and nodded. "When I inherited the place, I had grand ideas about making an observatory out of the cupola. But really it's just a place to keep my telescope and flask for stargazing on clear winter nights."

Shane raised his eyebrows and looked around, letting the unspoken question hang between them: *How do you get up there?*

Mr. Williamson indicated a cherry-stained door with a scrimshaw knob. "It used to be an open ceiling and staircase for ventilation through the cupola, but when Jonah was born, I had a contractor close it off so we don't have to worry about finding him climbing around on the roof. It's the only room in the house that we keep locked." He clapped Shane on the shoulder. "If we weren't short on time, I'd take you up for a look at the sunset. Maybe next time."

Mrs. Williamson stepped into view below, one arm in a black frock coat. "Cal, we're going to be late." She was a tall, pretty woman, her gray-streaked dark hair and red lipstick a stark contrast to her vellum skin.

"Coming," he said, rounding the balustrade and trotting down the creaking stairs. "Do we really need coats?"

His wife shrugged, slipping into the other sleeve of hers. "*You* might be fine, but I'm wearing one. It's always chilly on the water at night."

Shane descended the stairs and examined a bookshelf while Mrs. Williamson bent to kiss her son on the forehead. "Last chance for questions," she said to Shane, rising and plucking lint from her lapel.

"I think I'm good. Have fun."

"Cal gave you the supper instructions and cell numbers?"

"He did."

"Well then, we're off. We'll be home before the horses turn back to mice."

WHEN THE CAR had turned out of the driveway, Shane turned toward the sound of ripping paper rising over the crunch of tires on gravel. Jonah sat among paper scraps scribbled with color.

"Aw, what'd you do that for? You ripped up your artwork?"

The boy nodded, staring at a blank space on the floor as if he could see through it.

"Why? I wanted to see it." But Shane knew why. Jonah was venting anger at his parents leaving him with a stranger for the night. A typical and harmless act of destruction for a boy his age.

"It was sucky," Jonah said.

"Language, buddy."

"It wasn't like what I see in my dreams."

Shane laughed and resisted the urge to tousle the kid's hair. "Well, ain't that the eternal struggle of the artist? You wanna play a game?"

Jonah shrugged.

"It's a little early for your supper, so let's play something. What do you have around here?"

"Cards."

"Perfect. Go get 'em."

Jonah fetched a deck from under the lid of a piano bench beside an upright in the corner. Shaking the cards from the box, Shane was taken aback to find it was an antique French tarot deck, the grunge-speckled artwork and gilded edges dulled with age. The uncoated cards smelled of mildew and myrrh, their texture like dried skins between his fingers. One card caught his eye as he shuffled through them—a man falling from a tower into a roiling sea, a crudely painted black barracuda opening its jaws to devour him. A bolt of lightning threaded down from a cloud above to strike what looked like a stone idol in the tower window. Another card depicted a devil with the forelegs of a goat joined to the scaly, curling tail of a fish. Shane quickly dropped the cards back into the box.

"We can't play with these, Jonah. Do you have a regular deck with...you know, hearts and clubs and stuff?"

Jonah went to the kitchen and returned with a cheap pack of Bicycle playing cards.

"What games do you know?" Shane asked, idly shuffling the deck. "Got a favorite?"

"Goldfish."

"You mean *Go Fish*? Okay, cool."

They sat on the floor amid the shredded papers and played while the house grew dark. Shane's phone chimed with a text, but he only spared it a glance to make sure it wasn't Mr. Williams. When Jonah finally won a round, Shane decided it was a good time to call it quits and feed him. He rose from the floor with a cramp in his leg and fumbled with the beaded chain dangling from a stained glass lamp on a nearby end table. The room lit up a buttery shade of yellow.

Shane read the message on his phone while Jonah put the cards away. It was from Kelly, his girlfriend—though he was still getting used to calling her that.

> **KL:** *Hey nerd. R U really babysitting on a Friday night instead of taking me out?*
>
>   **SR:** *I'm making money so I CAN take you out. Tomorrow.*
>
>   **KL:** *Which house is it? I'll visit you.*
>
>   **SR:** *Don't. Please. It's my first time. If the kid tells, I'll lose the gig.*
>
>   **KL:** *Your loss. I'm \m'.*

Shane snorted at the homemade emoji for devil horns. Kelly was boldest when she knew she couldn't have him.

> **KL:** *What time do you put him to bed?*
>
>   **SR:** *Seriously. Save it for tomorrow. Gotta go feed him now <3*

Jonah was sitting at the dining room table, humming under his breath, when Shane placed a grilled cheese and a glass of iced tea in front of him. The kid wrinkled his nose at the food. "What's this?"

"The dish your mom left for you went bad, so I fixed you something else. Sorry, I'm not much of a chef, but you have to eat something."

"I don't want this. I want what Mama made. I want my Friday supper."

Shane sighed. "I don't know how it went bad in the fridge, but I couldn't feed it to you. Trust me, you wouldn't want it. It was rancid."

Jonah pushed the plate away, slid off his chair, and headed for the kitchen.

"Where are you going?"

"I'm getting my supper."

"You can't. It's in the trash."

But the kid was already gone. Shane scrambled after him, noting the rattle of the silverware drawer and the creak of the trashcan lid yawning open. He found Jonah lifting a chunky spoonful of the putrid mush out of the trash: chunks of shell-fish in a curdled sauce, trailing strips of green-black noodles that looked like kelp.

"Oh, God. Give me that." Shane seized the child's wrist and wrenched the dripping spoon away.

Jonah flashed his dirty teeth in defiance.

"Stop! Just...you can't eat out of the trash. That food will make you sick, Jonah. You don't like grilled cheese? Fine. Just tell me what you'll eat, and I'll make it."

Jonah burst past Shane. He bounded across the living room and up the stairs with the loping gait of an animal. The sound of his bedroom door slamming shut reverberated from the second floor balcony.

Shane heaved a sigh of frustration, then plodded into the living room. He plucked his knapsack from the staircase and carried it to the kitchen, where he settled down to unpack his notebooks and pick at the grilled cheese while he let the kid cool off. He was just beginning to find his focus when it was shattered by a knock at the door. Kelly stood on the stoop, her curled fists jammed into the pockets of a light hoodie, her foster mom's grimy Saturn parked askew on the gravel behind her.

"Kelly. I told you...I'm working."

She ignored the admonishment, stepping past him into the house. "Thanks for inviting me in. It's fucking frigid out there. I thought it was supposed to be spring."

"How did you find the house?"

"Your bike gave it away. In the future, when you're avoiding me, you might want to stow that somewhere."

"Keep your voice down. The kid's upstairs. And I'm not avoiding you." Shane, trying not to be annoyed, reminded himself that Kelly had abandonment issues. Her mother had committed suicide when she was eleven, just a little older than Jonah was now. She'd never known her father. And she'd never been big on rules about where she couldn't go or what she couldn't do. Shane still marveled that he was dating her. If she'd been in his class at Newburyport High, they'd never have connected. He was far too nerdy and straight-laced for her.

But they'd met as lifeguards last summer at Salisbury Beach, where the Harbor Schools program for at-risk youth placed her after paying for her Red Cross certification. Truth be told, he was slightly embarrassed that she was visiting him at a babysitting gig, but he was only taking jobs like this one to get through the off season until the beaches opened. Some parents were weird about hiring a male sitter, but his CPR certification usually sealed the deal. And the money was good.

"Is he asleep?" Kelly asked.

"No. He's just pissed at me about his dinner. I'll have to coax him out soon and get him to eat something before bed."

Kelly plunked down into an empty chair at the scuffed farmhouse table, her gaze roaming over Shane's library books, notes, and laptop. "Homework? On a Friday night? You are hopeless."

Shane resigned himself to sitting with her for a moment before giving her the heave-ho. Maybe, if she felt reassured that he'd rather be with her—and would be tomorrow after putting a little cash in his pocket—she'd leave of her own accord before Jonah saw her.

"We're going out tomorrow, and I don't want it hanging over my head on Sunday."

She picked up a book and knitted her brow at the cover art. "This is homework? Looks like Dungeons and Dragons. Are you sure I didn't crash your secret geek club?" She tossed the book on the table—a sea monster dripping black ichor glared up from the cover.

"It's for a local history paper. Find some obscure fact about the town and research it. I'm doing H.P. Lovecraft, the horror author?" Kelly liked horror movies, but the name brought no flicker of recognition to her cold green eyes.

"*Lovecraft*? What did he write, the Kama Sutra?"

"He was a pulp horror writer in the 1920s. Newburyport features in one of his longest stories. The character visits the library and the historical society and learns about a cult of like...fish people. They moved it—the historical society—but I visited the house where it is now on High Street, and the one where it used to be when Lovecraft visited. Turns out he was inspired to write the story by a train ride he took to Newbury-port back before the town got a facelift. Back then it was like a shantytown. The Towle silver factory was the only industry besides fishing. The rest of Water Street was just rotting shacks."

Kelly yawned theatrically.

"Well it's way more interesting than most local history. At least I get to read a horror story and write about how this racist, sex-phobic dude was fascinated by human/amphibian cross-breeding, right? Give me some points for style at least."

"So, it's like mermaid porn?"

"Would that make it cooler to you?"

Kelly planted her elbows on the table, raked clawed fingers through her hair, and shook her head in dismay. "What am I doing with you?"

Shane dangled his pen over his notebook, looking for the last line he'd transferred to the laptop. But it was no use. He couldn't concentrate with her sitting there bored, restless, and all kinds of hot in that pink halter-top. He needed to get her out of here, needed to work on coaxing Jonah out of his room and back to the kitchen where they could negotiate a meal.

As if reading his mind, Kelly sat up, sniffed the air, and frowned. "Did something die in here?"

"It's the food I threw out. It went bad."

She wandered into the living room, waving a hand in front of her face. Seeing the paper scraps on the floor, she knelt and sifted through them, assembling the shredded drawing like a jigsaw puzzle.

Shane closed his laptop lid in resignation and flipped random kitchen cabinet doors looking for cereal or peanut butter, anything he could offer the kid. He found a can of tuna and set it on the counter. When he came up behind Kelly to see if he could get her to leave, his throat constricted at the sight of the reconstructed drawing on the floor. In a riot of ocean blue, mossy green, and shadow black, it depicted the ruins of a sunken city. Cartoon fish swam between cyclopean columns rising from winding terraces. It was an unsettling combination of a child's crude effort and a veracity of detail that might be almost accidental—his brain interpreting scribbles and random white spaces as barnacles and wavering fronds of kelp.

"How old is he?" Kelly asked.

"Eleven."

"He's gifted, huh?"

"I guess. I think he might be on the spectrum. I don't know."

The hollow sound of a flute floated down over the balcony railing, mournful and faint, with a minor note that reminded Shane of soundtracks from movies set in Egypt or Persia. The melody and technique were crude, not unlike the drawing, with flourishes that could have been discordant accidents or an intentionally unnerving tune.

Kelly touched the hollow of her throat and laughed. "Well *that's* creepy as shit."

"I need to feed him, Kel. You can't be here when I do." His eyes lingered on the drawing as he spoke to her. Something about the style was vaguely reminiscent of the tarot cards he'd seen earlier.

Kelly looked up at the second floor railing, her eyes following the haunting tune. "Where's the door to the widow's walk?"

"If I don't get fired tonight I'll show you next time. Anyway, it's locked."

"Ooh, a secret room? I bet I can find it," she sang, springing from the floor and prancing up the stairs on tip toes. Shane fumbled to his feet and gave chase, almost shouting after her, but catching himself.

The flute melody haunted the upper hall as Kelly crept along the row of doors. When she reached Jonah's bedroom, Shane waved his hands, brushing the air at his waist in a *leave it alone* gesture. With a glint of mischief in her eyes, Kelly scurried to the narrow cherry door with the scrimshaw handle. Shane could see now that the design etched into it was a giant squid. He watched as she rattled the unmoving knob.

"Okay, you found it," Shane whispered. "You win. Now let's go."

Kelly was up on her toes, feeling along the upper edge of the lacquered trim. When her hand came down, it held something the pewter color of a thunderhead. She slotted it into the key plate before he could move to snatch it from her. The door clicked open and swung inward, and she turned a broad smile on him, bobbing her upper body with pantomimed laughter.

"How did you know the key was there?"

She answered with a *Do you even know me?* expression of mock scorn. "Where do you put something you don't want a kid to find?"

The sound of Jonah's flute had ceased. Was he listening to their hushed exchange, or just pausing between tunes? Shane reached past Kelly and seized the knob, intending to pull the door shut, but as he did so, Jonah's door clicked open. Shane pushed Kelly through and closed the door to the cupola before hurrying to Jonah's bedroom.

"Mama?" Jonah said through the gap between door and frame, his face out of view.

"No, buddy, your mom and dad are still out. It's just me."

"Then who were you talking to?"

"Nobody. It's just me. Hey, I'm sorry about your dinner. What can I get you to eat? You must be hungry."

No reply. But the door remained open.

"You like tuna? Can I make you a tuna sandwich?" The casserole had been seafood, so Shane was hopeful this suggestion might score, but now the door did swing shut with a slow creak. At least the kid hadn't slammed it in his face. A moment later, the flute melody resumed. He put his hand on the knob and found it locked. For a moment, he debated knocking, mustering a firm tone, and threatening to call the boy's parents if he didn't open the door and come out to eat. But the sound of the mournful melody, gradually took the wind out of Shane's sails. He decided that as long as he could hear the flute, he knew what Jonah was doing, and that was good enough for now.

He turned to the door he'd pushed Kelly through. She'd taken the key with her, but—to his great relief—the ivory knob turned in his hand when he tried it. He slipped through and closed the door carefully behind him.

Looking around, he was surprised to find not a staircase leading directly to the cupola, but rather a small room lined with bookshelves, a leather armchair on a Persian carpet in the center, and an iron spiral staircase ascending to the octagonal glass room above.

Kelly sat perched on the ledge, her legs swinging idly, the cherry of a joint burning in the shadow that fell across her face, her form dusky beside the silhouette of the telescope. She hadn't turned on a lamp, and the light had drained from the sky. Candle light lapping at her throat played a trick that made it look like she had a scar he'd never noticed before. The effect was unsettling.

"I thought you'd never come," she said, her voice a laconic drawl.

Shane felt a flash of anger and struggled to contain it. How had he lost all control of the evening? He climbed the spiral stairs to her level and glared at her. "Seriously? You're smoking in my teacher's house. In his private room that's supposed to be locked. You're leaving the smell of weed in the one forbidden room of the house where I'm getting paid to watch a kid?"

"Oh, will you just chill? It's not mine. I found the dude's stash. The place already smells like it. He'll never know." She offered him the joint, but he waved it away and she tilted her head with an expression of...was that sympathy? It was hard to tell in the dark, but then the green glow he'd seen from the driveway traced a sine wave across her jawline, frosting the ends of her hair.

"You could use a hit, Shane. You're wound so tight tonight."

He looked past her for the source of the illumination. A statue of a woman carved from what looked like a block of granite squatted on a pedestal beside the antique brass telescope. Or was it a woman? The curves glimmered with a phosphorescent glow, different lines shifting in and out of prominence—some human, others serpentine. A hybrid of the erotic and the grotesque, equal parts woman and dragon.

"I thought it was a lava lamp from outside."

Kelly nodded "It's beautiful," she said, and exhaled a plume of smoke. "How does it do that?"

"It's chemical," Shane said absently, climbing the remaining stairs and approaching the statue. He was dimly aware of the panoramic view of the island through the windows of the cupola—the waves sweeping the beach below, the moon rising from a cloudbank, the white embers of Salisbury Beach scattered in the distance. But the stone figure drew his focus like a magnet. As he stepped closer to the pedestal on which it was perched, he felt a tightening in his sternum, as if he were passing through some kind of magnetic field or invisible current in the air. When ne tried to push through it, his body rejected its proximity to the idol, his bladder sending urgent signals and his skin prickling with gooseflesh, every sense urging flight.

"It's like something out of that book you were reading," Kelly said.

"Yeah." Shane moved back toward the stairs.

"This teacher you're sitting for, is he the one who told you to read Loveshaft?"

Shane forced his gaze from the idol, focused it on Kelly. She looked so ambivalent. Was she really not feeling the palpable malevolence radiating from that thing? "I found the Love-craft/Newburyport connection on my own," he said. "Mr. Williamson didn't tell me to read anything. Why?"

She leaned forward into the light, eyebrows raised, the joint hanging from her upturned hand. "Because he's obviously into this, like, fish worship stuff you were ranting about earlier."

Shane blinked. "I wasn't ranting."

Just like that, she'd yanked him from the borderland of a trance back into their dysfunctional dynamic. Sometimes he really couldn't remember why they were dating except that it was incredible when they *stopped* talking. "It's just a statue," Shane said.

Kelly laughed and jutted her chin toward the book-lined chamber at the bottom of the iron stairs. "Check out teacher's desk."

He followed her gaze to the source of the wavering light: a fat candle burning on the desk beside an open book, a massive leather-bound tome too big to be shelved. Even from his high vantage on the stairs, Shane could make out the rough lines of a woodblock illustration nested among the text. He descended, approaching the book like a sleepwalker, the illustration coming into focus with each reluctant step. It depicted the same coral terraces as the drawing Jonah had made with his pencils. Something vast lurked in the silt-clouded water beyond the towering columns. A shape reminiscent of the idol that glowed and pulsed like a psychic beacon at the peak of the house. The caption under the illustration read: *Pth'thya-l'yi, she that dwells amidst wonder and glory in Y'ha-nthlei.*

Shane projected a smile that didn't quite reach his eyes. "He's a scholar. There's probably all kinds of weird stuff in these books. You're not freaked out, are you?"

Kelly scoffed. "No, but you look like you are. I actually think mermaid porn is kinda hot."

Shane climbed the stairs again. Something nagged at him, something that had nothing to do with the unsettling illustration or the bad energy of the statue. Not a presence, but an absence. Kelly, her legs still draped over the edge, leaned back on her elbows and unbuttoned her jeans. Shane climbed past her, ignoring the invitation. He reached the top step and continued past the statue, making a deliberate effort not to look at it. His eyes were drawn to the shoreline below where waves darkened the sand in retreating cycles, leaving strands of ruddy seaweed behind.

Something pale clambered over the grassy dunes, flopping toward the water. It was the size of a dog, and for a moment Shane thought it must be a harbor seal, its pelt bleached by moonlight. But then he caught the shadow shapes of vertebrae down the creature's back. His gut rolled over as he identified the absence that had been nagging at him. There'd been no sound from Jonah's flute for...how long?

He tilted the telescope toward the figure as it reached the surf and felt Kelly's hands on his hips as he bent to peer into the eyepiece. Her slender fingers slipped around his waist from behind. Shane's pulse throbbed in his carotid artery, propelled more by what he saw than what he felt.

The naked figure lunging for the waves was Jonah.

"Oh, my God." Shane reeled around, knocking the telescope over and fumbling past Kelly. He was halfway down the stairs when she leaned over the railing and called after him, "Is that the kid you're supposed to be watching?"

Shane careened across the little library, thinking as he went that he should put out the candle—it was beside a book, probably a rare one, and Kelly was too messed up to be trusted in here with an open flame—but there was no time. He had to get to the waterline before Jonah did.

The door to Jonah's bedroom was wide open when Shane flew past it. He turned his head without slowing, just on the off chance he might see the boy in there, sitting on the bed with his flute or sketch pad, but the room was empty. He tore down the stairs and slipped when he hit the polished floor, then managed to regain his balance and avoid a wipeout. The front door was open, a gaping maw of terrible possibilities, inviting the salted night air into the house and setting the curtains to shiver at its kiss.

Shane leaped across the threshold and hit the sand running.

FROM THE CUPOLA, Kelly watched Jonah wade into the surf. He lurched with an awkward gait against the force of the waves, but also from the transformation of his bones, his limbs flapping and elongating as the water rolled over and around him, the brine awakening something amphibious that had slumbered until now under his skin. He moved fast despite his ungainly transient form. When the water reached his waist, he stooped and dove into the foam of an incoming wave, the fins that had sprouted on his calves and spine slicing the water and vanishing under the moon-frosted foam.

Shane splashed into the spot where the boy had been only seconds ago and was knocked backward by the next wave. He managed to stand, staggering against the weight of his wet clothes, and swiveled his head, searching the dark water, treading deeper toward the shelf where the bottom dropped off. He must have spotted a sign of Jonah because he dove through a wave and swam along a vector that spoke of clear purpose.

Kelly couldn't see what he moved toward, but she knew he wouldn't miss. He was a good lifeguard. She'd seen him lock in on drowning people in worse conditions than these. She picked up the fallen telescope and set it on its feet, but squinting into the brass eyepiece, she found only wavering shadows.

She was resigned to abandon the device when Shane's head popped above the grainy surface of the water. Had he tried to rescue Jonah from below? No, he'd been pulled under, and no sooner had he gulped a breath of air than it happened again. When he came up the second time, it was for just long enough to expel what remained of his breath in a ragged scream, thrashing against a predator she couldn't see until it pulled him under for the last time.

Kelly pressed her cold hands to her throat as the icy headlights of a car splashed over the house below.

CALVIN WILLIAMSON SAW the front door hanging open before he'd turned off the car. He touched his wife's hand as she reached for the seatbelt release. "Wait here. I'll be right back." There was concern in Phoebe's eyes, but also trust. He snuffed the headlights, climbed out of the car, and headed for the beach.

He found Jonah crouched over the ravaged body he'd dragged away from the reach of the breakers. It almost looked as if he were trying to perform CPR on Shane—a black irony, considering the babysitter's training. The hallmarks of a Deep One were receding from Jonah's flesh, withdrawing now that he'd been out of the water for a few minutes. Only his shark teeth were still prominent, stained as if he'd been caught gorging himself on cherry pie. His gill flaps and vestigial fins were already hidden, as they would remain until his molting next fall.

Calvin felt a pang of regret. He'd liked Shane, and hadn't wanted things to turn out like this. Not yet, anyway. The boy was a bright student. Calvin had hoped that he might at least have the chance to appreciate the hidden wonders of their town and its place in a secret history before the end of his brief span. But weren't all lives brief for folk who hadn't got out of the idea of dying? Who hadn't learned to breed it out of their bloodlines?

At his father's approach, Jonah looked up, his head slung low between his shoulders like a dog that had made a meal of something forbidden while its master was away.

"It's okay," Calvin said. "It's hard to resist the call of the sea."

"He threw my supper in the trash, Papa." A witness on the beach would have thought the words an incoherent gurgle, but Calvin Williamson was practiced at interpreting his son's vocalizations in the between state.

"You had to feed. Your mama would have been upset if you went to bed without supper."

The squeal of an unoiled hinge carried on the breeze and Calvin, recognizing it, followed the roofline of his house to the silhouette of a girl perched at the railing of the widow's walk. The aquamarine aura of the idol delineated her face, pulsing from the cradle of her arms, and Calvin hailed her. "Sister," he said in the old tongue, "do you wish to feast?"

By the time she'd returned the idol to its pedestal, her transformation was complete. Kelly L'Orne, Childe of the Deep, curled her batrachian fingers around the railing, climbed like a tree frog down the side of the house, and crawled through the tall beach grass and over the dunes. When she reached the body, she rose up on her hind legs and fanned her gills in a wet sigh of grief. Jonah slinked away, back toward the house and his mother.

"He would never have been one of us," Calvin said. "You know that."

Kelly blinked, translucent membranes sliding lazily over her bulbous eyes. They caught the moonlight with a tremulous shimmer.

"I'm sorry." Calvin tugged at his bow tie, pulled the black silk from his collar and stuffed it in his pocket. "If you're not going to feast, you should change. You can help me get his bicycle and backpack off the island. Leave them where they'll be found. Upriver, between here and his home. I'll dive with the remains down to the reef."

"Let me," she said, and before he could argue she'd knelt and slid her green-spotted arms under the dead boy's knees and neck, her fins slicing grooves in the sand. She lifted him with a gentle strength she could never have exhibited in her human form.

Calvin nodded, scanned the horizon for boat lights, then turned to follow his son over the dunes. When he looked again at the water, he saw her wading through the foam, guiding the floating corpse along a road that would lead to the moon, if silvered waves were white bricks.

"Give my regards to your grandmother," he said, though he knew his words would die on the wind.

THE GEOMETRY OF DREAMS

WENDY N. WAGNER

"You sure you don't want to put that bag in the backseat? You don't look very comfortable, Jaymie."

I wiggled my feet a little farther apart. Everything I owned fit in this garbage bag—I wanted to keep a good hold on it, even if something inside was jabbing my knee pit. Something clinked inside the bag as it shifted, and I hoped like hell it wasn't Mom's snow globe.

"I'm fine."

Ms. Schultz gave me one of her strained smiles. She wanted to like me, I think. I ought to be easy to like, compared to most kids in the system. No record, good grades, no psychological issues.

The smile wavered, and she tried again. "I think you'll like this family's house. It's one of the oldest in the city."

I'd noticed we'd headed into the West Hills. If I turned around, I could probably see all of Portland down there, except maybe my last place in Felony Flats. The houses got bigger every mile we climbed above sea level.

"It's just a couple, no other kids. They're very excited to have you."

Ah. The "we always wanted to have kids" type, well-meaning and obviously rich. I wasn't sure if that was worse than the kid farms or just more fake.

"You'll be happy to know Mrs. Marcus is a college professor. She teaches math of some kind. Doesn't that make you happy?"

The car slid into a driveway where the autumn sunshine filtered through an archway of yellow leaves. A tree tunnel, my mom would have called it. A tree tunnel. My fingers tightened on the makeshift handle of my garbage bag.

"I hate math."

"But you're in advanced calc—"

Then the house was in front of us; all brick and big timbers like some kind of English gamekeeper's lodge. The spiral topiaries framing the front door only added to the British accent.

Mr. and Mrs. Marcus stood between the topiaries, his arm around her shoulders. She stood with her arms folded across her stomach, her dark eyes focused on the ground. They both wore lightweight sweaters in neutral colors like something out of a Gap ad. He lifted his hand in greeting as we approached.

Ms. Schultz pulled to a stop. "They're already outside to welcome you. Oh, Jaymie, don't you feel good about this place?"

I glanced from one face to the other. Mrs. Marcus hadn't moved, but a smile stretched Mr. Marcus's lips taut over his blue-white teeth. I wondered if Schultzie noticed that it failed to reach his eyes.

Between the two of them, I had never felt less welcome in my life.

DINNER WAS SERVED "PROMPTLY AT 6:30," Mr. Marcus had told me when he'd left me and my garbage bag in my new room. I made sure to leave my new bedroom at 6:20 to give myself time to find the dining room. There hadn't been a grand tour or anything when I arrived; he'd just whisked me away to my bedroom suite. The bathroom was bigger than the kitchen in our old house; the marble and chrome fixtures like something out of one of those magazines Mom subscribed to.

Out on the second floor landing, I hesitated. The staircase, wide enough for four or five people, stood directly in line with the front door. If I really wanted, I could sprint downstairs, across the great room and the foyer, and out the door the before either of the Marcus creeps noticed I was late for dinner. I gripped the banister, wondering if it was a good idea. I'd learned a thing or two about trusting my instincts in the past few months.

Still. I took in the vast bookshelves on the left side of the great room, the green marble fireplace on the right. The suit of armor in the corner. There was always the chance that what really creeped me out was the presence of all this wealth. I hadn't exactly grown up around money. Was I mistrusting my new foster parents or their bank account?

I'd have to be some kind of idiot to just walk away from all this without even getting to know the Marcuses.

I marched my feet downstairs and followed my nose to the kitchen. Mrs. Marcus stood at the stove with a wooden spoon in one hand, a pot steaming up at her. She'd put on an apron and rolled up her sleeves. A pen stuck out of the messy bun on the back of her head.

"What are you doing here?"

"Isn't it dinner time?"

She looked confused. "Yes, but we eat in the dining room."

"Do you need any help?"

She looked from me to the pot. "I...you don't mind?"

There were lines around her eyes, and with her crazy red hair and apron, she looked more like a tired elementary school teacher than a country club snob. I noticed the soup box laying on its side on the counter and realized we had something in common.

"I'm a pretty terrible cook, but I can schlep things."

She pulled a bag of garlic bread out of the oven and shook it into a basket. "Can you take this? Salad's already out there." She held the basket out to me. Purple bruises marked her wrist, the size and shape of a man's hand. Her eyes followed mine to her arm and she slid her sweater sleeve back down. "Please?"

So much for getting to know the Marcuses.

I took the basket. "Which way to the dining room?" More like, which way to Schultzie's office? My phone was upstairs, so calling her for a ride was out until after dinner. Then I remembered it was Saturday, and that I only had her office number. I was stuck here until Monday.

Mrs. Marcus pointed to the kitchen's other doorway, her finger trembling a little. I did not want to go into that dining room, where Mr. Marcus undoubtedly waited.

"He's not a bad man," she whispered. "Really, he's not."

I leaned closer to her so she could hear me. "Look, Mrs. Mar—"

"Carol."

"Carol." I set my jaw. "I don't take shit. If he touches me, he'll need an ambulance. And I *am* leaving this place as soon as possible."

Then I carried the garlic bread into the dining room and took a seat. I couldn't trust either of these two, but I was stuck with them for the weekend. I needed to learn what I could about Mr. Marcus so I'd be ready for whatever he threw at me.

I smiled across the table. "Good evening, Mr. Marcus."

He glanced up from the thick book resting on the table. "Dinner's ready?" He closed the book carefully. "Carol? What's keeping you?"

She appeared in the doorway. "Soup's on!" She'd taken down her hair, and now it lay around her shoulders in copper waves.

"Excellent." He pushed the book farther from his place setting. It looked very old, its leather binding cracked and worn. The gold letters, spelling out its title in some inexplicable alphabet, had mostly flaked off. "When does Georgette get back from vacation?"

"Another week, John," Carol murmured. "Our cook," she added, as if I had asked.

"Another week to ourselves," he said, and he beamed at me. "What a way to get this little family settled in before the Dunwich Book Fair."

Carol shot me a look of pure terror.

I LAY in bed in the dark, breathing as quietly as I could so my ears could pick up any stray creak in the hallway. I'd gone to bed early and braced the antique desk chair under the door knob for protection. The snick of the lock about an hour later only confirmed my bad feelings. I couldn't wait around and work with the system. I had to get out of this place.

If this was a story I was reading with my mom, she would have laughed. The poor orphan who always dreamed of a house in the glamorous West Hills finds herself imprisoned and endangered, more miserable in her costly surroundings than the cramped apartment where she'd grown up. But if this was a story, I'd close the book and make mom put on a horror movie, and I'd eat popcorn and cuddle up with her instead of laying here missing everything about our old life.

How the hell had she gotten hit by a bus and left me alone like this? I blinked back angry tears.

The lock *snicked* a second time. The door shook, but the chair kept it closed.

"Jaymie!" Carol hissed. "Jaymie, open up!"

I got out of bed and crept to the door. "Why should I?"

The door rattled again. "Jesus, Jaymie, just let me in!"

I slid aside the chair.

She closed the door behind her and sagged against the wood. "I heard him moving around upstairs," she said, her voice so low I could barely hear it. "We don't have much time." She pulled a tiny flashlight from her pocket and scanned the floor. "Good, you didn't unpack."

"What are you talking about? What's going on?"

She locked the door and pulled me closer to the bed. "You're not safe here. I wasn't sure, but I was looking through one of his notebooks after dinner, and I saw."

"Saw what?"

"A...a *ritual*. He's got to get it done before the book fair if he wants to—" she broke off, flapping her hands. "Just grab your stuff and come on!" Carol hoisted my garbage bag and jerked her head toward the door.

I slipped on my sneakers and grabbed my coat off the writing desk. The desk looked like something out of a museum, all carved wood and furniture polish. It was the prettiest thing I'd ever had in any bedroom. Just my luck it belonged to a couple of nutjobs.

"Isn't it a little late to be going somewhere?"

Mr. Marcus's poisonous voice froze me in mid-motion. My coat slid down my arm and dangled from my wrist.

"John." Carol stepped in front of me. "Jaymie couldn't sleep. I thought a walk—"

"Shut up, Carol." He smiled as he said it, that white-toothed smile that failed to reach his eyes, and his hand swung up, his fingers closing on the front of her hair. He turned the smile on me. "I know my iniquitous wife is trying to rescue you."

She whimpered as his grip tightened on her bangs.

I took a step backward, trying to search for an escape without losing sight of him. The window lay on the far side of the vast acreage of the writing desk. "Screw you," I spat, and ripped the desk drawer out of its case. It flew past his head, splintering on the door frame.

He laughed and yanked Carol closer to him. "Boys," he called, without taking his eyes off me. "Come downstairs and meet my amusing new daughter."

Just like that, two men appeared at the end of the hallway. Black robes shrouded them, their faces swallowed up by vast hoods.

I launched myself at the desk and reached for the lock on the window. A hand closed on the collar of my shirt, yanking me backward hard enough to cut off the air in my throat. Then I spun through the air until my head thudded against something black and solid. The blood rushed to my brain.

Queasy, I blinked at my upside-down world. My garbage bag leaked clothes and books onto the carpet. My black-clad captor shifted from foot to foot, knocking my head against his back. How had the men in black gotten all the way down the hall and into my bedroom so quickly? No one could move that fast.

I could see Mr. Marcus's Euro-boot tapping impatiently in the doorway.

"Take her upstairs. The woman, too," he added. "Let's get this party started."

MOONLIGHT STREAMED in through the attic's lone human-sized window as I gripped the bars one more time. I'd never been the fittest kid, but I set my teeth and strained against the wrought iron until spots appeared in my vision.

"There's no use," Carol said, her voice hollow with unhappiness. "If John does something, he does it right."

I kicked the wall. "Son of a bitch!"

"It's over forty feet to the ground, anyway. You'd kill yourself."

I plopped onto the floor beside her. "Even if I made it out alive, I'd have to come back for my stuff."

Her chin jerked up from where it rested on her knees. "Are you crazy? What do you own that's so important?"

For the first time, I realized her eyes were the same shade of hazel my mom's had been. "My stuff." I jumped back up to my feet. I couldn't stand the thought of just sitting here like she was.

I stepped over one of the spaniel-sized black stones set into the black planks of the floor and began pacing. Black floor, black stones. Black walls. Even the door was made from some kind of black wood—extremely strong black wood, too, as my shoulder could attest. "There has to be some way out."

"I doubt it. I've never been up here, but John's an architect. He knows the best contractors and engineers in the city. If he wanted an impregnable cave, he could make one."

"Shit."

"Do you always swear this much?"

"Do you always have rooms in your house your psychotic husband keeps secret from you?"

Carol got up and went to the window. "It wasn't like this at first. See that little cabin out there?"

I crossed the room to look out at the backyard. Only a thin finger of manicured lawn ran beside the house; the rest was filled with handsomely sculpted trees and graveled paths. One ran to a tiny house so sweet it could have been an elf's summer cottage.

"John built that for me. It's my studio. Not a lot of people appreciate esoteric math, but he always encouraged my work." She made a sound like a dry cough, and it took me a minute to realize it was laughter. "Of course, now I know why."

"What does math—" I broke off. I moved to the door and leaned my ear against it.

"What do you think that thumping was?" Carol whispered.

"I don't know." I listened for another minute, but the sound had stopped. Mr. Marcus and the men in black had been "gone for supplies" a lot longer than I'd expected them. I turned to face Carol again. "So, what does math have to do with John's freakiness?" I wouldn't have admitted it, but it was hard to call

Mr. Marcus by his first name. My mom and her archaic standards, I guess.

"We used to travel to these esoteric book fairs. John had all these friends who went to them, and he loved collecting old books. Plus, I knew there were certain ancient texts that could provide insight into some of my stranger projects. I didn't think anything of it when he bought the book for me. It was just another wonderful gift from my wonderful husband."

She folded her arms around her stomach. She looked genuinely ill, and I had to admit, I did sympathize with her. A guy that shared her interest in old weird books and gave her presents like her own little cottage—she must have thought her life was perfect. Well, I knew a thing or two about life being perfect one minute and turning to garbage the next.

"I found a formula," she blurted. "I'd been working on a theory that with the right tools, we could understand the way our universe adjoins with other ones. The book supported the idea. It claimed that a series of non-Euclidean geometrical equations could be used along with certain kinds of power sources to open a door to another reality."

"You're not trying to tell me that's true, right? Because that's crazy AF. Non-Euclidean geometry is still logical, even—"

A thud powerful enough to vibrate the floor sounded. Then a man screamed. My hand closed around Carol's. "What the hell was that?"

"Oh, no." She pulled me closer to her and put her arm around me. "He stole my formula. He—" she broke off as the scream sounded again, one sharp, tormented sound cut short. "He opened the door once before," she whispered. "That's where the men in the robes came from."

Then we heard the footsteps, the booming stride of a man's boots, accompanied by a strange pattering sound.

The door flew open, and the silhouettes of three men stood framed in the doorway, the harsh light of the hallway making me blink.

John Marcus stepped inside, a glow stick in his hand. The sickly green light made the spatters on his beige sweater look like ink.

"I've got the supplies and you've got the brain, dear foster daughter. Looks like we're ready for the big time!"

A THICK LEATHER strap dug into the skin of my forehead, pressing my skull into the hard table the men in black had set up in the center of the room. One stooped over me, checking the buckles on each strap. Wrists, ankles, waist, chest, forehead: there was no way to even wiggle. The man gave the chest strap's buckle a tug, and I saw his fingers for the first time. Dark gray hair covered each knobby knuckle, and the purplish-black nails tapered to a tip, like a talon. I still couldn't see his face, but the tap-tap-tap of its feet—like the tapping of a goat's hooves as it pranced around its pen—made me doubt his humanity.

Was Carol right? Had these...*things*...come from some other world? It would explain their impossible speed and their strange, inhuman hands.

John swooped into my field of vision. "I am so excited." He pressed his hands to his chest. I'd seen theater nerds behave with less melodrama. "The first time I tried this, I used myself as the dream vessel. Carol did the math and performed the ritual, although her lack of enthusiasm may have contaminated our results."

One of the goat-things began painting designs on the walls with an oversized paintbrush. The misshapen stars and impossible shapes clotted on the fine wood paneling. My stomach churned at the stench of blood. I had a horrible feeling about the origin of that scream Carol and I had heard.

Carol's muffled voice sounded off to my left. John had gagged her after she'd bitten one of the robed men-things. Now she was strapped to a chair as tightly as I was strapped to my torture table.

"But you!" He pressed his cold hands to either side of my face, leaning over my forehead so his eyes looked into mine. I wanted to squeeze shut my eyelids to hide from the insanity of his face. "You're the solution. Your precious, youthful brain. Your dreams are what I need."

He stood up, disappearing from view. "Goros, Mishak, begin the ritual!"

A gong struck, and the smell of sulfur filled the room.

Then John reappeared, practically beaming as he slipped into his own black robe. "Did I tell you you're going to dream me up a two-way portal to another world? Aren't you excited?"

He pulled a syringe out of his pocket. "The drug will make you very sleepy, so I won't have long to wait." He uncapped the needle and jabbed it into the side of my neck. "Your brain will melt during the process but I'm sure everyone will simply blame your circumstances for your mental collapse. After all, you've been through a lot."

His face began to spin. "Screw you," I said, or maybe only tried to say. The skin on my face felt heavy. My eyelids sagged shut.

"You see a door." The voice vibrated inside the depths of my ear. "A glowing door."

The stink of sulfur grew more powerful. Something cold and wet pressed against my forehead and squelched. Liquid dripped down my paralyzed face and into my hair.

A door.

He could stick that door right up his ass. If I was going to dream, I was going to dream my own dream. Blackness filled my mind, a soft blackness with folds that twisted open. My garbage bag. And right on top, my mother's snow globe. I could even hear the sound of its music box winding, the click of its little gears. The girl inside began to spin.

"What the hell is this?" someone asked, their voice piercing the drug haze for a moment.

Then I swooped into the snow globe. Sparkling crystal flakes swirled around me. The girl in the yellow dress spun in a slow circle, the bird on her finger growing larger and larger as I approached. Its beak curved, changing from a sweet yellow triangle into a raven's fierce hook.

"Nevermore," it squawked and then fluttered up to sit on her shoulder. "Never! Never!"

"Jaymie, it's so good to see you."

The girl in the yellow dress had finally turned to face me. But instead of the soft, painted features of Disney's Belle, my mother's face smiled back at me.

"Mom! Help!"

"I'm right here, sweetie. Together, we can get you out of this."

I threw my arms around her. "I've missed you so much. Everything's been horrible since you died. And this guy is using me to open a door to another wo—"

She pressed a gloved finger to my lips. "That's a tale as old as time, don't you think?" She smiled. "I'm more interested in you. How are you holding up?"

I shoved her away. "How am I holding up? Mom, you died! You left me all alone to live out of a garbage bag! Nobody gives a crap about me!"

She slowly rotated away from me. I chased after her, but she sped up. I grabbed a handful of fake snow and threw it against her back. It struck her dress and left wet spots.

The raven squawked again. It looked bigger than it had just a second ago.

A very muffled shouting came from someplace behind me. "What are you doing?" John Marcus shouted.

Mom circled around to face me. "It's okay to be mad at me. I shouldn't have left you. But don't let that stop you from living your real life."

"I don't have a life! I might as well be dead without you!"

The raven flew off her shoulder, its wings battering my face. Black feathers filled the air. It flew to the top of the globe, its beak clinking against the glass.

"I don't have much time," Mom said. "I love you, Jaymie."

The sound of shattering glass cut off anything else she might have said.

"Jaymie! Wake up!"

My stomach lurched and surged. I sat up, trying not to puke. I couldn't see. White shards and black feathers filled the air.

Fingers tugged on the waist strap. "We've got to get out of here." Carol sounded like she was crying. "Come on."

Her hand closed on mine. I swung my legs over the table's edge. "What happened? What's going on?"

A horrible squawk sounded behind us. Something roared.

"Come on!" Carol screamed. She yanked me down from the table and pulled me to the door. She slammed it behind us and stood gasping for a second. Feathers stuck out of her hair. Fake snow coated every inch of her. "You opened a door."

"But I tried not to."

"Just as John was going in, this bird thing came out—" Carol gave a little scream as something hit the door with a horrible crunch.

I didn't need any urging to run. We hit the stairs at the end of the hall and didn't slow down. A terrible splintering sounded.

"What the hell is that?" she asked.

The saurian scream sounded again. The door slammed and then the tapping of hooves echoed behind us.

I wasn't sure what I was more scared of: the raven I'd brought out of my dream or John Marcus's creatures. We hit the landing at the top of the grand stairway. The house looked so ordinary down there, the couches and the fireplace and the beautiful bookshelves like something from a universe where Martha Stewart made the laws, not non-Euclidean magical geometry.

A thudding sounded behind us, and we couldn't help but turn to face it.

The man-thing in the black robe raced down the hallway. Its hood had fallen back, and I could see its shaggy head with two knobby horns and an inhumanly wide mouth. Pointed teeth, nearly tusks, showed as it panted desperately. It headed right for us.

The raven behind it filled the hallway. Its eyes flashed yellow. Then it stretched its neck, its black beak closing on the man-thing's middle. There was a crunch.

The top half of the man-thing flew forward, arcing up and over Carol and I. It hung in the air above the grand staircase for a few seconds and then plummeted down, bouncing from one step to the next until it landed in a wet heap at the bottom of the stairs.

The raven kept running toward us.

"Come on!" I shouted. I pulled Carol down the stairs, skidding on blood spatters.

The raven soared over us. It spun in a lazy circle and landed right in front of the front door.

It opened its mouth. "Where are you going?" John Marcus's voice came from somewhere inside it.

The raven made a croaking sound. Its beak opened wide as if it meant to puke up something terrible.

"It swallowed John," Carol whispered.

The raven's throat began to pulse and throb. A hand appeared in the back of the raven's open mouth.

"No," she whispered. "Please, no."

John's face appeared, grinning wildly.

"I don't know what kind of dreamworld you took me to,

foster daughter, but I'm more than man enough for it. When I get out of here, I'm going to make you and my pernicious little wife very, very sorry."

He slithered over the raven's tongue and grabbed onto the edges of its beak, ready to pull himself completely free. The raven shook its head wildly.

There had to be a weapon somewhere. Something I could use to protect Carol and I. The suit of armor was on the far side of the raven, but I could make it to the fireplace. I'd never had a fireplace, but in the movies, a fire poker always made a great weapon.

The raven twisted so its yellow eye met mine. It wasn't an animal shade of yellow at all, but the color of daffodils in sunshine; the same color as Belle's dress in *Beauty and the Beast*, the one she wore in my mom's snow globe.

The raven winked.

Then its beak snapped shut on John's neck.

His head dropped to the floor and rolled toward me, his eyes round and startled. For once, he wasn't smirking or cold-eyed or in any way in control of what his face showed. For some reason, that made me happy.

The raven pulled its wings in tight to itself and began to shrink. Carol came to my side.

"Entropy is increasing," she whispered. "With John dead, there's no energy to power the door."

The raven became horse-sized, then sheep-sized. Its feathers faded from black to purple to blue. Its beak shrank to a yellow triangle. For a moment, the blue bird fluttered in the foyer, and then it went still. It crashed to the floor and shattered into a thousand bits of painted porcelain.

"It's over," I said. I burst into tears. "Please tell me it's over."

She gave me a fierce hug "It's over. For now, at least."

"For now? What does that mean?" My head hurt, and my stomach still wanted to escape my body. If I let go of Carol, I'd probably fall down.

"John's friends will expect him at the book fair next week. When he doesn't show up—well, everyone knows I was the brains of the operation." She made a sound that might have been a laugh or the beginning of a sob.

"Will they come after you?"

"Don't worry, we've got a few days. Ms. Schultz will have you in a new family before anything happens."

I pulled free of her grip. "Is that what you want? To get rid of me?"

"What? No!" She shook her head so hard her hair swatted me in the face. "Jaymie, you're the bravest person I ever met. And one of the only people outside the university system who knows anything about non-Euclidean geometry. But if you stay with me, you could get hurt. I can't let that happen."

I put my hands on my hips and narrowed my eyes at her. I remembered the bruises on her arms, the meek way she'd talked to Mr. Marcus. That quiet, mousy woman was gone. She'd put herself in danger to get me out of this house, and that had taken some kind of strength. She was even willing to keep fighting her husband's creepy pals.

The thought of facing down more ancient-book-loving-monster-raising psychos scared the crap out of me. But was it really so much worse than another shitty foster placement?

"Well, I can't let you get hurt, either. I'm already bored in my advanced calculus class, and you seem like you just might have something to teach me." I grinned. "Besides, I'm a lot tougher than you. Being in the system will harden up a girl."

Something thumped upstairs. We both jumped.

"Maybe we should get out of here for a little while? I'm not sure that other goat-monster is dead."

"Good idea," she said, her eyes suspiciously bright.

"No mushy stuff," I warned. "I am not a hugger."

The thumping sounded again, this time louder. She glanced upstairs, then back at me. "We can hit up a twenty-four-hour restaurant and figure out what to do next. You want to get your stuff?"

"No," I said, and began walking downstairs, "I don't need it. You like pancakes?"

"I love them," Carol said.

Maybe we had more in common than just being good at math. And maybe that was reason enough to stick around.

After all, my mom had been a fried eggs kind of gal.

BEING EMILY-CLAIRE

JONATHAN MABERRY

Emily-Claire had monsters in her closet.

But then, who didn't? That's what closets were for. Well, mostly. The closet also had a lot of clothes in darker earth tones, grays and black. She wasn't Goth like a lot of the girls at school, or didn't think she was. Emily-Claire was just herself and she wasn't interested in relating to the other kids. Those colors let her fade into the background. Where it was quiet. Where it was safe.

There were shoes in there—old sneakers she wore in gym, heels her sister said she could save for prom. As if. And she had some good walking shoes because Emily loved to walk. Hiking shoes, ditto. Lots of old toys in there as well; stuff people gave her when she was little. Back when they thought she was the kind of kid who played with those sorts of toys. Her aunts and grandparents stopped giving her Barbies and Baby So Sweet when they saw what happened to them.

There were shouts after that, Mom crying; Dad on the phone to therapists. Whispers behind closed doors. Tests and scans. Emily-Claire told a pack of lies and after a while they stopped looking at her like she was a new species of toad. Not that being a toad would be a bad thing, but since people like her parents didn't like toads, the looks weren't happy ones.

She didn't tell them that there were monsters in her closet. Even when she was little—six or seven—Emily-Claire was too smart to make that mistake. Young did not mean stupid. Not for her.

So, yes, she had monsters in her closet. Once in a while one of the monsters would hide in the curbside mailbox, waiting for her to reach in and get the mail. That was nice.

She was so happy they were there. Without the monsters, where would she be? It was a question that weighed on her. Because, truly, without them, where *would* she be?

The real problem was that there was a monster in her school locker, too, and that thing wasn't one of *hers*.

-2-

Emily was thirteen, an age she wished she could be for the rest of her life. Thirteen was, after all, her lucky number. Fourteen was looming, though. Fourteen would be dull. Fifteen, too. Maybe sixteen would be okay, though, because she planned on getting her license at the earliest possible moment. Old Mrs. Willow three doors down said that she would sell her car to Emily-Claire for a dollar and a crow feather when she got her license. Emily-Claire had tried to give her a crow feather on account, but the crone asked for the dollar instead.

"Crow feathers are special things, little witch," said Mrs. Willow. It didn't matter that Emily-Claire was not a witch. The old lady called her that because *she* was a witch. Not a pointy-hat kind, but a real one. Positive magic, crystal energy and wisdom that ran miles deep. *Wicce* was an Old English word for sorceress. A word people always got wrong, using wicca instead, but that was the masculine. On the other hand, the Middle English word *wicche* could be used for men or women.

But no one ever used it. In either case, 'witch' was just—according to the old lady—a 'term of convenience.'

"What's that mean?" Emily-Claire had asked. She was nine at the time.

"It means that there isn't any word in English that really fits," said Mrs. Willow. "There's no word in any language you could fit into your mouth that suits who you are. Or what you are."

Even at nine, Emily-Claire thought she understood that. Even so, she didn't call herself 'witch.' Instead, she preferred another of the old lady's favorite words.

A *sensitive*.

Yes. That fit her very well.

The car the old lady said would be hers was an ugly, lumpy AMC Gremlin that hadn't been pretty when it rolled off the assembly line in 1978. Some maniac had painted it a lurid shade of dark orange that was nearly, but not quite, pumpkin. Emily-Claire thought it was magnificent. Named for a monster, and as ugly as a gargoyle. Despite its age, Mrs. Willow whipped around town in it way too fast. A few times Mrs. Willow had taken Emily-Claire out to strange little stores in parts of the city she could not afterward find on a map.

There, on side alleys off of Boundary Street, Mrs. Willow and Emily-Claire had gone shopping in tiny, crowded stores filled with crystals and dried herbs and decks of hand-painted tarot cards, and cones of incense that smelled like memories rather than smells. The owners of the store were always old ladies like Mrs. Willow. Some were so ancient their faces looked like collections of wrinkles rather than skin. Except for the eyes. All of them had young eyes. Or...maybe it was that their eyes were so old they looked young. Emily-Claire rather thought that was the right way to think about it.

She wanted to go find those stores on her own. In that car. She was certain the Gremlin would remember the way. She wanted to get to know those old ladies. Maybe grow up and grow old and be like them. That sounded wonderful to her, and she was sure her closet monsters would approve.

If, of course, she lived that long.

Right now, things weren't looking good.

Even the monsters had their doubts.

-3-

She first realized that there was a problem when something in her locker at school tried to eat her. Well, maybe not eat. But grab. It definitely took a grab. And it wasn't at all nice about it.

It was a Thursday, which was no surprise to Emily-Claire. Thursdays tended to suck on a regular basis.

It started in the girls' bathroom.

Emily-Claire was washing her hands after a really fun biology class, where they dissected pig fetuses. She'd told Mr. Boykin that she 'forgot' to wear the blue protective gloves. Really, she liked to feel the skin and the organs. Even though the pig had never been born it had a lot to tell her. Memories borrowed from her mother and from other pigs going way back. Like as far back as when there were no people and the pigs were being hunted by saber-toothed cats—*Smilodon Fatalis*.

She always learned so much from blood and skin. Nearly as much as she learned from rotting vegetables and decaying trees. They were fading away and wanted to tell her their stories; and she always wanted to listen. Though, it was listening with touch and smell and sometimes taste. It wasn't an ear thing, and, for some reason, smell didn't connect her to anything except what it was in the moment. If she smelled a chocolate chip cookie it told her it was a chocolate chip cookie. She had to actually break it up between her fingers before she learned about the fields and forests where the wheat and cocoa grew.

So, her hands were messy, and Mr. Boykin told her to clean

up before her next class. Emily-Claire always washed slowly and thoroughly, because good soap broke the connection and let her come back to the now. Otherwise she'd be jumping at shadows thinking a saber-toothed cat was about to eat her.

The two other girls in there were at the far end of the line of sinks. Unlike her, they were Goth, though not the same kind of Goth as each other. Cynthia Harper—who demanded that people call her Syn—was a full-blown traditional Goth who only listened to Goth punk from the 1980s. She wore a lot of chains, fishnet stockings—often hidden under her jeans so she didn't get yelled at for dress code stuff—and had bats and skulls on every item of clothing or personal possession she owned. She was a ninth grader, which made her a senior at John Paul Jones Junior High. She began applying a fresh layer of black lipstick while talking to Naomi Pelembe, who was still a Baby Goth. Naomi hated that people called her that, but she was a seventh grader who still wore Disney princess t-shirts on the first day of school. Syn had very pale skin that Emily-Claire figured was mostly makeup. Naomi's parents had emigrated from Mozambique before she was born, and she had beautiful dark brown skin.

Emily-Claire tried not to look like she was eavesdropping, but she caught a name that made her want to hear. Syn mentioned something about Jonah.

That really caught her attention. Emily-Claire had only recently started thinking seriously about boys. Well...*boy*. Jonah Allyn was the best-looking human being she had ever seen. Tall and thin and pale, with icy blue eyes that looked like he'd not only seen things but had spent enough time thinking about them to understand what he'd seen. That mattered a lot to her. When he looked at her, which he did more and more often this year, his eyes seemed to open up a little door in her head and peer inside. Like he not only saw her, but wanted to see more. To know more. About her.

Her.

The fact that he had curly blonde hair, great teeth, and smelled good had absolutely nothing to do with anything.

They had spoken a bunch of times. Always about books. He was one of those guys who didn't read fiction. It was always nonfiction stuff. History and philosophy and geography. Jonah said he wanted to become an archaeologist, digging up the bones of history to understand why people did what they did. His blue eyes turned kind of misty gray when he talked about the past. It made her wonder if he was a sensitive, too. Not with dead or dying things, but with old stone and wood and things people owned when they were alive. It was a question she'd been working up the nerve to ask, but hadn't gotten there yet.

"...said they saw him in social studies," Syn was saying, "but then he just like bugged out. Left his bookbag and even his cell phone."

Naomi gasped, horrified. "He left his *cell*?"

"I know, right?"

"So, where'd he go?"

"That's just it," insisted Syn, "nobody knows. That skanky old backpack he uses as a book bag was on the floor by his locker. Door was closed and locked and all. His cell was in his backpack. But he wasn't there, and nobody's seen him."

"And he didn't come back for his phone?" Naomi seemed unable to get past that part of the story.

Syn, who was always looking at Jonah—like *all* the time— seemed hooked on the strangeness of it all. She looked around to see if anyone was listening even though it was only the three of them in the bathroom. Syn looked right through Emily-Claire. People did that a lot. Maybe it meant that it didn't matter if someone like her heard, because Emily-Claire didn't have any friends. Probably, but she didn't care. School friends were never a priority for her. There were other conversations worth having. Mrs. Willow. The ladies on Boundary Street. The trees in the yard. Dead pigs and crushed beetles. Something was always dying in the world, and dying things always wanted to share. They were better conversationalists, too. They spoke about old things, deep things. Important things.

In an exaggerated conspiratorial whisper Syn said, "I heard that they called his mom and she freaked out because Jonah never came home. And my friend Jilly who's an office aide told me that Jonah's folks are going to file some kind of missing persons thing."

"Why?" asked Naomi, clearly confused. "He's not missing. He just didn't come home."

"That's the same thing, genius," snapped Syn. "They think maybe he ran off."

"Ran off? That's crazy," cried Naomi. "Who would run away and not take their phone?"

Emily-Claire wanted to tell her to shut up about the phone, but she kept her mouth clamped shut and listened.

"I don't know," admitted Syn, "but it's really weird, don't you think? It's not like Jonah was a freak or anything. I don't think he was into anything. He's not a druggie or any of that."

"I still don't understand why he'd up and take off without his phone," muttered Naomi as the two girls walked past Emily-Claire like she was a hole in the air.

The door closed with a bang and then it was completely silent in the bathroom. No water dripping, no sounds at all from the hall.

Emily-Claire frowned at herself in the mirror.

"What?" she asked her reflection. The short, pale, thin, wisp of a girl looking back at her had no answers.

-4-

Emily-Claire began asking questions.

As she saw it, the whole school was weird. There were very few of what might be called 'normals.' Only a handful of the cheerful kids in trendy clothes and this year's hair. The school dances were mostly played out with clumps of kids standing talking about other clumps while a DJ played EDM that like four people danced to. The whole school vibe was fringe, but not in a fun way. There were more varieties of Goth than anything else—vampire Goth, metal Goth, fairy Goth, Candy Goth, J Goth... A long list, but none of them mixed, except for a few Baby Goths, who were sucked into one tribe or another by the end of seventh grade. There were the retro grunge skater kids. There were the ghosts, the ones who drifted through the halls without saying a word to anyone. Like...ever. There were some in the hip-hop crowd, but they usually had earphones in, even at dance parties. There were the school cliques—choir, chess, art, band, stage—who seemed to view anyone outside of their circle as beings from another world.

Then there was Emily-Claire, who was not a ghost or a Goth, and did not consider herself a freak or a geek. She was who she was and liked being exactly that.

She talked to some people. She had no actual friends, but there were other kids she sometimes talked to. They, unlike she, were actively withdrawn. Either because of social anxiety issues or being told too many times that they were freaks, they'd washed up against the fringes of school society. Saying little, not even to one another. Pale or dark, skinny or fat, pretty or plain. It didn't matter. They were different in all the ways that mattered to kids like Syn and Naomi.

The people who she knew would talk to her didn't have a lot to tell her. The story spread that Jonah was missing. There were rumors that he'd been abducted, though why and by whom changed from one story to the next. Drug cartels, human trafficking, a death cult, the government, and aliens were all suggested. Emily-Claire didn't think any of those theories made sense.

She sought out Syn's friend, Jilly, who worked in the office. Jilly was the kind of person who got high on gossip, and Emily-Claire guessed that's why she volunteered to be an aide. Jilly liked to vaguebook and sly-tweet all sorts of stuff. Most of it was all hype and no meat, but she was sometimes right.

"Hey, Jilly," said Emily-Claire, catching up with her going into another bathroom. Jones had a lot of bathrooms and all of them looked like the one from Harry Potter. Emily-Claire suspected that all school bathrooms were haunted, and that was fine. "Did you hear about Jonah?"

Jilly turned, already smiling, eyes alight with secret knowledge. She was in the same Goth clique as Syn, but dressed more 'normal' because of working in the office. Even so, it was black on black on black. No dark lipstick or eyeliner, though, and she had auburn hair that wasn't dyed black.

"What did *you* hear?" Jilly asked as they went inside. It was her standard opener, wanting to know what someone else knew so she would never get hit with a "Yeah, I know" response.

Emily-Claire told her what she overheard from Syn, and some of the theories floating around school. Jilly made a face of haughty disdain. "Oh, girl, you're way behind the times. Jonah isn't just *missing*; the police were here twice and sent one of those CSI teams to check out his locker."

"Why?"

"Because of the blood, silly," said Jilly with a happy leer. "Why else?"

"Wait...blood?" Emily-Claire's heart slammed to a frozen halt in her chest. "What blood?"

"On the inside of the locker." Jilly managed to say everything as if the other person was somehow mentally deficient. Emily-Claire never minded; that was Jilly's thing. Jilly took a breath and explained that the vice principal and the school security officer decided to open Jonah's locker to see if there was anything that might provide a clue as to what happened to him. The locker, however, was completely empty. No textbooks or papers, no smelly gym clothes or pictures. "You know what was in there?" Jilly added.

Emily-Claire's heart was an icy stone. "What...?" she asked, her voice hollow and small.

"*Three drops of blood*," said Jilly with ghoulish triumph.

"Three...?"

"Drops of blood. Yes. That was all, but I mean...it means something nasty happened."

Jilly said more, but Emily-Claire wasn't sure she heard any of it.

Blood.

"No," she whispered.

Jilly sniffed indignantly. "What, you think I'm lying?"

Emily-Claire jerked upright. "What? Oh! No, that's not—"

"I don't just make stuff up," snapped the other girl, clearly offended.

"No, sorry, I—"

But Jilly went into a stall, banged the door shut and locked it.

Emily-Claire fled.

-5-

The next thing Emily-Claire did was go straight to Jonah's locker. It was in a corner of the basement hallway, down the hall from the boys' gym. The lockers were a million years old, with dented doors covered in band stickers, scratched graffiti, and grime. She did not have to look hard for 117, but she couldn't get to it.

There were five orange traffic cones set in a wide half circle around it, and the locker itself was sealed with black and yellow tape. Crime scene tape, though there were no words on it. The tape sealed all four sides of the locker and clear plastic had been placed over the dial combination. Signs were taped up that read: *POLICE: DO NOT TOUCH*.

She edged close, leaning over a cone, reaching out to touch.

A locker was a closet, and closets had shadows. Monsters

lived in shadows, and they were her friends. Were there monsters in Jonah's locker? If so, would they know what happened to him?

She knew his combination because they'd been talking once while he opened it, and Emily-Claire noticed things like that. Left three, right fifteen, left thirty-seven.

She was beginning to reach for the knob, sure she could turn it even with the plastic cover, when she smelled it.

The stink.

Such a stink. Like rotting fish. It was awful. The kind of smell from a cellar where something bad happened. Worse than the smell of a beach after something washed up. This didn't have a normal odor. It was wrong. Very, very wrong.

Then something thumped inside of the locker. She jerked back, staring.

But there was only silence now.

Did that just happen?

There it was again. It sounded wet and heavy and the fish stink was worse. Not just stronger, but the stink no longer felt quite dead. No. Now it felt completely alive, and in all the wrong ways. She yelped and nearly ran.

Nearly.

What stopped her was the voice. It spoke in a soft whisper, like the way her closet monsters did. But it wasn't the same. This voice was lower, deeper. Sneakier.

"Open the door," it said.

"Wh-what?"

"Open the door," repeated the voice. "I know you want to. I know you can..."

It was like a closet monster voice, but she knew—she sensed—that it was a lie. A trick. Her own monsters had coaxed her into opening her closet door when she was little, speaking in soft whispers, too. She'd been too young to be really afraid of monsters. The unknown was never scary to her. She always wanted to touch it and listen to it and taste it.

Once she'd opened her closet the monsters had reached out with their strange hands. Claws and scales and fur. Touching her small hands. Touching her face. They could have torn her to pieces because closet monsters are very, very strong. But none of them ever left so much as a scratch on her. Not then, and not since. She'd spent so many hours on so many days and nights, sitting in the open closet doorway, listening to their stories in their whispery voices; and she telling them her own stories.

But this was different. She could feel that without even touching the locker. And yet she wanted to dial that combination and open the door and ..

And what? she asked herself.

Jilly said they'd found blood. She'd touched human blood before. It spoke to her the way those kinds of things often did. Telling the things that happened to the body in which it used to race like red fire through the veins. There had never been a reason to touch the blood of someone who'd died. She'd only done that with animals. Like the pig fetus in biology.

Jonah's not dead, she shouted inside her head.

"No," agreed the silky voice, as if it could hear her thoughts. Or, that one at least. "Jonah's not dead. He's in here with us."

With us.

Us. Now it was saying that there was more than one thing in the locker. How many? And what kind of monsters were they? She knew, from the stories her monsters told her, that not all creatures were kind, even though they were all dangerous. Most were not dangerous to little girls. Or to teenage girls. Or to boys, for that matter. Not unless those kids were mean to the monsters. They never forgot and never forgave, but they were loyal and kind, too.

"Open the door, E.C.," said the voice.

Emily-Claire nearly screamed. Only one person ever called her E.C..

"J-Jonah...?"

"Yesssss," hissed the voice, drawing the word out so that it turned to hot steam. It kind of sounded like Jonah, too.

She backed up a step and was about to go when she saw something that made her pause. There, on the lower corner of the door, was a smudge. It was dark and nearly invisible against the band stickers. She saw it, though. She knew that the CSI people had missed it.

Blood.

The tiniest smear of it. Not quite dry.

"C'mon, E.C., go ahead and open the door. It's cool," suggested the voice, and now it was talking exactly like Jonah.

She stuffed her fist into her mouth and stood there, wide-eyed, wet-eyed, shivering.

Then she reached out a trembling finger toward the smudge.

"What are you doing, E.C.?" asked the Jonah-voice.

"N-nothing," she lied, though her voice quavered.

"Don't touch that," said the voice. "There's a metal splinter there. You can't see it, but it's there. Touch it and you'll get cut."

It sounded so reasonable now. No longer slippery, but the real Jonah. Reasonable, normal. It made her doubt for a long moment, the vulnerable pad of her finger only half an inch from the smear.

"Why don't you open the locker instead," said the voice. "That way you can have whatever you want."

She didn't move.

"You can have me, E.C.," said Jonah. "We can—y'know—hang out and stuff."

"I...."

"You know the combination," he said. "I saw you watching...."

A tear broke from the corner of her eye and rolled like acid down her cheek.

"Jonah," she breathed.

"I'd love to hang out, E.C.," he said. There was such

warmth, such kindness in his voice. "You're pretty cool, you know that? I think you're hot and—"

She touched the blood.

It did not speak to her.

It *screamed.*

Then a teacher came out of a side room, saw her, began walking toward her, and she whirled and ran away, trying to outrun her horror. Trying to outrun her broken heart.

-6-

She ran upstairs and down the empty halls and back to the bathroom. Into a stall. Door slammed, lock turned. Emily-Claire stood wide-legged as if the floor tilted under her and she did not want to slide down into a screaming place. She braced her hands on the metal walls and clamped her teeth shut and squeezed her eyes closed.

The horror, though, and the heartbreak was in there *with* her.

It was Jonah's blood. She was absolutely sure of it. Positive beyond any doubt. But it was wrong, too. The blood was—she fished for the word—*polluted.* His and not his. Jonah's but not completely Jonah's. She wasn't sure if she could explain it, even to herself, but she absolutely knew. Something had happened to him, and whatever was in his locker had taken him. Or... taken him over. She wasn't sure. His blood was mixed with something else. It stank of fish and rot and life and—

Not death, though.

Jonah was gone, but she did not think he was dead. He was *gone.* Taken. Something had stolen him away, maybe pulled him into his locker when he opened it. Tore him through that narrow opening, leaving behind nothing except a few drops of polluted blood.

She did not ask herself why. 'Why' was a stupid question. It was naïve, because monsters didn't have the same wants or needs as people. They were, after all, monsters. And this one was a kind she'd never encountered before. Not in dreams and not in any of the closets in her family's big house. None of them smelled of fish and wrongness. Her monsters smelled of compost and rich earth and worms and skin and old bones and darkness.

Bells rang and suddenly the whole world seemed to be doors banging out, sneakers on floorboards, laughter, gossip, hurrying, shouts and yells, the ringing of cell phones. The noises swirled around. Girls came into the bathroom, chattering like pigeons, used the facilities, left. Then silence fell again.

She wanted to be home. To fly there. To suddenly *be* there. Home where the shadows were her friends. Home where the monsters in the closet were.

She wasn't.

Emily-Claire was in school and something was horribly wrong.

-7-

It took her a long time to come out of the bathroom. The halls were silent and empty once more. The old, polished floors gleamed with light that slanted down through the big windows at each end of the hall.

Emily-Claire hurried along like a small ghost, sticking to the shadows, until she reached her own locker. She wanted to get her stuff and then go home. Maybe talk to Mrs. Willow and see if she had any idea what to do.

She dialed her combination and pulled open the door. She never stopped to consider the smell. The wrong smell. The fish smell.

As the lock clicked, the door suddenly whipped open and something dark and green lashed out at her. Something that glistened wetly. Something that uncurled from the shadows inside her locker. For a moment she thought it was a snake, but it wasn't. Snakes did not have big suckers in rows on their bellies. Suckers rimmed with rows upon rows of sharp little teeth.

One of the tentacles slapped across her face as she dodged away. It did not catch her, but it did cut her. She felt it burn, but even that was wrong. It burned too much for so shallow a cut. It was more like an actual burn—intense and shocking. She backpedaled all the way to the opposite wall as the thing chased her, reached for her, and only when she slammed against the soccer team trophy case did she realize what it was. Not a snake. Not an arm.

It was a tentacle.

Long and swollen and slimy, with suckers on the bottom and barnacles on the top, as if it had lived deep in the water for a long time. Way too long.

A second tentacle wriggled behind it, trying to crowd through the narrow opening. And a third. More.

Back there, deep inside the shadows that stretched much farther than her shallow locker, was a beast of some kind. Incredibly huge. Ugly. Obscene. It wanted her. It wanted to drag her inside, the way it had dragged Jonah. The way it might eventually take all of the kids here. One at a time.

What then? What would happen when it had fed on all of the kids in her school? Would it be strong enough to break through the whole wall of lockers, tearing its way from wherever it lived down so deep that sunlight couldn't reach it?

"No!" she shouted.

"Yesssssssss," it whispered, no longer pretending to be Jonah. Being itself. "Come inside, child of flesh and bone. Let us show you the infinite stars. They go on forever and forever and forever. We will open your skin and fill it with stars. We will—"

"No!" she bellowed again then whirled and ran.

It was two miles to her house, and Emily-Claire ran all the way.

-8-

No one was home. Mrs. Willow was out, too. Emily-Claire called the numbers for the little shops on Boundary Street, and no one answered.

She pounded up the stairs to her room and lunged for the doorknob of her closet.

But there she froze.

What if it was *here* now, too? What if it followed her home, just like it followed from Jonah's locker to her own? What if it chased away all of her own monsters? Or worse, hurt them. Killed them. Just to get to her?

Hopelessness was a punch to the stomach and her knees buckled. She dropped down so far her knees thumped painfully on the rug.

"Please...," she begged.

She reached up to the knob. If her monsters were gone, then what?

Then I'll let it take me, too.

The thought was a knife in her mind. Cold and sharp. She looked around the room as if she could see the whole house. No one was home. Where had everyone gone? Had they opened the wrong doors, too? Was that how it was all going to end? People opening doors to lockers and closets and offices and bathrooms, expecting things to be what they ought to be. Not expecting ancient monsters. Who would be prepared for that?

Had her family already been taken? Had Mrs. Willow and the old witches on Boundary Street? Was everyone she cared about gone?

Something shifted inside the closet. Heavy. Soft.

Fresh tears rolled down her cheeks. She wiped at them and

her hand came away red, and for a moment she couldn't understand it. Then she remembered her sliced cheek.

Another thump.

"Please," she said again, and reached for the doorknob.

If they're all gone, then it can have me, too.

The knob turned easily with a nearly silent click. She held the door shut still, dangling on a moment of terrible doubt.

Then Emily-Claire opened the door.

-9-

The thing inside reached for her. It had a long, long reach because it was stretching out from much farther away than the clothes hanging inside her closet. It reached through worlds of shadows.

The reaching hand had long, long fingers and each one was tipped with sharp, sharp claws. Those claws were black as midnight and sharp as thought. Those talons spread wide as it reached for her shoulder. She bowed her head as tears fell onto her thigh.

The fingers closed on her shoulder.

Very, very gently.

-10-

Emily-Claire went back to school. She had a fresh Band-Aid on her cheek. It had little pictures of the Bunny Beasts from the Blood C anime she liked. Her hair was brushed and pulled back into a ponytail and she wore clean clothes.

She carried a box with her. Small, wooden. Something she'd made in an arts and crafts class. A shadow box. The teacher had tried to explain to her that it wasn't a shadow box because real shadow boxes were actually very deep picture frames with glass lids. They were for putting 3-D stuff into, like dried flowers and dinosaur bones and swarms of dead butterflies. Emily-Claire had only smiled and built the box her way.

"But," said the exasperated teacher, "it's just a *box*."

"With a hinge," she said.

"Well, sure, but—"

"And it's full of shadows," Emily-Claire told him. The teacher gave in, because he was wise enough not to argue about such things with a girl like Emily-Claire.

The shadow box was made of maple and hickory and painted with images of night-blooming jasmine. The wood was heavy, but she managed. It did not have dinosaur bones or dead insects in it.

When she got to the front steps of the school she stopped and looked up. They looked the same, as did the school itself, but the world had changed for her. Her cheek tingled; not so much with pain but with a reminder that Jonah was gone and there was something in there, hiding in the beautiful shadows, that was ugly and wrong. Something that didn't belong. Something she now knew was actually sleeping and only *dreaming* that it was here in her school.

That's what the monsters in her closet had told her while she sat there, weeping, resting her cheek against the scaly wrist of the thing that lightly gripped her shoulder. It was her first monster, the oldest one. The one she'd met when she was three. It whispered to her of things even older than itself. Creatures so incredibly old that people thought they were immortal. Beings so strange and powerful that whole civilizations on dozens of worlds worshipped them as gods.

Except they were not gods. They were monsters and they were aliens, but not gods.

The monster in her closet was very specific on that point. Once they were servants of vastly-powered elder gods and over time came to believe that they were gods themselves. Some of them rebelled and committed terrible sins across a thousand worlds. To the civilizations they conquered they were the Great

Old Ones. Feared as demons and worshipped as gods, they drove their own worshippers insane.

The Elder Gods smashed them down, but even they were not powerful enough to destroy the creatures they had created. So, they locked them away. One of the most powerful of the Great Old Ones was an incredibly powerful and evil being who embraced the terror of his aspect and fed on the fear that his monstrous form and incredible power created. Whole worlds died for him—sometimes in war, sometimes in waves of mass suicides.

When Emily-Claire heard that, she wept. Strange as she was, and as in love with the voices of dead things as she'd come to be, suicide was the worst thing she could imagine. Being alive meant that there were so many things to see and know and learn and sense and taste and experience. Even a girl as alone as she was—or maybe because she spent so much time alone—she was in love with life. The idea that a creature with so much power enjoyed tricking billions of people into killing themselves for him made her so furious that she got up and walked round her room and kicked things, punched things, screamed at the top of her lungs.

The monster, patient, waited for her to sit back down.

"What's the thing's name?"

The monster paused as if unwilling to speak it aloud, then he drew a breath and whispered the name. "Cthulhu."

The very sound of that name hurt her ears to hear it and her brain to know it, and she shook her head, sorry she'd asked.

When she could speak—and it took a while—she asked, "If this thing is that strong, then what can we do? It's going to eat all of us!"

"The universe was born from chaos," whispered the monster in a voice as soft as rabbit fur, "but there is a beautiful balance to it. Cthulhu, for all his power, was thrown down and imprisoned in a city beneath the waves. In the nightmare corpse-city of R'lyeh he sleeps and only dreams that he is awake."

"Wait...*what*? That makes no sense at all."

"Life is a dream," whispered one of the other monsters from deeper in the closet, and others picked it up and chanted it for a few moments. The line from the old nursery rhyme came to her: *Row, row, row your boat, gently down the stream...merrily, merrily, merrily, merrily...life is but a dream*. It had been a silly song when she was little, but now it chilled her.

"We are all dreaming," said her patient monster. "When we believe that our dream is the only reality then we stay asleep forever. But when we open our inner eye to look around, we see that the universe is like the ocean and we, in the bubbles of our dreams, swim there. Together sometimes, or alone. Cthulhu believes that his dream is the only one, and he is so old, so powerful that he is trying to force that dream into *your* world, Emily-Claire. Into this world. Jonah has already become lost in that dream. Cthulhu fed on his dreams, and he wants to feed on yours. On the dreams of your friends at school. If he feeds enough then the sleeper will awaken, and the dream of this world will become a nightmare."

She shivered as if a cold, damp wind was blowing through her bedroom. She fumbled for the monster's hand and clutched it, pressing it to her hammering heart. "What can we do? How do we fight something that strong? I mean, how was he even stopped before?"

"With magic, of course," said the monster. "With magic so old the names for the spells were lost before your sun caught fire. Old, *old* magic. The Elder Gods had many servants and not all of them rebelled. Cthulhu used evil and ugly magic, but the magic of the loyal servants was cleaner. It was a terrible fight, though, and worlds were destroyed in the conflict. In the end, their dream of beauty was enough to overcome his dream of horror."

"Clean magic? Like the Jedi?" suggested Emily-Claire.

The monster in the closet chuckled. They had watched those movies together when she sat in the open doorway and played the films on her laptop. Many other monsters had clustered around.

"Like the Jedi," it agreed, "though ten billion times more powerful."

"And this Cthulhu thing was like the Sith?"

"If you like," said the amused monster. "The struggle was terrible and lasted for a thousand years, but in the end the loyal servants cast a great spell that sent Cthulhu into a deep, deep sleep. They imprisoned him beneath the ocean where no one could find him or free him. There the evil has slept for thousands of years."

She remembered the stink of rotting fish and wrinkled her nose.

"But Cthulhu dreams," warned the monster. "Oh, he dreams, and his dreams are so deep, so powerful that they intrude into *this* world. Into many worlds, and many times."

"He's asleep and he's that strong?" asked Emily-Claire, amazed.

The monster made a sound. Maybe it was a laugh. "Coming here, to your school, stealing your friend, attacking you...that is not power, my little princess. That is a whim in a dream. But if he feeds enough to wake up...then you will see power. Then worlds will fall as his rage awakens."

"But...but...what about those good guys? Won't they just—I don't know—knock him out again?"

"The universe has changed much since then," said the monster with a sad shake of his head. The others in the closet shifted and muttered. A breeze like a dry wind blew out of the closet door. It smelled of sadness and fear, which she had never felt before here.

"We have to do something," insisted Emily-Claire.

"Yes," said the monster. "You do."

It took her a half second to realize that he said 'you.'

She asked, "What...?"

"There is a reason evil has come to your school, your friends, to you..."

"But...I'm just a girl. I'm only *thirteen*, for Pete's sake. What can I do?"

The monster said nothing.

"You're all monsters," she yelled. "Can't you fight him for me?"

"We are sent to watch by the Elder Gods, but the world as it is now is vastly different from the world as it was when we were brought here. Our shadows once roamed free beneath a ceiling of clouds, but your kind rose up and built structures—tombs and temples, castles and houses, and in their rooms we became trapped, retreating from the clearing skies, fleeing from the sun, finding safety in rooms without windows."

"Like closets...?"

"Like closets," said the monster. "We live in your closet, Emily-Claire. The shadows here are the darkness in which *we* dream. And so, we remain, monsters in your personal shadows. Bound to you, Emily-Claire."

"But...but..."

In the open doorway, the shadows roiled and swirled as the other monsters clustered to watch.

To watch her.

She stared back at them. At their forms, which changed constantly as if moved by winds only they could feel.

And she smiled.

Then she said, "Ah."

And all the shadows swirled faster and faster.

Which is why Emily-Claire went back to school.

-II-

It was late, and the last class was about to let out.

Emily-Claire went to the auditorium, which doubled as the

theater for school shows. She'd worked crew for two productions and knew every inch of the backstage area. There were prop rooms and changing rooms, and rooms for pieces of set and band instruments. She snuck into a costume room, locked the door from the inside, set the box on the floor, then sat down to wait.

She heard the bells and the banging open of doors and the herds of footsteps. She heard the building come alive and, gradually, fall quiet again. There was no window and the only light was from her cell phone.

Waiting was hard. It was scary. But it was also exciting.

The minutes gathered into bunches and slowly—so slowly —withered and fell away. She texted her mom, who—to her incredible relief—responded. Everyone was back home now. Emily-Claire lied and said she was staying late for a school thing.

Well, not really a lie. This was the school and there was a thing.

Her mom filled the screen with emojis, told her to be home as soon as it was over, and that was that.

"Over," echoed Emily-Claire. "Sure. If I can."

-12-

When she was sure the building was completely empty— there were no night watchmen at John Paul Jones Junior High —Emily-Claire unlocked the door and crept out, carrying the heavy box.

The halls were dark and so quiet that even her careful footfalls made a racket. Echoes chased her as she tiptoed down the stairs and along the hallways to her locker. A spill of yellow light from one of the sparse security lamps fell across the floor, and she saw—scuffed by a hundred shoes—a few smears of her own blood. She set the box down and touched her cheek.

She left the box on the floor and went to the janitor's closet around the corner, returning quickly with a long-handled push broom.

"Sorry," she said to the school as she swung the broom with all her might and shattered the security light, plunging the hall into nearly total darkness. Emily-Claire tossed the broom away and knelt to touch the spots of blood. Sniffed it, rubbed it between her fingers. There was nothing to learn from it because she was still alive. Living things didn't speak to her in the same way. She was relieved to find that there was no fish smell, either. Not that she expected any, but it was a relief nonetheless.

A sound made her jump and she whipped around to see her locker door jiggling. It was weird to her that the small hinges and cheap combination lock could trap a monster like that.

"Cthul—" she began and bit down on the last syllable. Even so, a tentacle slammed so hard against the locker door that cracks whipsawed up the wall above it and two acoustic tiles fell from the dropped-ceiling. Emily-Claire yelped and clamped her hands over her mouth.

The hinges on her locker creaked ominously.

Emily-Claire felt sweat burst from her pores and soak her clothes. She had never been this frightened before. What if she was wrong? What if her plan was stupid? What if the thing who lived in the shadows here had fed on more than Jonah? What if all he needed was one last Emily-Claire-sized bite?

She licked her lips, set her teeth, and walked carefully over to the locker.

The combination was twelve...two...thirty-seven. She dialed right, then left, and then past zero to the right and all the way to thirty-six before she paused. The locker trembled, but not as if struck. More like the thing was right there, directly behind the thin metal, trembling with the anticipation of that last click.

"Please," she said aloud. It was not a prayer. It was a plea. The kind one would make to a friend.

She took a breath and turned the combination lock one tiny bit to the right.

Click.

The door burst open as three massive tentacles squeezed out, coiling in the air to try and wrap around her. If they had caught her she would have been dead—or lost—on the spot, but by then Emily-Claire was moving. As soon as she turned the dial to thirty-seven, she whirled and threw herself into a long dive. One full semester of gymnastic club hadn't taught her much, but she could tuck and roll. She tucked, and she rolled, and the tentacles crushed the empty air inches above her.

Emily-Claire came out of her roll badly, rising too fast and pitched too far forward. She tried to grab the sides of her wooden box and missed completely, hitting the top with her chin, biting her tongue and nearly breaking her jaw. Blood welled in her mouth and she gagged, but she fumbled for the box, grabbed a corner as she fell, clawed it toward her as one of the tentacles smashed down on the floor. The old polished floorboard cracked apart in a spray of splinters. The shock knocked the box out of her hands again and it went sliding down the floor. With a cry she scrambled to her feet, ducked under another tentacle, and dove again.

A fourth lashing tentacle caught her, lifted her and smashed her against the base of the trophy case. The display glass shattered, showering her in glittering razor-sharp debris. She covered her face with her arms, but felt a dozen burning points of pain ignite on her skin.

Then she lunged again, throwing herself along the floor like a seal, reaching for the box. One tentacle tried to curl around the box—maybe sensing its danger—but Emily-Claire clamped her hands on the lid, gritted her teeth, and tore it open.

All of the shadows in the box spilled out.

All of the monsters who lived in those shadows—her monsters—spilled out, too.

The monsters she had gathered into her light-proof little shadow box and carried all the way to school. A simple act that she could do, and they could not.

Emily-Claire had brought her shadowy friends to school with her, and in the darkened hallway, she let them out to play.

The tentacles paused, confused as the shadows spread out and grew and expanded, because size does not mean the same thing in all dimensions. Not at all in a world of shadows. Emily-Claire snatched up the broom and held it like a war club, but she knew that it was not the weapon to win this fight.

Her monsters were here. With her. For her. *Because* of her.

Her monsters.

Hers.

She faced the waving tentacles. "You took my friend," she said. "You can't have me. And you can't have my school."

The shadows gathered around her. The tentacles whipped back and forth, furious and threatening.

"This is *my* world," she growled. Emily-Claire reached up a hand and touched the shoulder of her first friend. He was a thing of horror and of beauty. Tall, covered in scales and spikes, with enormous fangs and eyes that blazed like black fire. "And these are my friends."

Her friends howled as they attacked.

-13-

School was closed the next day. It was on the news. Someone had broken in and smashed the trophy case, broken some lights, tore open a whole row of lockers and even ripped up floor boards. The police were called in. The principal was on the news to growl about hoodlums and gang members.

Emily-Claire sat on the floor in the open doorway of her

closet and watched. Her laptop was propped atop her shadow box. She was eating a bowl of fresh sweet strawberries, and every now and then a hand with long claws would reach out of the darkness of her closet to pluck a fat one. Monsters liked strawberries, too.

ABOUT THE AUTHORS

Chesya Burke is a doctoral candidate in the Department of English at the University of Florida. She has written and published nearly a hundred fiction works and articles within the genres of science fiction, fantasy, noir and horror. Her story collection, *Let's Play White*, is being taught in universities around the country and her novel, *The Strange Crimes of Little Africa*, debuted in Dec 2015. Poet Nikki Giovanni compared her writing to that of Octavia Butler and Toni Morrison, and Samuel Delany called her "a formidable new master of the macabre."

Chesya received her Master's degree in African American Studies from Georgia State University. Her story, "Stormy Monday," examines the existence of monsters inside of us all.

J.C. Koch is scared by horror stories but writes them anyway. J.C.'s stories have appeared in *Arkham Tales*, *Necrotic Tissue*, and *Penumbra* e-zines, and a variety of excellent anthologies (like this one) including *The Mammoth Book of Kaiju*, *A Darke Phantastique*, *The Madness of Cthulhu Vol.1*, *Out of Tune II*, and *Submerged*.

"Pickman's Model" is one of J.C.'s all-time favorite Lovecraft stories, so it only seemed right that the story of "Pickman's Daughter" should now be told. Keeping the family business going, so to speak.

In addition to writing about scary things, J.C. also likes to do scary things like pay attention to politics, keep up with the Kardashians, and play the stock market. With no time to actually do any of those things, though, J.C. tends to stay hidden under the bed, letting more of the terrors of the mind bleed onto the page, both metaphorically and literally. Reach J.C. (otherwise known as Gini Koch) at *Going Bump in the Night*. (http://www.ginikoch.com/jkbookstore.htm).

Jonathan Maberry is a NY Times bestselling suspense novelist, five-time Bram Stoker Award winner, and comic book writer. His vampire apocalypse book series, V-WARS, is being produced as a Netflix original series, starring Ian Somerhalder (LOST, VAMPIRE DIARIES) and will debut in early 2019. His other works include the *Joe Ledger* thrillers, *Glimpse*, the *Rot & Ruin* series, the *Dead of Night* series, *The Wolfman*, *X-Files Origins: Devil's Advocate*, and many others. His YA space travel novel, *Mars One*, is in development for film; and his novel *Glimpse* and the *V-Wars* shared-world vampire apocalypse series are being developed for TV, as is his bestselling *Joe Ledger* thriller series.

He is the editor of many anthologies, including the *X-Files*, *Aliens: Bug Hunt*, *Nights of the Living Dead* (co-edited with zombie genre creator George A. Romero), and others involving murder ballads, variations on Sherlock Holmes, young adult horror, and the upcoming *New Scary Stories to tell in the Dark*. His comics include *Captain America*, the Bram Stoker Award-winning *Bad Blood*, *Black Panther*, *Punisher*, *Marvel Zombies Return*, *George Romero's Road of the Dead*, and more. His *Rot & Ruin* novels were included in the Ten Best Horror Novels for Young Adults. His first novel, *Ghost Road Blues* was named one of the 25 Best Horror Novels of the New Millennium. A board game version of *V-Wars: A Game of Blood and Betrayal* was based on his novels and comics. He was a featured expert on the History Channel's *Zombies: A Living History* and *True Monsters*. He is one third of the very popular and mildly weird *Three Guys With Beards* podcast. He is a board member of the Horror Writers Association and the president of the International Association of Media Tie-in Writers.

His story for this anthology, "Being Emily-Claire" combines his love of the Cthulhu Mythos—something he was introduced to at a house party when he was thirteen by Harlan Ellison and L. Sprague de Camp—and tales of disenfranchised teens discovering their power. It is entirely likely Emily-Claire will find her way into other stories in the future.

Jonathan lives in Del Mar, California with his wife, Sara Jo. www.jonathanmaberry.com

Seanan McGuire is the author of more than forty full-length books, as well as dozens of short stories spanning multiple genres. As Mira Grant, she also writes biomedical science fiction thrillers, which is a fancy way of saying "like Michael Crichton, but with more zombies." She also writes for Marvel Comics, primarily for *Ghost-Spider* (Gwen Stacy of Earth-65) and *The X-Men* (proving that childhood dreams do actually come true). When not writing, she enjoys travel, Disney Parks, and not getting enough sleep. We bet you can guess why.

Seanan's series of stories focusing on a cheerleading squad called the Fighting Pumpkins has always taken the girls in orange and green to terribly dark places. Now, with "Away Game," she's taking them a step deeper into the darkness...and they may not all make it out again. Find her at www.seananmcguire.com, or on Twitter as @seananmcguire.

Premee Mohamed is an Indo-Canadian scientist and speculative fiction author based in Canada. Her short fiction has appeared in *Analog*, *Automata Review*, *Mythic Delirium*, and many other venues. In her spare time, she enjoys painting and annotating her paperback copy of *The Necronomicon*. She can be found on Twitter at @premeesaurus.

In this anthology's story, "Us and Ours," a pair of mismatched teens rely on the power of their friendship and the strength of the land to fight back against the abrupt intrusion of ancient gods into their protected valley. This story shares the world of previously published stories "Willing," "The Evaluator," and "Below the Kirk, Below the Hill."

Lisa Morton is a screenwriter, author of non-fiction books, and award-winning prose writer whose work was described by the American Library Association's Readers' Advisory Guide to Horror as "consistently dark, unsettling, and frightening." She is the author of four novels and more than 130 short stories, a six-time winner of the Bram Stoker Award®, and a world-class Halloween expert. She co-edited (with Ellen Datlow) the anthology *Haunted Nights*; other recent releases include *Ghosts: A Haunted History* and the collection *The Samhanach and Other Halloween Treats*. Lisa lives in Los Angeles.

For "Holding Back," I wanted to explore the notion that it's not a long way to go from the classic Mythos-style cultist to the modern-day bully. I was also intrigued by the idea of setting that cult in the middle of American suburbia.

Weston Ochse (pronounced oaks) is a writer of thirty books in multiple genres. His military supernatural series *SEAL Team 666* has been optioned to be a movie starring Dwayne Johnson and his military sci fi trilogy, which starts with *Grunt Life*, has been praised for its PTSD-positive depiction of soldiers at peace and at war. His shorter work has appeared in DC Comics, *IDW Comics*, *Soldier of Fortune Magazine*, *Cemetery Dance*, and peered literary journals. His franchise work includes the *X-Files*, *Predator*, *Aliens*, *Hellboy*, Clive Barker's *Midian*, and *V-Wars*.

His most recent novel, *Burning Sky*, has been called both the "Pinnacle of Military Horror" and "a Masterpiece." Booklist said *"Ochse's writing finds the beauty in the language of brutality, which will appeal to fans of Blood Meridian by Cormac McCarthy."* In the story, "The Icarus Club," Weston wanted to bring some of this beautiful violence and brutality to the young adult page, remembering that to the Elder Gods, we are little more than insects, and slightly less interesting than a forgotten toy. He invites you to fly with him, if only during a single storm.

Stephen Ross. My short stories and novelettes have appeared in the *Ellery Queen Mystery Magazine*, the *Alfred Hitchcock Mystery Magazine*, several Mystery Writers of America (MWA) anthologies, and many other publications. I have been nominated for an Edgar Award (2011, Best Short Story), a Derringer Award (2011, Best Novelette), a Thriller Award (2015, Best Short Story), and I was a 2010 Ellery Queen Readers' Award Finalist.

I am delighted to have a story appear in this anthology. For a long time, I've wanted to write a boy-meets-girl story that features a Lovecraft spin. And I've always wanted to write about a lighthouse; there's something inherently creepy about these tall structures, whose sole purpose is to glow in the dead of the night.

Lucy A. Snyder is the five-time Bram Stoker Award-winning author of over 100 published short stories. Her story "Visions of the Dream Witch" focuses on a pair of shoggoth-fighting teenagers who must do battle with the Dream Witch Yidhra in Louisiana. Can they resist the wiles of a goddess who promises them everything they could ever imagine?

Snyder's most recent books are the collection *Garden of Eldritch Delights* and the forthcoming novel *The Girl With the Star-Stained Soul*. She also wrote the novels *Spellbent*, *Shotgun Sorceress*, and *Switchblade Goddess*, and the collections *While the Black Stars Burn*, *Soft Apocalypses*, *Chimeric Machines*, and *Installing Linux on a Dead Badger*. Her writing has been translated into French, Russian, Italian, Spanish, Czech, and Japanese editions and has appeared in publications such as *Asimov's Science Fiction*, *Apex Magazine*, *Nightmare Magazine*, *Pseudopod*, *Strange Horizons*, and *Best Horror of the Year*. She's faculty in Seton Hill University's Writing Popular Fiction MFA program; you can learn more about her at www. lucysnyder.com.

Josh Vogt has been published in dozens of markets with work covering fantasy, science fiction, horror, humor, pulp, and more. He also writes and edits for a wide variety of RPG developers and publishers. His novels include *Pathfinder Tales: Forge of Ashes* and his humorous urban fantasy series, *The Cleaners*, with *Enter the Janitor*, *The Maids of Wrath*, *The Dustpan Cometh*, and the forthcoming *Fellowship of the Squeegee*. He's a member of SFWA, the International Association of Media Tie-In Writers, and a Scribe Awards and Compton Crook Award finalist.

"The Art of Dreaming" was inspired by Josh's fascination with lucid dreaming and how our sleeping realities can intertwine with our waking lives in strange, inspiring, and often disturbing ways.

You can find him at www.JRVogt.com or on Twitter @JRVogt.

Tim Waggoner has published over forty novels and five collections of short stories. He writes original dark fantasy and horror, as well as media tie-ins, and his articles on writing have appeared in numerous publications. He's won the Bram Stoker Award, the Horror Writers Association's Mentor of the Year Award, and he's been a finalist for the Shirley Jackson Award and the Scribe Award. He's also a full-time tenured professor who teaches creative writing and composition at Sinclair College in Dayton, Ohio. His story, "Just Imagine," is about a teenage girl who stops at a coffee shop after school to get some homework done, only to discover that monsters from another dimension have something else in mind for her.

Wendy N. Wagner is the author of more than forty short stories and two novels for the *Pathfinder* role-playing game. Her third novel, the SF eco-thriller *An Oath of Dogs*, came out 2017 from Angry Robot Books. She is also a Hugo award-winning editor. You can learn more about her work at www.winniewoohoo.com

A long-time resident of Portland, Oregon, Wendy credits Portland's legendary HP Lovecraft Film Festival for introducing her to Lovecraft's work. Nearly half of her fiction has grappled with his creatures or themes. "The Geometry of Dreams" was inspired not only by H.P. Lovecraft, but also by her family's running bad luck with snow globes.

Douglas Wynne is the author of five novels, including the SPECTRA Files trilogy (*Red Equinox*, *Black January*, and *Cthulhu Blues*). His short fiction has recently appeared in the anthologies *Tales From the Miskatonic Library*, *I Am the Abyss*, and *Shadows Over Main Street 2*, and his writing workshops have been featured at StokerCon, the Peabody Essex Museum, and the New Hampshire Writer's Project at SNHU. Originally from New York, he attended Berklee College of Music in Boston and worked as a recording engineer before settling down with his family near Newburyport, Massachusetts, the town that inspired both H.P. Lovecraft's novella, *The Shadow Over Innsmouth* and Wynne's story in the present volume, "The Mouth of the Merrimack." You can find him online at www.dougwynne.com.

ABOUT THE EDITOR

Jennifer Brozek is a Hugo Award finalist and a multiple Bram Stoker Award finalist. Winner of the Australian Shadows Award for best edited publication, Jennifer has edited sixteen anthologies with more on the way, including the acclaimed *Chicks Dig Gaming* and *Shattered Shields* anthologies. Author of the *Karen Wilson Chronicles*, *Industry Talk*, *The Last Days of Salton Academy*, and the acclaimed *Melissa Allen* series, she has more than eighty published short stories, and is the Creative Director of Apocalypse Ink Productions.

Winner of the Scribe, Origins, and ENnie awards, Jennifer's contributions to RPG sourcebooks include *Dragonlance*, *Colonial Gothic*, *Shadowrun*, *Serenity*, *Savage Worlds*, and *White Wolf SAS*. She is the author of the award winning YA *BattleTech* novel, *The Nellus Academy Incident*, *Shadowrun* novella, *Doc Wagon 19*, and the *Arkham Horror* novella, *To Fight the Black Wind*. She has also written for the AAA MMO, *Aion*, and the award winning videogame, *Shadowrun Returns*.

Jennifer has been a freelance author, editor, and tie-in writer for over ten years after leaving her high-paying tech job, and she's never been happier. She keeps a tight schedule on her writing and editing projects and somehow manages to find time to volunteer for several professional writing organizations such as SFWA, HWA, and IAMTW. She shares her husband, Jeff, with several cats and often uses him as a sounding board for her story ideas. Visit Jennifer's worlds at jennifer-brozek.com.